WHAT COMES AROUND (2)

An Allison Parker Mystery

Adair Sanders

ISBN: 1518835058
ISBN 13: 9781518835056
Library of Congress Control Number: 2015918242
CreateSpace Independent Publishing Platform
North Charleston, South Carolina

To My Readers

This book is a complete work of fiction. While there may be similarities in the names of some of the characters, and some of the locales and businesses may, in fact, exist, the story told is one that was created solely by the characters themselves as they appeared to me through the Muse that directs my writing.

Adair Sanders
Brevard, North Carolina
November, 2015

CHAPTER ONE

The wind howled with the voice of a thousand demons, heavy breaths bending the tall pines, snapping in half those who dared to resist, rushing over the rural landscape, monstrous shapes roiling just above the tree line, jagged thrusts of lightning heralding the imminent birth of destruction. A small structure appeared in the distance, its shape briefly illuminated. Ramshackle would have been too gracious a description. No larger than a shed, with faded remnants of color peeling in strips from the wooden siding, the hovel began to shake as a long, narrow finger reached towards it from the maelstrom above.

She should have been terrified. But nothing was more terrifying than the man who had bound her, who had tortured her, and who had left her here alone, laughing as he locked the shed door shutting her into darkness. Hearing the roar of the approaching tornado, the girl smiled and willed her limbs to relax into the chains that held her to the concrete floor. Soon, she knew, she would be free.

The black finger of her deliverance pierced the shed's roof, flinging splinters of wood and roofing towards the sky, blasting the flimsy walls to unrecognizable debris. The storm's violence hammered the girl's frail body, its vortex fighting to pull her into a wild embrace. An agonized scream escaped from the girl's lips as the core of her body was sucked towards the storm's open jaws, her arms and legs remaining shackled to the grey concrete beneath her, causing her body to arch unnaturally. Her last thought, the one that came seconds before her body was ripped from her arms, remained a question for someone else to answer. *Why?*

⊷⊶

Tobias "Toby" Everett Trowbridge came from a long line of lawmen. Isaiah Trowbridge, Toby's great-grandfather on his father's side, was a figure of historical significance in the family tree. Born into the post-Civil War insanity of the South, Isaiah Trowbridge had incurred the wrath of the white citizens of Pickens County, South Carolina by refusing to arrest a local black man who, by the simple act of making eye contact upon passing, had supposedly offended some prissy white woman on the streets of Easley.

When ejected from his office in the next election, Isaiah Trowbridge had moved his family north to Louisville, Kentucky where Isaiah hoped to find people of a more tolerant disposition. There, after establishing himself with community service and employment in local law enforcement, Isaiah eventually ran a successful campaign for Sheriff of Jefferson County, holding that position well into the sixth decade of his life.

Isaiah and his wife raised two sons, both of whom were expected to follow their father's steps into law enforcement. The older boy, Samuel, never made it, meeting his demise at the end of a German bayonet in World War I. The younger son, Esau, too young to serve in the war, but nevertheless wanting adventure of some sort, applied to the Louisville Police Department at the age of 18 and was hired as a beat patrolman. Well suited to police work, Esau rose through the ranks of the police department, ending his working days as a veteran homicide detective among Louisville's finest.

Esau's son Luke, Toby's father, had been the only boy in a brood of four girls delivered by Esau's wife.

Luke spent his growing up years living between the front and back covers of a book where, if bad things happened, it was only to other people. A quiet and introspective boy, Luke had showed no inclination towards any sport requiring physical activity, much less the life of a law enforcement officer like his father and grandfather before him. Eventually Esau gave up trying to change his son's nature, assuming Luke would choose an undemanding career, maybe as a teacher or a writer.

But life, intervening in the body of an itinerant drifter, had other plans for Luke Trowbridge.

Imogene Trowbridge was Luke's youngest sister, a surprise late-in-life baby for Esau and his wife, born when Luke was thirteen years old. From the day his parents brought Imogene home from the hospital, Luke had been entranced by his dark haired, green eyed little sister. By the time Imogene reached school age, she and Luke had developed an irreplaceable and inexplicable bond. No child could have had a more devoted guardian than Imogene had in her big brother Luke.

When Imogene entered first grade, Luke adjusted his class schedule at the local community college so he could walk Imogene to and from school each day, not because of any inherent danger - the Trowbridges lived in a safe neighborhood only three blocks from Imogene's school- but rather for the sheer pleasure of spending time with his little sister. Until one day in early spring when Imogene's school let out earlier than expected, and the child headed home alone.

Imogene's body was found not far from the family's house. Working on a tip from an elderly woman who had been walking her dog and had seen a suspicious stranger hurrying from a wooded area near where Imogene's body had been found, authorities tracked a drifter to a nearby hobo camp. There, amidst other discarded detritus, they discovered Imogene's torn pink sweater stuffed in the man's knapsack.

The murder of Imogene Trowbridge caused a psychic shift in Luke's world, a change that would shape and direct him for the remainder of his life. Shedding his easy-going ways as easily as a snake sheds a skin it has outgrown, Luke abandoned a life of books and academia for one of finding and incarcerating those who would murder, rape, and commit violent crime. A year after the Trowbridge family laid their youngest to rest in the family plot Luke graduated first in his class from the Louisville Police Academy.

Luke started his law enforcement career in his home town, but found that too many memories of his sister haunted him in the familiar surroundings.

Adair Sanders

When a job opening came available in the Calhoun County, Alabama Sheriff's Department Luke packed his belongings and moved his family to Ft. Charles, a medium sized town, situated between Birmingham and Atlanta in eastern Alabama. The years passed, and by the time Luke's family received word that Imogene's murderer had been killed in prison by another inmate, Esau was close to retirement, Luke had been a homicide detective for ten years, and Toby Trowbridge was a young teenager who wanted nothing more than to join law enforcement as soon as he graduated high school.

Insistent that her son be the first Trowbridge with a college degree, Toby's mother convinced her son that a degree in criminal justice from the university would stand him in good stead in the career he wanted. Avoiding fraternities and carrying as heavy a caseload as the school would permit, Toby graduated cum laude, criminal justice degree in hand, just three years after he first walked onto the campus in Tuscaloosa.

The Calhoun County Sheriff's Department had gladly hired Luke Trowbridge's son. Toby applied the same hard work and focus that had served him well at the university to his job in the Sheriff's department. Over time, the citizens of Calhoun County, comprised mostly of residents of Ft. Charles, learned that Toby Trowbridge solved cases. Fifteen years after he joined the department, Toby was elected Sheriff in an uncontested election.

Walking through the debris field in front of him, Toby Trowbridge reflected on his genetic history. Even had some other occupation presented itself, Toby knew there would have been no way to ignore the whispering call of the three generations that had preceded him. Law enforcement was a part of Toby Trowbridge as surely as was the hand that he had, by habit, placed on his holster as he approached the crime scene that Tom Spencer had discovered this morning.

911 calls came straight to Dispatch in the Calhoun County Sheriff's office.

"You better listen to this" the department's emergency operator told Toby before transferring a tape of the call she had just received. "I've already dispatched a black and white to the location."

"Mother of God" Toby heard, immediately recognizing the voice of his neighbor Tom Spencer. "Tell Toby.." Toby listened as Spencer's words were interrupted by the sound of violent retching. "Tell Toby to get out here. Fast. I don't know where the rest of the body is."

A lifetime of living in southern Alabama had accustomed Toby to the vagaries of the spring storm season. Aptly named, Dixie Alley regularly produced tornadoes ranging anywhere from a F1 to the F3, with an occasional F4 or F5 monster. Modern technology had improved the warning time, giving the locals a head's up with broadcasted tornado watches and warnings, but most residents of Ft. Charles and Calhoun County could predict bad weather simply by looking at the color of the sky and noting the "feel" of the air preceding an approaching storm.

The experts at the National Weather Service had pegged yesterday's tornado as an F3, a medium sized monster packing winds of close to 200 mph when it crossed Calhoun County. Fortunately for Toby's constituents, the tornado had missed Ft. Charles, raging instead over mostly unpopulated rural areas in other parts of the county. Trees and a few barns had been decimated, but no homes had sustained damage, and no deaths had been reported. Until the 911 call came from Tom Spencer.

Approaching the group of men, Toby watched as Andy Dabo, Calhoun County's Medical Examiner, peered underneath a large blue tarp that covered a small portion of a building's slab foundation.

"What've you got, Andy?" Toby asked.

Acknowledging Toby's question without looking up, Dabo replied "Two arms, part of one leg and foot, nothing else. Storm took the rest."

"Any way to identify sex?" Toby figured he knew the answer but asked anyway.

"Well, given the painted toenails on this foot, I'd say female" Dabo opined, "but you never know nowadays."

"What was here?" Toby asked Tom Spencer.

"Just an old shed. Back in the 50's there was a sharecropper house over yonder" Spencer pointed to a spot several yards to the north where the remains of a stone foundation peeped through the pasture grass. "Guess this was an outbuilding of some sort for those tenants."

"When was the last time you came out here?" Toby pulled a spiral notepad and pen from his jacket.

"It's been a while" Spencer reflected. "Probably a month or so ago. Had a couple of cows get through a fence in the south pasture and I figured they would head this way."

"Did you look inside the shed?" Toby probed, recording Spencer's replies in the personal shorthand Toby had developed over the years.

"No. No reason to." Spencer shook his head. "But nothing seemed odd or out of place to me either - you know, nothing that would have caught my attention."

"I don't recall any missing person report for a female, do you Rob?" Toby turned towards the young deputy who had been dispatched in response to the 911 call.

"No, Sir" the deputy replied. "Last one of those was when old man Gibbs wandered off from the nursing home last summer."

"Anything other than body parts?" Toby asked as the ME finished his preliminary examination.

"Looks like fabric or thread imbedded in the ankle tissue. I'll know more once I get the remains to the lab." Dabo stripped latex gloves from his hands. "Might tell us the kind of clothing the victim was wearing. It's a long shot, but…."

"It's the only clue we're likely to have unless you can pull prints off those hands" Toby interjected. "Do the best you can, Andy. Let me know what you come up with."

"I will, Toby" Dabo replied grimly. "Two of my staff are on the way out here as we speak. We'll get everything bagged, tagged and in the lab by mid-afternoon."

Toby nodded his approval. Dabo was a thorough and competent medical examiner. If there was evidence to be found, Dabo would find it. In the meantime, Toby would post what details he had on the National Crime Information Center network and hope for the best. Somewhere, a mother had lost a daughter, or a child had lost its mother or a husband his wife. Toby's job was to bring closure to the family, justice to the victim, and punishment to the offender. Driving back to Ft. Charles, Toby began to plan his investigation.

CHAPTER TWO

Dropping her briefcase beside her desk and kicking off black stiletto pumps, Allison Parker flopped her slim body onto the sofa which hugged the back wall of her office.

"Oh Lord" she exhaled. "What a week."

"Did the jury return a verdict?" Allison's secretary Donna Pevey inquired, following her boss into the private space.

A satisfied smile accented Allison's face. "Sure did. Defense verdict on all counts." Pushing herself to a sitting position, Allison continued. "I knew we had a strong case, but when the jury was out more than two hours I got a little concerned."

"Well, I wasn't worried. Susan called after you gave your closing argument." Donna replied, referring to Susan Teal, a paralegal and the newest employee at Parker & Jackson. "She said you nailed it, had the jury eating out of your hand by the time you finished."

Allison laughed. "Susan's got a lot to learn about juries. I've watched jurors nod and smile at counsel for one party during closing argument and then return a verdict for the other side. The playing field changed when Congress amended Title VII to allow for jury trials" Allison replied, using the shortened acronym for The Civil Rights Act of 1964. "When that law was first enacted all those cases were decided by the judge. Lots more defense verdicts back then." Allison continued. "Juries are an unknown factor. No matter how many experts are hired to help with jury selection, there's just no way to truly predict what part of the evidence will resonate with any particular juror."

"Guess that's right" Donna acknowledged. "Didn't one of Jack Striker's clients pay a bundle for a jury expert in that Westinghouse case he had a couple of years ago?"

Jack Striker, a local Ft. Charles attorney, was one of Allison's biggest competitors. Events which had led to Allison leaving Johnson & Merritt, her previous firm, had given Allison a new respect for the lawyer. Most attorneys would have ignored the red flags that led Jack Striker to contact Allison with concerns about one of his clients. Although careful not to breach the attorney - client relationship, the information Striker did share with Allison provided a necessary puzzle part in the mystery Allison was investigating at the time.

"Yes. And it didn't do Jack or his client any good, either." Allison explained. "Westinghouse got hit with a big judgment, plus another $250,000 in punitive damages. So much for jury experts, huh?"

Allison glanced at her desk where the red flashing light on her phone's display pad indicated a waiting message. "Who called?" she asked her secretary.

"Oh" Donna smacked her forehead with her hand. "I totally forgot - too interested in hearing about the verdict. Frank Martin called. Said he'd leave you a message. Something about a new case. He wanted to talk to you today if possible."

Allison checked the time. "It's right at 5:30. I'll give him a call, but knowing Frank he's gone for the day."

"I don't know." Donna frowned. "Frank seemed pretty excited. Bet he's waiting on your call." Changing the subject, she added "If you don't need anything else I'm going to head on home."

"Have a good one" Allison called to the back of her retreating secretary. "See you Monday."

Allison skimmed the pile of mail that had accumulated during her week in trial while she waited for Frank to answer. No fires burning, she decided, relieved that the upcoming weekend could be one of leisure rather than work. If it was warm enough, maybe she and Jim would take out the boat. Charlotte and Mack, their children, would love a day on the Reservoir, and Allison knew she and her husband needed a few hours of down time.

"You have reached Martin Investigations. Our business hours are nine to five, Monday through Friday." Allison listened as the voice of Frank's secretary politely instructed the caller to "please leave a message".

"Frank, it's Allison Parker" the words had barely left Allison's mouth before she heard a click on the line, quickly followed by Frank Martin's gruff reply.

"Been waiting on your call" Frank chastised Allison. "I was about to give up on hearing from you."

"Didn't Donna tell you I was waiting for the jury to come back?" Allison sighed. Frank was an excellent private investigator, but patience sometimes seemed a foreign concept to him. Allison had given up trying to figure out how Frank could be so good at his job while sometimes lacking that particular virtue.

"Yeh, she did" Frank grumbled in reply. "You win?"

"Yes, and now I'm getting ready to head out for a few days of R&R with my family." Allison informed

Frank. "But, since I know how you are, I stopped to return your call before leaving."

Chastened, Frank replied "I appreciate that, and after you hear what I have to tell you, you'll be glad you did."

"If it's going to interfere with my weekend, you can save it 'til Monday." Allison warned.

Ignoring Allison's comment Frank began. "Got a call from Sheriff Trowbridge this afternoon. You remember hearing about the human remains Tom Spencer found out in his north pasture yesterday?" Hearing no response from Allison, Frank continued. "There's not much to go on. DNA, some fabric threads found on part of the body, but no other potential identifiers. Andy Dabo was able to pull some prints from the hands. Be good luck if they're in the system. Anyway, the reason I called is this - the Sheriff's Department is short staffed right now, so Toby asked if I had time to assist in the investigation, try to develop some leads as to the perp's identity."

"That sounds gruesome and interesting at the same time" Allison laughed. "and right down your alley. I must have missed something, though, because I don't see how that concerns me? You know I don't do criminal work."

"Could have fooled me" Frank laughed a reply. "Since when is blackmail and murder not a criminal offense" he asked, reminding Allison of the case they had been involved in the previous year.

"Really, Frank" Allison shuddered as the memory of events which almost killed her and her husband, Judge Jim Kaufman, filled her mind. Ben Johnson, Allison's boss at her old law firm, had conspired with an ex-con to have her, Jim and Allison's partner David Jackson killed in an attempt to cover up blackmail and a murder-for-hire plot Johnson had been involved in years earlier. "That was my first - and hopefully last - foray into the world of sick fucks like Ben Johnson and his cohorts in crime. And it surely doesn't qualify me as a criminal attorney."

"I'm not asking you to take a criminal case, Allison" Frank replied. "Toby hired me to try to find the perp, not defend him in court. It's just that we worked well together on the McNair investigation, and I think we'd work well together on this case, too."

Allison smiled. "We did work well together, Frank, but I still don't see how I can be of any help to you, at least at this point. I don't have a P.I. license, and you know the state has tightened up on regulating your profession. I don't need an ethics complaint filed charging me with engaging in P.I. business without a license."

"Not to worry" Frank assured Allison. "Right now all I anticipate is your agreement to look over the file as we develop information. If we are dealing with someone not from around here, and I think that is likely, odds are he's done this before. Two sets of eyes are better than one, and your eyes are pretty damn sharp."

Allison glanced at her watch. The stress of a week in trial and the long hours that accompanied such had just about done her in. Jim and her children were waiting on her at the house. Interesting case or not, Allison had heard enough.

"Let me think about it over the weekend, talk to Jim, get his take on my involvement in something like this" Allison told Frank. "Oh, and I guess this is pro bono, right?"

"Yep, it's a freebie" Frank admitted. He hoped that fact wouldn't queer the deal. He wanted Allison's cooperation on the case. "Look, Allison, I really need your help. I'll owe you P.I. time gratis on your next case." That offer was the best Frank could think of on short notice.

A tired sigh prefaced Allison's soft reply as she terminated the call. "I'll talk to you Monday, Frank."

The Farm at Serenity Hill was all that its name implied. Run down and almost forgotten when Allison and Jim first saw the original house, the lure of its setting on gently rolling hills had temporarily blinded them to the rigors of rehabbing and then maintaining a house built in the late 1800's. The couple had decided to stay as true to the home's roots as possible so that the modern additions they added blended imperceptibly to the untrained eye. Comfortable and rambling, the farmhouse had become a loving place of respite for Allison and her husband from their busy lives as trial lawyer and judge. A large pond on the property enhanced the home's country appeal, evidenced by the jon boat tied to the pond's small dock.

After the birth of their two children, Allison and Jim had added a barn and two ponies. "What's a farm without ponies and livestock?" Allison had asked her husband, as chickens and then goats were added to the family's growing menagerie. As might be expected, The Farm at Serenity Hill had become a favorite retreat not only for Allison and her family, but a popular gathering place for their children's friends and parents.

Heading out of town, Allison was glad that they had not scheduled any company for the weekend. She needed some serious down time with her family, something she was more and more aware of the busier her law practice had become. Allison had known, intellectually, that opening her own firm with David Jackson would be different from being a partner in a large firm like Johnson & Merritt where all of the back room details were handled by competent support staff. But, intellectual knowledge was never the same as reality, and Allison had quickly learned that even a small law practice required a larger portion of her time and attention that she had anticipated. Fortunately, Allison's secretary Donna Pevey, who had followed her from Johnson & Merritt, was a natural at organization and had taken on the lion's share of back room work at the fledgling law firm. If the firm continued to be successful, Allison knew she would eventually have to hire more staff to relieve Donna of her additional duties.

Wasn't that the goal? Allison asked herself as she signaled her turn from the main highway to the two lane road leading to her home. *Or was it?* The call from Frank Martin had brought forth that troubling question, one that had been creeping around Allison's awareness for some time, and one that Allison had, to date, been pretty good at deflecting. *It's time to take a look at this, my girl* Allison's alter ego intoned. *You can't ignore this itch any longer.* Stepping from her car, Allison heard her children's voices coming from the swimming pool behind the house. The weekend beckoned. Just like a Southern girl from another era, Allison would worry about the troubling questions tomorrow.

CHAPTER THREE

David Jackson whistled driving to work, even though it was Monday and he had a stack of unworked legal files waiting on him at the office.

"Don't forget to make reservations at Nick's for Wednesday night" his wife had reminded David as he left his house that morning. Nick's, a local restaurant that David and Sarah Jackson often frequented, was owned by one of David's best friends in Ft. Charles. Offering French inspired food with a uniquely Southern twist, Nick's provided intimate dining and excellent service, perfect combinations for special evenings like this coming Wednesday.

"It's on my calendar" David had smiled his reply. "Don't forget to line up a sitter."

"Already did" Sarah called to her husband. "Mom's taking the kids for an overnight. We'll have the entire evening to ourselves."

A grin replaced David's whistling as he replayed the morning's conversation. Eighteen months ago he wouldn't have bet even a nickel that he and Sarah would be eagerly anticipating a night celebrating their wedding anniversary. Divorce court would have been a much more realistic prediction. But the suicide of Sarah's father, Ben Johnson, and the subsequent discovery of the man's secret life had been a shocking and surprising game changer in the lives of David and Sarah Jackson. Therapy, both individual in Sarah's case and together as a couple, had played a big part in getting David and Sarah Jackson to where they were now. No doubt about that. But driving to the office David knew that the real reason his marriage had survived was due to his wife's ability to face and accept very painful truths about her father, and in turn, about herself.

Sarah's willingness to be brutally honest with herself had motivated David to do the same. As a result, their lives had changed completely. With Sarah's blessing he had left the safety of an established law firm to open his own practice with Allison. Terrifying and thrilling at the same time, launching Parker & Jackson had definitely been the right move. Not to be outdone, Sarah had taken some of the money she had inherited from her father and opened a design studio, following a dream she had nurtured since her teen years.

"I know it sounds crazy" Sarah had offered when she first shared her idea with her husband. "But I think I'd be good at design, and I want to give it a shot."

"I like the new Sarah" David had replied. "Not afraid to take a chance."

Sarah laughed. "More accurately, not afraid of daddy's disapproval. I think I'll give Dr. Franklin's office a makeover as a thank you for working with us" she replied, referring to the family therapist who had helped them through the emotional minefield that had once described their marriage.

"Don't get carried away" David replied in a teasing tone. "Just give him a good discount. We still have bills to pay."

The crunch of the car's tires interrupted David's reverie as he pulled into the gravel lot adjacent to the offices of Parker & Jackson. A silver Porsche sporting Louisiana plates was parked in the slot closest to the sidewalk. Detouring on his way to the office's rear entrance, David's attempt to garner clues about the car's owner was prevented by the heavily tinted windows blanketing the car.

Using the firm's employee entrance allowed Allison and David to circumvent the firm's waiting area when they arrived at the office after a client or returned from court midday, and out of habit David used that entrance this morning. Neither lawyer regularly scheduled client meetings on Mondays unless circumstances dictated no other option or they were preparing for trial.

"I like to think of Monday mornings as "re-entry time" Allison had explained when she and David first opened their firm. "For some reason, taking those few hours at the beginning of the week to organize and plan makes me much more effective the remaining four and a half days. So, unless I have to be in court, my calendar is blocked off from 8 to noon every Monday." Allison's reasoning had made sense to David, and he had agreed to do the same. The passage of time had proved the benefit of Allison's "re-entry time" in David's work life. Reflecting on their joint habit, David was fairly certain he didn't have any appointments that morning and he didn't think Allison did either.

Tossing his briefcase on a nearby chair, David settled his lanky frame into the leather backed chair that had belonged to his father-in-law. He and Allison had actually argued about having the chair in the office.

"The man tried to kill us. Why in the Hell would you touch anything belonging to him?" Allison had demanded. "It's bad juju."

"The chair didn't try to kill us, Allison" David had retorted. "Besides, don't you think there's some poetic justice in this? It's a great chair, an expensive chair, and it saves me from having to spend the money on a new one."

Allison had reluctantly agreed and eventually more of Ben Johnson's belongings than just the leather desk chair had ended up in David's office. Sarah Jackson did indeed have a flare for design, and David's office had become an eclectic and pleasing mix of antiques and contemporary pieces.

"There's a man here to see you." Donna Pevey walked into David's office and handed him a client intake form. "He said he didn't have an appointment but hoped you would see him anyway."

David glanced at the form. Precise handwriting identified the writer as Jefferson Boudreaux. David recognized the address listed on the form as that of a local bed and breakfast he had represented a few months earlier in a dispute with an unhappy guest. "Any idea what he wants?"

Donna shook her head. "He said he was new in town and you had been recommended to him. Beyond that he refused to say why he needed a lawyer, said he'd prefer to talk privately with you." Motioning towards the paperwork in David's hand Donna added "He left that part of the form blank."

"Well, let's see what he wants" David tossed the intake form on his desk. "Bring him on back and I'll see what I think."

David had barely taken a sip from his morning coffee before the potential client was escorted into his office. Tall, slender, with light auburn hair thinning a bit around the temples, Jefferson Boudreaux looked like a model for *Esquire*. An off-white cashmere sweater was casually draped around his shoulders, a typical preppy contrast to the pink polo shirt and knife sharp khakis adorning Boudreaux's elegant frame. What appeared to be real alligator mocs covered the man's sockless feet, and a gold Rolex graced the wrist of the hand that reached out to shake the one David proffered. *A lefty*, David noted, seeing the watch on the man's right arm.

"Mr. Boudreaux, I'm David Jackson." Introducing himself, David motioned to a chair indicating where the well-dressed man should sit. "What brings you to Parker & Jackson this morning?"

"Thank you for seeing me without an appointment" a cultured voice replied. "I apologize for this irregular request, but time constraints and urgency required this intrusion."

David nodded, encouraging his visitor to continue.

"I was born in Ft. Charles fifty-two years ago. A bastard, the unwanted offspring of Rebecca

Fairchild and Geoffrey Montclair." A tightness appeared around Boudreaux's eyes. "The day I was born my parents sent me to an orphanage over in Texas. Dumped me like last week's garbage." Boudreaux paused, crossing one khaki-clad leg over the other. "I was adopted. Twice. Once by a couple who decided when I was four years old that being parents wasn't what they wanted after all. And then after being in the orphanage for another year, by a family over in Abilene."

David shifted uncomfortably in his chair. This was a sad tale, no doubt about it. Maybe he could refer the guy to Dr. Franklin. It sounded like Jefferson Boudreaux might need a good therapist.

"I empathize with you, Mr. Boudreaux. You certainly had a difficult beginning. But I'm not sure why you've sought me out this morning, or what I can do as a lawyer to assist you."

Unruffled by the slight rebuff, Boudreaux continued. "The Miller family saved me, in all ways that the word can be interpreted. But my salvation was, unfortunately, short lived." Boudreaux retrieved a folded sheet of newsprint from a tan satchel that screamed money, unfolded the faded paper and handed it to David. "When I was fifteen years old our home burned to the ground. I had gone to a baseball game with a friend and decided to stay over at his house for the night. My adoptive parents, my adoptive sister and brother - they were all killed in that fire." Boudreaux paused to return the paper to its leather case. "This time I refused to return to the orphanage. I left town, got a job on one of the off-shore rigs out of Galveston. No one asked how old I was. The only thing the oil riggers wanted was a hard worker."

"I find it difficult to imagine you as a laborer on an oil rig" David's tone implied a modicum of disbelief at the tale he was hearing. The sooner he could get this man out of his office the better.

"You and many others, Mr. Jackson" Boudreaux replied softly "But looks can be deceiving, can't they?"

Enough of the charades David thought. "Mr. Boudreaux, this is a law office. While what you are sharing with me about your early life certainly is heartbreaking, you haven't told me anything that is illegal. Your birth parents may have acted immorally, but there is nothing illegal about giving up a child for adoption. Likewise, as despicable as they were in returning you to the orphanage, the first couple who adopted you didn't break any laws either. If the fire that killed the Millers was arson, the statute of limitations on arson would have expired years ago, although murder charges would remain viable. Is that why you're here Mr. Boudreaux? Do you think the Millers were murdered?"

Jeffrey Boudreaux picked a speck of invisible lint from the crease of his soft cotton pants, flicked it from his fingers, and then inspected his fingernails for any leftover detritus. "No, Mr. Jackson, I do not think my adoptive family was murdered. The Fire Marshal's investigation revealed a plethora of wiring problems in the old house - that fire was just a matter of time. For once Fate was on my side - but for a last minute invitation to stay over at Johnny Mack's house, I would have burned up with everyone else that night." All of Boudreaux's attention fixed upon David Jackson. "No, Mr. Jackson, I relate my life history solely to ensure you will fully understand, and appreciate, my motives in hiring you."

"Why do you want to hire me Mr. Boudreaux?" Time to get this meeting over with David thought behind the words he asked.

Once again ignoring the posed question, Jefferson Boudreaux continued as if no interruption had intervened. "I am sure you are a perceptive man, Mr. Jackson, and you would be correct in assuming that notwithstanding my dire beginnings I have done very well for myself financially. People change, and I soon realized that owning an oil rig was a much better way of making a living rather than working on one. It's been a long road, and not particularly pertinent to my visit to you today, but suffice it to say that I ended up a wealthy man, far removed from the infant who was dumped in that Texas orphanage." Boudreaux rose from his chair and walked to the window. With his back to David, the tall man asked "You're not from around here are you Mr. Jackson?"

Surprised by the change of subject, David gave a startled "No."

"Didn't think so" Boudreaux continued, talking to the window. "You never flinched when I mentioned the name Fairchild. If you'd been born and raised here that name would have gotten an immediate response." Turning away from the window, Boudreaux leaned against the sill. "Rebecca Fairchild died last month. She and my father" Boudreaux's lips curled as if he had eaten something sour "never married, and she didn't have any siblings. According to my sources, she left her entire estate to several charities. No one knows the real numbers for certain, but a year ago my mother broke the Forbes 500 list as one hell of a wealthy woman."

As Boudreaux continued to expound on his birth mother's wealth David racked his brain for the name Fairchild. It sounded familiar, but he was pretty sure he'd never met anyone in Ft. Charles by that name. Then he remembered an article he had seen in the Ft. Charles Gazette a few years back. Something about the old Montague estate being brought back to life by a distant relative. Wasn't the name of the new owner Fairchild?

"Her mother was a Montague." Boudreaux's continuing commentary confirmed David's musing. "Rings a bell now doesn't it?" Boudreaux asked seeing David's attention shift from boredom to interest. "Her maternal grandmother willed the estate here in Calhoun County to my mother maybe twenty, thirty years ago. It sat empty and decrepit until 2009 when my mother renovated the place and moved in with a hand full of servants."

"How do you know all of this, Mr. Boudreaux?" David Jackson wondered just who the man in his office really was. "And again, what do you want me to do for you?"

"I want what is due to me" Jefferson Boudreaux answered in a voice that dripped with ice. "I've done my research, or rather paid to have it done by experts. I'm sure a sufficient amount of money greased enough palms to ensure there was no record of my being handed over to that orphanage. But there was another record. My birth certificate. And it names Rebecca Fairchild as my mother and Geoffrey Montclair as my father. My mother never severed her parental rights, and she didn't disinherit me. As I understand the law, I have an excellent chance of overturning my mother's Will and inheriting her estate in its entirety. That's why I'm here

Mr. Jackson. That's why I want to hire you. Are you game?" Seeing David's hesitation, Boudreaux added "I'll pay double your going hourly rate."

"If I take your case, I'll set a reasonable fee based on the level of difficulty I estimate the case to involve. The current beneficiaries of your mother's bequests will certainly vigorously contest your claim. I've never handled a Will dispute case of this magnitude, and while I am confident of my ability to do so, full disclosure demands that I let you know this upfront." David was intrigued, but wary.

"You have a reputation as a good lawyer, Mr. Jackson. A hard working lawyer and an honest one. That assessment is more important to me than whether or not you have handled one Will dispute case or hundreds." Reaching once again into his leather case, Boudreaux handed David a thick stack of documents. "Please review my case, Mr. Jackson. If, after looking at these documents and the information I've gathered, you don't want to take my case I'll go elsewhere."

David mused. It would probably be easier to get rid of the man by agreeing to his request. "Alright. I'll take a look at what you've got. I may need to do a bit of research before making a decision about taking your case. I'll bill you at the rate of $225 an hour for a preliminary review, and I'll give you a written assessment of your claim even if I decide not to take your case." Seeing Boudreaux's nod of approval David instructed "If you'll wait in the reception area my secretary will bring an initial fee agreement for you to sign. I'll have an answer for you within the week."

CHAPTER FOUR

1981

He stroked his engorged penis with his left hand, a groan escaping from his lips. Moving languidly, no reason to rush such pleasure, the man positioned himself over the prostrate form of the frightened girl. *Just like tying a hog* he thought, admiring his handiwork. Thick rope encircled his captive's wrists and ankles, its straw color now stained with blood from the girl's attempts to free herself. The stain was a nice touch to his diorama. Maybe he should have tied her arms straight above her head instead of splayed open like her legs. Really, he couldn't decide which would be better.

He wouldn't be able to wait much longer. Lowering his body so that his penis lightly touched the girl's face he commanded "Open your mouth". Eyes wide with fear, the girl rolled her head from side to side and strained at her bonds. Forcing the girl's jaw open with a rough hand, the man shoved his throbbing penis into the girl's small mouth. His victim gagged, then whether by reflex or in fear, clamped sharp teeth onto the meaty intruder.

The man's shriek of pain filled the barn as he tried to disengage his member from the torture being inflicted upon it, but like a snapping turtle ensnaring a meal, the girl's jaws simply tightened around the now flaccid weapon. In desperation, the man began to pound the girl's face with his fists. Blood, skin and finally teeth covered the man's chest as the repeated pummeling released the battered penis from its prison. Rage replaced pain as the man ripped away the girl's clothing. *Punish her* instructed the reptilian part of the man's brain. *Punish her.*

The autopsy conducted on the girl's body after it was found determined that blows to her head had caused a massive brain hemorrhage, rendering the girl unconscious and likely unable to process any external stimuli. *Thank you, God*, the young forensic pathologist had murmured. A wooden rod has been jammed so far up the victim's rectum that it had punctured multiple internal organs. He hoped the authorities would soon catch the maniac who had done this.

They did not.

CHAPTER FIVE

Present Day

Toby Trowbridge skimmed the medical examiner's report Andy Dabo had prepared. Hopefully, some of the information contained in the report would be useful in identifying his victim. Andy hadn't had much to go on - dismembered arms and the lower portion of the victim's left leg, foot attached, plus some threads of what appeared to be cloth of some kind imbedded in the skin around the victim's ankle. But modern forensic detection had come a long way since Toby's great-grandfather had entered the field of law enforcement. And, thankfully, Andy Dabo had not hesitated to call in assistance from the state crime lab where there was access to considerably more sophisticated testing than in the labs of the Calhoun County Medical Examiner.

While it had seemed obvious to those at the crime scene that the tornado had done the damage to the victim's body, inaccurate assumptions had more than once been the downfall of an otherwise pristine investigation. Toby noted Dabo's finding from the Precipitin test: the blood found on the victim was human, not animal, establishing that the injuries to the victim had not been made by an animal attack either pre or post mortem. One of the reasons the ME had sent blood samples to the state crime lab was to confirm the victim's sex. Based on microscopic testing, the blood samples revealed the presence of Barr Bodies, establishing with scientific certainty that the victim was female.

Given the dearth of evidence at the crime scene, Toby was both pleased and amazed to have the information at the end of the report. Dabo had been able to type the victim's blood and to pull readable prints from the fingers of both hands. An AB blood type was rare, and Toby hoped that running the prints through AFIS, the national fingerprint database, would return a hit yielding the identity of the poor girl who had died such a terrible death in his county.

"Beth" Toby yelled out his office door to get the attention of his secretary Beth Robinson. "Come here, will you please?"

Two years shy of being an octogenarian, Beth Robinson had worked for the Calhoun County Sheriff's Department for almost sixty years. A legend of her own sort in the county's law enforcement history, Beth Robinson had informed Toby on his first day of work that she knew where all the bodies were buried, both literally and figuratively, and he would do well never to forget that fact. Although Beth had laughed after scaring the new deputy with her pronouncement, the passage of time had convinced Toby that there might actually be some truth in what Beth had said to him all those years ago.

Handing his secretary the attached fingerprint record, Toby offered Beth a grim smile. "Andy pulled good prints off the tornado vic. Let's run these and see if we can get lucky."

Nodding in agreement, Beth replied "That poor girl. It is a girl, right?"

"Yes, the serology testing shows our vic is female. An AB blood type will narrow the field some if needed, but being able to ID her fingerprints would give us a place to start."

"I've seen a lot of crime come through this office, but this is the absolute worst" Beth shuddered. "Creeps me out to think whoever did this may still be around here."

"This is a small county. If the perp is local I think we'll pick up a lead sooner rather than later." Toby began to examine a stack of papers which had taken up a haphazard residence on his desk. "In the meantime, run the prints. Maybe we'll get lucky."

Administrative tasks consumed Toby's attention while he waited to hear the results of the AFIS search. *Thank God for the AFIS system,* Toby thought, reflecting on what his father and grandfather could have done with such easily accessible data. Launched in July, 1999, AFIS was the largest criminal database in the world. Prior to its implementation, the processing of fingerprints was a time-consuming, manually intensive process which could take as long as weeks or months to produce identification. AFIS stored fingerprints from criminals, arrested as well as convicted, plus the prints of any person who had either served in the military or worked for the Federal government. Not only could AFIS produce results within 24 hours and usually much faster than that, the system also provided corresponding mug shots, scars and tattoo photos, plus physical characteristics like height, eye and hair color.

"Must be your lucky day" Beth announced as she hurried into Toby's office. "Your vic had a record. And a picture."

Taking the proffered printout from his secretary, Toby eagerly scanned the information AFIS had provided. Marilee Wingo was a prostitute. Arrested on a solicitation charge in New Orleans in 2013, Wingo had served six months at the Orleans Parish penal farm.

"Way too young" Toby commented, automatically doing the math on the girl's date of birth. "Barely eighteen when she did time on the solicitation charge. She'd have been twenty next month."

"Probably been turning tricks for a while." Beth had read the AFIS report before handing it to her boss. "Born in Amarillo, no info on family, no missing person report. Whatever family she had was more than likely glad to see her go."

"That's cold, Beth, even for you" Toby reprimanded his secretary. But Beth was probably right. Too many runaways ended up selling their bodies in order to survive. "But how did she end up in a shack in Tom Spencer's field?"

"Hitchhiking?" Beth offered a theory.

"Maybe." Toby reflected. "But Tom's property is a couple of miles from the interstate. Seems an odd place to pick unless the perp already knew about that shed." The girl's identity was helpful, especially having her mug shot from the New Orleans' arrest, but Toby knew it wasn't nearly enough information. "I think I'll get Frank Martin to check out the truck stops off I-20, say between Birmingham and Vicksburg, Mississippi. Show our vic's picture around. Maybe someone will remember her."

CHAPTER SIX

Kilby Correctional Facility was located on 154 acres just outside Montgomery, Alabama in an unincorporated community known as Mt. Meigs. Opened in 1969, Kilby was one of the state's maximum security prisons. Escape from Kilby was prevented by a double fence of 18-foot tall chain link mesh topped with razor wire, with armed guards manning five tall towers overlooking the prison yard. In the unlikely event that an inmate made it past those deterrents, Kilby's well-trained dog tracking system generally caught and returned the escapee in short order.

All prisoners entering the Alabama prison system started their incarceration at Kilby where they were evaluated, classified and then generally assigned to other correctional facilities within the state. A smaller portion, those who had committed the crimes that might put them at risk in larger prisons, remained at Kilby. The Alabama Department of Corrections, aware of the negative publicity the state had suffered over the years, tried hard to live up to its mission statement of "providing rehabilitative programs for convicted felons in a safe, secure and humane environment". Thus, during a stay at Kilby prisoners were encouraged to take advantage of the various inmate programs offered such as anger management, sex offenders therapy, and 12-step alcohol and drug counseling. In addition, for many inmates, incarceration at Kilby meant access to benefits such as medical, dental and mental health treatment that had previously been beyond their reach. All in all, other than being deprived of their freedom, the majority of the inmates at Kilby enjoyed a standard of living far superior to the one they had known on the outside.

Allison pondered the information she had gathered on Kilby. She would see the lock-down facility for herself when she visited her brother Rice tomorrow. Child killers never fared well in prison. In the hierarchy of incarcerated criminals, the lowest and most despised placement was saved for pedophiles and child killers. Men or women who had committed those crimes often never survived inside.

Deemed scum by their fellow prisoners, more than a few exited the system in a black body bag, the recipient of a shiv or beating by persons unknown. Would Rice be targeted, even though he had not intended to kill his children?

Once again, Allison was grateful for her husband Jim's influence. Every defendant received a fair trial in her husband's courtroom. But if a guilty verdict was returned by the jury, it was well known that Judge Kaufman tended to impose tough sentences, particularly where a violent crime had been committed. Fifteen years her senior, Allison's husband had been on the bench for over twenty years, consistently re-elected by citizens who appreciated a law and order judge. Judge Kaufman's respect for the penal system had not gone unnoticed by either law enforcement or the staff of the state's correctional institutions. Thus, Jim's call to Kilby's warden had ensured heightened security for Rice, at least temporarily. Allison wasn't sure about the long term.

"You got a minute?" David Jackson's inquiry interrupted Allison's reverie. "I've been asked to take a Will contest, and I want to get your thoughts on whether or not to accept the matter."

"Since when do we turn away business?" Allison's raised eyebrows emphasized her reply.

Taking Allison's question as an invitation to enter her office, David headed for the green corduroy sofa which hugged the back wall. "If I had a sofa in my office I'd be in trouble" he observed, making himself comfortable by arranging the sofa's decorative pillows behind his back.

"No reason to have a boring, sterile office" Allison replied. "Besides, that sofa has done double duty more than once as a napping spot for Charlotte and Mack." A wistful smile turned up the corners of Allison's mouth. "You have to admit, being able to bring our children to the office when we need to for personal reasons has been an unsuspected plus of having our own firm. But enough of that" Allison paused to take a sip of coffee. "What's the problem with taking a Will contest case?"

"It's not the case, per se" David replied, lapsing into legal lingo. "A Will contest is like any other litigation matter. Get the facts, do some discovery, take depositions, go to trial if I can't settle the claim, which by the way is doubtful with this case given the amount of money allegedly at stake. A settlement, that is."

Allison was puzzled. "Sounds like the case itself isn't the issue. What's the problem?"

David reached for the yellow legal pad lying on the sofa next to him and flipped through a couple of pages. "It's what I've discovered, or rather haven't discovered, about the potential client that is bothering me.

David's comment immediately grabbed Allison's attention. Prior to the McNair case eighteen months earlier, Allison would have dismissed David's gut feeling without a second thought. But following her own gut feelings about events surrounding the McNair case had not only proved Allison correct about that case, but haphazardly following those feelings had almost cost her, her husband and David their lives. That lesson well learned now caused Allison to lay aside her pen and direct her full attention to her partner.

"Tell me more" she instructed.

"You know that big estate out on the highway towards Montgomery?" David asked.

"The old Montague place?" Allison had a vague recollection of a decrepit house covered in ivy and kudzu." "Somebody went in there and cleaned that place up a while back, didn't they?"

"Yes. A very wealthy woman named Rebecca Fairchild. Old lady Montague was a relative. Bequeathed the house to the Fairchild woman. Is this ringing any bells yet?"

Allison turned to her computer and typed in a brief search command. "Wow" she exclaimed, skimming the search results. "Rebecca Fairchild was a very wealthy woman. Looks like she left an estate valued in the billions." Allison gave her partner a bewildered look. "I've never heard much about the woman. How could someone like this be living right down the road and it not be news in Ft. Charles?"

"I have no idea." David shrugged his shoulders. "But Rebecca Fairchild's billion dollar estate will be the target of the Will contest case if I take on Mr. Boudreaux as a client."

"Well, that could make for a nice payday for the firm" Allison grinned.

"I know," David agreed "but I don't want a potential big fee to override caution. I've got some questions about Jefferson Boudreaux that make me hesitant to take his case. On the other hand, if I don't take the case he'll just hire someone else, and we miss out on what is likely the biggest fee we might ever get."

"What worries you about this Boudreaux guy?" Allison asked. She was curious about David's reluctance. A Will contest could be messy, but it was still just a civil matter – no killers lurking around the corner – and weird client or not, Allison was surprised that David was debating whether to take on the matter.

"That's the problem" Chagrin covered David's face. "There's nothing really definitive that I can point to. He gave me a large retainer simply to review his case. I had Donna check with the bank and the check's good. Boudreaux listed The Old Fort Inn as his current residence so I called up Ed

Mitchum to see what he thought about the guy. Ed said Boudreaux had been in town about 10 days, was gone during the day, had paid cash up front for a month's stay, and was polite to the other guests. Ed said he wished he had more guests like him."

"How'd Boudreaux find our firm?" Although the United States Supreme Court had given its blessing on attorney advertising in 1977, Allison had always found the notion of professional advertising rather tacky. Thirty years later, many attorneys had taken the ruling by the Supremes as a license to inundate the public with television and billboard ads that had, in Allison's opinion, given the legal profession the credibility of a county fair carney. "One call, that's all" had become a licensed trademark of at least two lawyers in Southern states, promising clients a big payout, but the absolute worst piece of lawyer advertising Allison had ever seen was the gigantic billboard on the I-20 loop around Birmingham. Allison shuddered remembering the assault on her eyes the first time she saw the large solicitation – a blond-headed woman of color in a business suit proclaiming in large letters above an 800 number "Your sister, in law". Determined to keep her firm's advertising to a minimum, Parker & Jackson paid for a simple ad in the Ft. Charles telephone directory listing the firm as providing 'general legal services'. Even the firm's website wore a minimalist brand. Reputation and referral were Allison's preferred methods of obtaining business.

"Boudreaux told me Ed had given him my name" David replied. "Ed confirmed the same story. Said Boudreaux asked him for the name of a good lawyer, and Ed gave him mine."

"So, Boudreaux seems like an ok guy, on the up-and-up." Allison observed. "I haven't heard any reason not to take the case. Besides, you've only committed to review his case. Do that, and make a decision about going further after you've finished the preliminary evaluation."

David flicked his pen between his fingers, contemplating his partner's suggestion. "Guess you're right. I'll take a look at Boudreaux's claim, review the documents he's given me, and see how I feel. Maybe I just got up on the wrong side of the bed today." David's left knee made a popping sound as he stood to leave. Too many years on the basketball court he thought, favoring the knee as he headed for the door. Stopping, David remembered the other reason he had come to see Allison. "Hey, aren't you going to see Rice tomorrow?"

"Yes" Allison replied shutting down her office computer and gathering her purse. "I'm heading over to the nursing home now to check on Mary Louise, then home for an early dinner with Jim and the children. Tomorrow will be long day, and I want to get in some family time before I go."

"Still can't believe Rice accepted that plea deal." David recalled the events of the preceding year. Rice Parker had been charged with first degree murder in the deaths of his three children, with an added attempted first degree murder charge for Rice's intended victim, his wife Mary Louise.

"I know." Allison replied. "Jason Brownlow finally convinced Rice that he was most likely looking at the electric chair if he didn't make a deal before trial." The arguments between Rice and his criminal defense lawyer had been heated. "But I think a lot of what changed Rice's mind was the time he spent in rehab over in Jackson. Rice told me dying was the easy way out. That he had a lifetime of amends to make, and prison was one way to start."

"That doesn't sound like the Rice I know" David replied. "But miracles never cease, do they?"

Giving David a gentle shove through the open doorway, Allison flicked the office light to its off position and followed him into the hallway. "I just hope the next miracle keeps Rice alive in prison."

CHAPTER SEVEN

A shiver ran up Allison's spine as she heard the "thunk" of the heavy steel door behind her. Rationally she knew she could leave Kilby any time she wanted. Still, the pat down by the guards, the rifling of her purse and briefcase, and the unsmiling demeanor of the guard who had directed her to the private room where she would meet with her brother had served to put her a bit on edge.

From time to time, as part of a probation order, her husband would order a juvenile offender to take a "tour" of one of the state's correctional facilities. "It's an eye opener for some of them" Jim had once remarked when he and Allison were discussing a gang shooting that had made the news. "If a dose of prison reality keeps just one of those kids from a life of crime, it's worth the time and expense it costs the state to put together those trips."

Waiting for Rice to be brought from his cell, Allison wondered if something as simple as a prison tour as a teen would have deterred her brother from the actions that had resulted in three life sentences. Probably not, she thought. Too many years of their father Matthew protecting Rice from the consequences of his bad decisions had lulled Rice into a false sense of entitlement. Until the unthinkable had occurred.

"Hey Sis." The light tenor of Rice's voice belied his tired and drawn face. "Thanks for coming."

A uniformed guard standing behind Rice nodded at Allison. "Visiting's limited to thirty minutes. Knock on the door if you're finished before then."

"You've lost weight" Allison observed as her brother pulled out a straight-backed metal chair and gingerly lowered his body to a seated position. "And you're hurt. What happened?"

A tight smile barely raised the corners of Rice's mouth. "My mouth is what happened." Seeing Allison's raised eyebrows, he continued. "Don't look so surprised. I may be a slow learner, but eventually even I can figure out cause and effect."

"Have you been to the infirmary?" Leaning towards her brother, Allison carefully turned Rice's face to examine a fading purplish and yellow bruise. "I'm going to talk to the warden about this."

"No, Allison." Rice jerked his head from his sister's grasp. "I have to handle this myself."

Allison stared at the man sitting across the table. Was this her brother? "Rice, I'm serious. How did this happen? You're supposed to be in a protected cell."

"I told the warden I didn't want any special treatment. I'm in the general population now." Rice reached for Allison's hand. "I can't change the past. I know that. But I need to live with the consequences of my actions, even if that means getting beat up in prison." Releasing Allison's hand, Rice leaned back in his chair and smiled. "It only hurts when I chew."

Shaking her head at Rice's attempt at humor, Allison considered the importance of her brother's words. No doubt about it, six months in residential drug rehab had wrought a world of change in her brother. Not only had Rice agreed to the plea bargain brokered by his criminal lawyer - three consecutive life terms in exchange for the state not seeking the death penalty at trial – Rice's honest display of remorse at his sentencing had convinced everyone in the courtroom, including the judge, that a different Rice Parker would be entering the state's prison system.

All of this and more passed through Allison's consciousness as she studied the man still seated across the table. Gone was his thick blond hair, shaved into the prison buzz cut required of new inmates. A bright orange jumpsuit hung on a body that had lost close to forty pounds since Rice's incarceration months earlier. For a man who had valued appearances and nice clothes, Allison thought, Rice seemed remarkably content in prison attire. And, she realized, absent the bruised face Rice looked a lot healthier than she had seen him in a very long time.

"How are you spending your time, Rice?" Allison asked. "Have you been assigned a job?"

"I work five days a week in the prison library" her brother replied "and I attend AA meetings as often as I can. Usually 3 or 4 a week. It helps."

"That's made a difference, hasn't it?" Allison asked, referring to the Alcoholics Anonymous meetings held at the prison.

"It's given me a reason to live" Rice replied quietly. "How's Mary Louise" he asked, changing the subject.

A sad smile prefaced Allison's response. "About the same. She's awake, but she doesn't talk and the doctors don't think she's really aware of her surroundings." Rice's wife Mary Louise had survived the fiery car crash that had killed their children. Or rather, Mary Louise's body had survived, although badly scarred from extensive burns over fifty percent of her body. "She's well taken care of, Rice." Allison continued. "And frankly, it's a blessing she doesn't know about the children."

Allison saw a tear silently slide down her brother's hollow cheek. "I appreciate you coming to see me, Allison" her brother answered, wiping the wetness from his face as he moved towards the steel door at the side of the small room. "More than you can know."

"Visit over?" a guard asked in response to Rice's knock. Showing his hands to the guard, Rice turned back to Allison as he stepped into the hallway. "Love you, sis."

"I love you too" Allison responded, surprising herself by the truth of the words she had just uttered. "I'll see you in a couple of weeks."

CHAPTER EIGHT

T he green exit sign displayed the logo for a Pilot Flying J truck stop just a mile down the road. Signaling his shift to the interstate slow lane, Frank Martin tried unsuccessfully to relieve the knot in his lower back by repositioning his large frame in the undersized driver's seat of his truck's cluttered cab. As much as he hated to spend the money, the excursion that Frank had undertaken for Sheriff Trowbridge had convinced him of one thing. He was going to buy the biggest damn truck he could find as soon as he got back to Ft. Charles. One with cushioned leather seats, reinforced springs, cruise control and every other freaking upgrade he could afford.

The packed parking lot of Pilot Flying J was no surprise. The largest purveyor of over-the-road diesel fuel in the United States, the Tennessee-based truck stops were Frank's number one choice for interstate pit stops. In addition to servicing commercial long-haul rigs, the clean restrooms, good food and overall safety offered by the successful chain appealed to the average recreational traveler, a fact demonstrated by the number of family cars parked in the non-trucker area. Frank pulled next to a white SUV with Arkansas plates, turned off the motor, and eased his stiff body out of the mobile torture chamber that had been his prison for the past four hours.

"Shit!" Frank jumped involuntarily as his ears were assaulted by a barrage of fierce barking to his immediate left. A quick glance inside the white SUV identified the source of apparent canine anger. Shaking his head, Frank left the teeny white fluff to vent its frustration through the two inch opening the little hellion's master had left in the passenger window. Noting the pleasant drop in temperature as he stepped from the heated asphalt lot into the air conditioned comfort of the truck stop's interior, Frank figured the dog in the SUV was just pissed about being left in a hot car.

"'Scuse me, miss," Frank leaned on the checkout counter nearest the front of the store. "There's a dog in some distress out there in that white SUV with Arkansas plates. Y'all got any kind of public announcement system in here?"

"Yep. It's called a loud voice." Dressed in jeans and a t-shirt which proclaimed the wearer's loyalty to a band Frank had never heard of, the young attendant nimbly jumped to the top of the stool that had minutes before cradled her posterior and hollered "Hey! Whoever's got that white SUV out there, your dog is dying."

"Well, that worked" Frank observed as a woman holding the hand of a crying five or six year old rushed to the parking lot. "Just don't know what people are thinking, leaving animals in a hot car like that." Frank addressed his comments to the dog's savior.

"They don't" the girl replied. "Think" she added seeing Frank's hesitation. "Anything else I can do for you?"

Frank pulled Marilee Wingo's picture from his jacket. "You ever see this girl around here?"

Suspicion replaced the girl's friendly demeanor. "You a cop?"

"P.I." Frank replied.

"Why you lookin' for her?" the girl's eyes narrowed as she looked more closely at Frank. "She in some sort of trouble?"

Frank returned the picture to the inside of his jacket. "She was. Now she's dead. You know her?"

A sharp intake of breath preceded the clerk's nervous glance towards the back of the store. "I can't talk to you here."

"I'll wait" Frank replied softly, his curiosity on high alert. "Where can I meet you?"

"There's a diner next exit west. I'm off at 7:00."

"I'll be there" Frank turned to leave, then stopped. "What's your name?"

"Francine Turner" the girl replied. "Marilee's my cousin."

⊨⊨ ⊨⊨

Frank Martin had waited three hours for Francine Turner to show up at the diner. *Should have gotten her cell number* he chastised himself. At 10:30 Frank decided to backtrack. Maybe someone on the next shift at the truck stop could tell him where Francine lived.

By the time Frank had driven back the ten miles to the correct exit the clock on the truck's dash glowed 11:15. Even if he could get Francine's address Frank wondered about the wisdom of showing up at her house close to midnight.

The parking lot of the Flying J was half full on the commercial trucker side, but empty on the side reserved for regular folk. Frank figured the less people in the store the better chance he had of getting someone to share information with him.

Entering the door he had exited some hours earlier, Frank quickly observed he was alone in the retail side of the store. A young man who didn't look old enough to be legal lounged on the front check-out counter, elbows supporting his skinny body, cigarette hanging from his lips, and eyes locked on the glossy contents of a magazine which was spread over the glass top of a display case filled with candy.

"Harummp" Frank cleared his throat. "Got a minute?"

The object of Frank's question raised his head just high enough to cast bored eyes Frank's way. "What cha' need?" he asked, the teen's reply garbled by the wad of gum he continued to smack.

"I had a date with Francine after she got off her shift" Frank improvised. "We were meeting down at Nathan's Café around 7:30 but she never showed."

"Yeh?" Counter Boy replied. "What do 'ya want me to do about it? I ain't Francine's keeper." Returning his attention to what Frank had determined was a graphic sex rag, Counter Boy laughed. "You don't really think I believe Francine had a date with an old man like you, do you?"

Snatching Counter Boy's greasy hair in his fist, Frank jerked the teen's head to attention. "I don't give a flying fuck what you believe, you little shit." Frank released his prisoner and wiped his hand on his jeans. A grim smile claimed Frank's face. "Let's start over" he told the teen.

A flush of red crept up Counter Boy's neck, settling uncomfortably on the teen's pockmarked face. "That hurt" came a sullen reply.

"Nothing like it can" Frank smiled in response. Pulling a twenty dollar bill from his wallet Frank pushed the bill across the counter. "But like I said. Let's start over."

The twenty was gone in a flash. "What do you want?" the gum clogged mouth replied.

"I need Francine's home address" Frank pulled out a small notepad and looked questioningly at Counter Boy.

"She stays out Rt. 4, two miles west of here. White frame house. Turner on the mailbox." Counter Boy reached a grubby hand to rub his head. "You like to have pulled my hair out" he complained.

"Learn to respect your elders" Frank advised as he pulled out the picture of Marilee Wingo that he had shown to Francine a few hours earlier. "You know Francine's cousin?"

The bravado that had continued to reside on Counter Boy's face suddenly vanished, replaced by a look of fear. "Who are you, man?"

"Not the cops" Frank replied. "You know this girl?" A slight nod gave Frank an affirmative response. "When did you last see her?"

"That's worth more than twenty bucks." Counter Boy's response was barely audible.

Frank pushed another twenty across the counter-top. "When?" he asked again.

"Couple of days ago." Counter Boy was nervous, and Frank thought he knew why.

"Was she turning tricks out of this place?" Frank asked softly. "I know that's her trade. Not trying to bust her. Just trying to get some information from her." Frank didn't see any reason to tell Counter Boy that Marilee Wingo was dead.

Counter Boy pushed the twenty back towards Frank. "This ain't much of a job, mister, but I can't lose it. We're done talking."

Pulling out of the parking lot Frank noticed a couple of women leaning against the door leading to the trucker's lounge area inside the truck stop, their bodies gently illuminated by the neon lighting over the entrance to the restricted area. Frank debated whether he should stop to talk to them, show Marilee's picture, see what they might say or reveal, but a niggling feeling in Frank's gut told him that he needed to check on Francine.

Twenty minutes later, Frank's headlights bounced off silver lettering which identified 'Turner' as the recipient of mail deposited in the rectangular metal box leaning haphazardly on the side of the road. Pulling onto a grass shoulder, Frank cut the truck's engine and removed a pair of binoculars from beneath his seat. The wooden farm house was set back a good way from the narrow asphalt highway. Although now almost 1:00 in the morning, light blazed through the home's front windows. *Not good*, the warning flashed in Frank's mind. Frank exchanged the field glasses for his Glock and opened the car door.

Gravel crunched under Frank's weight as he neared the house despite his attempts at a stealthy approach. The home's front windows were open, thin curtains wafting gently in a light breeze, filtered light exposing a faded pattern against a white background. Frank figured either a window or door in the back of the house must be open causing the cross breeze. A few feet from the house Frank stopped and listened intently. An owl hooted, its location close by, but no human noise broke the normal night sounds of the rural area.

Creeping as quietly as possible Frank climbed the three steps on the front porch and moved towards the closest open window. Frank pressed his body against the home's wooden exterior and gathered a stilling breath. *No time like the present* he lectured, forcing himself to look inside the window. At first nothing seemed out of order. All the lights were on, but other than that the room seemed merely to lack inhabitants. Then Frank noticed a dark puddle on the floor near the corner of the sofa. And the fingers that were barely visible, touching the glistening liquid. *Fuck* Frank cussed. Retrieving his cell phone from his jacket pocket, Frank punched in 911.

Two hours later, sitting in the bullpen at the Lauderdale County, Mississippi Sheriff's office, the Deputy who had responded to Frank's 911 call handed Frank a cup of what Frank hoped was fresh and not day old coffee.

"Ran your P.I.license Mr. Martin. Talked to Sheriff Trowbridge, too." Seeing Frank's look of surprise the Deputy explained. "Just making sure you are who you said you are. You know the routine."

"Yeh, I do" Frank admitted grudgingly.

"Sheriff Trowbridge told me you were trying to track down information on a vic. What were you doing out at Francine Turner's house at 1:00 in the morning?"

"I've been canvassing the truck stops along I-20," Frank took a sip of his coffee. It wasn't bad. "When I showed the picture to Francine Turner she told me our vic, Marilee Wingo, was her cousin. Francine was supposed to meet me after she got off work. She never showed."

"So how'd you end up at her house?" the Deputy inquired.

"I got worried. Went back to the truck stop and one of the employees gave me her home address." The Deputy didn't need to know the particulars of how he had actually obtained Francine's address.

"Helpful staff, huh?" The Deputy tossed a doubtful look Frank's way.

"Yeh, surprised me too" Frank bluffed. He didn't know this Deputy, the Sheriff or where any of their loyalties lay. If Flying J had any hinky stuff going on, it was a big enough enterprise to pay off the local constabulary to look the other way. Frank wasn't giving up any information voluntarily. "I'd appreciate it if you'd keep me and Sheriff Trowbridge in the loop if you get any leads on who killed Francine."

"You think that's related to your murder investigation over in Ft. Charles?" the Deputy probed.

"Can't see how" Frank lied, trying to look as nonchalant as possible. "Still, I'm sure Sheriff Trowbridge would appreciate the professional courtesy."

The Deputy eyed Frank thoughtfully. "Sure" he nodded, "I'll pass on the request to Sheriff Gilbert."

Shaking hands with the Deputy, Frank headed towards his truck. Even though he'd been up almost twenty-four hours he was too keyed up to drive. Someone had slit Francine Turner's throat ear to ear. Frank didn't believe in coincidences. Just a few hours after he had shown Francine Turner a picture of Marilee Wingo, a killer had silenced the young woman. Driving towards Ft. Charles, Frank felt the weight of Francine's death on his conscience. The investigation Toby had hired him to conduct had just become personal.

CHAPTER NINE

Yawning in an attempt to banish the sleep hang-over that was the unfortunate side effect when-ever she allowed herself more than six or seven hours of sleep, Allison followed the smell of cooking bacon.

"Morning, Babe." Jim Kaufman smiled at his wife, then returned his attention to contents of the heavy cast iron skillet resting on the largest eye of the stainless steel monster in front of him. A mutual love of cooking, coupled with their desire for a com-mercial grade stove and refrigerator, had resulted in a trip to Greenwood, Mississippi during the kitchen's remodel a few years earlier.

Located in the middle of the Mississippi Delta, the once wealthy plantation town of Greenwood, Mississippi had suffered an economic decline in the

1960's as the town found itself in the cross hairs of Civil Rights activists and those who preferred the status quo. Over the next couple of decades many businesses closed and the town took on a sort of seen-better-days façade.

In 1989, however, things began to look up for the small town. Fred Carl, Jr., hometown boy, founder and CEO of Viking Range relocated his company's corporate offices and production unit to Greenwood. In addition to offering jobs to locals, Viking's presence and subsequent expansion into the hotel and spa business resulted in an unexpected boon. Greenwood, Mississippi became a tourist destination. The Alluvian, a high end boutique hotel, was opened as a Viking subsidiary in 2003 followed in 2005 by a spa, cooking school and bakery. The monstrous yet sleek six-eyed gas range which currently hosted a cast iron skillet full of sizzling bacon had been but one of the Viking appliances which had found its way to the farm outside Ft. Charles.

Allison grinned as she watched her husband cook. "You making pancakes too?"

"Of course" Jim replied. "What would Saturday morning be without pancakes. Charlotte and Mack ate the first batch an hour ago. They're up in the game room watching cartoons."

Fifteen minutes later, two short stacks of pancakes with blueberry syrup and a side of bacon had disappeared from Allison's plate. "Oh my lord" she groaned, leaning back in her chair and patting her belly. "I'll have to do two spin classes Monday in penance for this meal."

"Enjoy it while you can" Jim replied. "Eating plain Greek yogurt for breakfast is the pits."

"I know." Allison leaned across the table and kissed her husband. "But I appreciate you changing your diet. One stent is enough."

"Your turn will come" her husband laughed. "But seriously, you said last night you had something you wanted to run by me. What's up?"

"I got a call from Frank Martin about a week ago. Sherriff Trowbridge hired Frank to help on the murder investigation of that woman found out at Tom Spencer's place."

"That was a nasty piece of business" Jim reflected. "I heard down at the courthouse that they ID'ed her based on fingerprints. Why's Frank involved?"

"Toby is still short staffed because of losing a deputy last year when Lucien Pounder moved to Charlotte. He's got Frank doing out-of-town leg work on the theory that the woman might have been picked up by her murderer while she was hitchhiking. Frank's been showing her picture around truck stops on I-20" Allison explained.

"Sounds reasonable." Jim poured another cup of coffee. "Want a refill?"

Shaking her head, Allison declined the offer. "Anyway, Frank has called me twice now. Once before he went on the road, and then late yesterday. He wants me to help him on this investigation."

"Doing what?" Jim was curious.

"Well, right now he just wants me to agree he can use me as a sounding board." Allison took a sip from Jim's coffee.

"I thought you didn't want any?" Jim moved his cup beyond Allison's reach.

"Just a sip. That's not wanting more." Allison explained. "Anyway, I told Frank yesterday I'd listen to what he'd discovered, but there were no guarantees I'd have the time to do more than that. David Jackson's taken a Will contest case that's going to keep him busy, and I've agreed to cover some of his pending hearings."

"Okay." Jim nodded. "Why the need to run this by me?"

Pushing her chair from the kitchen table, Allison walked to the white farm sink and poured a glass of water from the tap, keeping her back and her face away from her husband. Jim watched silently. He knew his wife. Something was bothering Allison and she was trying to decide what and how much to share. A minute or so passed before Allison lowered the now empty glass to the counter and turned to answer her husband.

"Leaving Johnson & Merritt was the right thing to do. I think opening my firm with David was too. We've got plenty of business, so much in fact that we really need to add another attorney and another secretary." Allison hesitated.

"But" Jim offered.

"I'm bored." Allison shrugged her shoulders. "It's crazy to say that" she acknowledged, returning to her seat and facing her husband. "Even though I nearly got both of us killed, taking on the McNair investigation was energizing and exciting. This week, thinking over Frank's request that I join him on this murder investigation, I've come to realize just how much I enjoyed" *yes, that's the right word Allison realized - enjoyed* "solving that mystery."

"And you want to get involved in this one, too. Is that right?" Jim asked even though he knew the answer.

"Yes" Allison replied. "I do. I don't know where it will lead, or how it will affect Parker & Jackson. I'll have to let David know, of course, but I wanted to get your input on this first. Have I lost my mind?"

"Just be careful, Babe" Jim cautioned. "A cat may have nine lives but I'm pretty sure humans don't. Talk to me before you do anything other than review case files and Frank's reports." Jim gave Allison a stern look. "Promise?"

"Promise" she replied. "I promise."

CHAPTER TEN

Monday morning, substituting a cold Coke Zero for a cup of coffee, Allison exited her firm by the back door and walked the twenty feet to the back entrance to Frank Martin's office.

"Morning, Allison" Frank grinned, opening the door in response to Allison's knock. "I've got donuts in the conference room, and a fresh pot of coffee."

"Don't tempt me" Allison laughed, following Frank down the hall. "I'm trying to be good. I've even switched caffeine sources."

"Not me" Frank replied, grabbing a chocolate covered donut from the box on the conference room table. "Besides" he continued, taking a bite of the sugared confection, "this is the only sugar I get anymore."

Allison smiled, ignoring Frank's innuendo. "So, what's up with the murder investigation?"

Frank slid a typed report across the table. "We've got more than one murder. Take a look."

Concentrating on the document in front of her, Allison studied the report from the Lauderdale County Sheriff's office. Noting Frank's name and that of a Sheriff Gilbert at the bottom of the report, Allison gave Frank a puzzled look. "Who is Francine Turner?"

Two more chocolate donuts disappeared as Frank related his meeting at the Flying J with Francine Turner. "When she didn't show at the diner I went back to the truck stop and convinced one of her co-workers to give me Francine's home address."

"Humm" Allison replied as Frank stopped to wash down the remains of his third donut with a sip of coffee. "Bet my definition of 'convinced' is a bit different from yours."

"Whatever" Frank dismissed Allison's comment with a wave of his hand. "By the time I got to Francine Turner's house she was dead. I'm waiting to hear from Lauderdale County on a time of death."

"You don't think this is a coincidence, do you?" Allison looked at Frank.

"Not in a million years. When I showed Francine our vic's picture the first thing she asked me was if I was a cop."

"Well, that makes sense" Allison interrupted. "We know Marilee Wingo had a prior for prostitution. There's a high probability Marilee was still in the trade and Francine knew it."

"It was more than that" Frank frowned. "You'd have had to be there, read Francine's body language. She was worried." Frank hesitated. "No, it was more than that. Francine was afraid. I should have waited for her at the truck stop."

"You aren't responsible for Francine Turner's murder." Allison laid a gentle hand on Frank's arm. "Hindsight is 20-20. You know that" she admonished. "You might have gotten yourself killed, too." Allison sat silently, watching Frank process her words.

"Something was going on at that truck stop" Frank drummed his fingers on the tabletop. "Whatever it was, Francine Turner knew enough about it to get herself killed for talking to me."

"You said no one was even near y'all when you and Francine were talking" Allison observed. "That means either Francine mentioned the conversation to someone she shouldn't have, or someone who saw y'all talking interrogated her about it before she left work."

"That's my thinking, too" Frank replied. "And whatever happened, she ending up at her house instead of meeting me at the diner like we had planned. I'm taking a closer look at that truck stop. Want to go for a ride?"

"I've got to take a pass on that offer" Allison hated to say. "I promised Jim I'd only review files, not actually do any field work."

Frank grunted his understanding. "Sounds like something the Judge would ask. I don't think he's gotten over your last near-death experience."

"Hell, Frank" Allison retorted, "I haven't gotten over that either. Besides, you don't need me for a simple field trip." Allison tossed her empty soda can in the trash and headed for the door. "Let me know when you've got some reports for me. In the meantime, I've got plenty of work needing attention at my office."

CHAPTER ELEVEN

1998

He had worked hard the past seventeen years. Physical labor that nearly killed him, hours sweating under a brutal sun, long days spent on the water, skin turning the texture of tanned leather, rough from the lash of salt water.

But he was smart, and he had known from the beginning that better things awaited him. Education, he realized, would be necessary, so he had begun correspondence courses – basic stuff at first, then a course in economics, later one in finance, and finally advanced business courses. And he watched people. People who had what he wanted. He noticed they talked differently, polished he thought, so he ordered elocution tapes and gradually lost the

Texas twang of his youth. He observed the way they dressed – conservative, understated – and slowly, as his pay permitted, he replaced Walmart with Belk. Eventually, a combination of hard work, luck and a geographic change had produced a fine return. Five years earlier, new identity fully integrated, he had obtained an office job with LaPierre Drilling, a medium sized off-shore drilling operation in Morgan City, Louisiana. No one at LaPierre Drilling questioned his resume, taking at face value the degree he had listed from a bogus college in west Texas. He had taken a chance, a carefully calculated risk, but he sounded and acted like the educated man he presented himself to be. All that had mattered to Charles LaPierre, the sole owner of LaPierre Drilling, was that his new employee earned the money he was being paid.

He had only been on the job for two weeks when Cynthia LaPierre came home from LSU for the summer after her first year in college. The apple of her daddy's eye, Cynthia LaPierre was an only child, a beautiful replica of the mother who had died giving birth to Charles LaPierre's sole progeny. There was never a doubt in his mind. She would be his.

He had not rushed his quarry. When Cynthia returned to Baton Rouge for her sophomore year, he had respectfully asked if he could write to her. She had agreed. At Christmas he had only given her a Christmas card. Nothing improper. Their correspondence continued, and by the next summer he felt emboldened enough to ask Cynthia to have dinner with him one evening.

He took his time, played the gentleman, and gradually let his intentions be known. By the time he offered the engagement ring with a small diamond to Cynthia the day after her graduation from LSU, he had ingratiated himself not only to Cynthia but to Charles LaPierre as well. In honor of his daughter's engagement, and in a display of largess, Charles LaPierre had promoted his daughter's fiancee' to vice president of LaPierre Drilling. "You're one of us now, son" the man had declared.

He smiled, remembering. It had been a long con, but a very successful one. Wiping his hands on faded jeans which hung loosely on his slender frame, he ground out the half smoked Marlboro with his boot and pushed through the underbrush to the dilapidated cabin. The smell of feces hit him as he opened the rickety door. He'd need to wash her down before he finished. Too bad this one had been so scared. When he'd spotted her at the Dollar General over in Houma she'd been arguing with another girl and he liked the spunk she had displayed. When he invited her for a drive she'd willingly hopped in his car, but her spunk had been all for show. All she'd done since she woke up chained in the cabin was cry and beg. The ones that fought to the end were a lot more satisfying.

Stepping outside he walked to the nearby creek, filled a rusty bucket with water and returned to the cabin. His victim shrieked as the ice cold water washed over her naked body. Pulling desperately at her restraints, the young woman struggled to free herself.

"Please" she pleaded. "Please don't hurt me." Her body began to shake.

Slowly he unbuckled the leather belt around his waist. A faint smile creased his face as he unfastened his jeans, dropping them to the floor, allowing his swollen penis to spring upward. He stepped towards the girl, kicking aside the crumpled jeans and pulling the weathered t-shirt over his head.

He circled the bound girl, stroking his member with one hand, cupping and squeezing his balls with his other. How long could he make it last this time? His breath quickened as he gazed at the girl's pussy. He had tied her legs open in a "V" shape exposing the lips of her vulva barely hidden under pale blond pubic hair. Kneeling between her legs, he placed his hands under her buttocks, lifted her opening towards him, and lowered his face into the wetness. Quickly he shifted his grasp, ramming three fingers into the girl's anus as he bit hard on the lips of her vulva. A scream filled the cabin.

Withdrawing his fingers from the girl's anus, he moved his body over the girl's shapely body. He wrapped his hands around his victim's throat as his penis slid into her pussy. Using the girl's throat for support under his hands, he began a slow and deep thrust. Harder and harder he drove his penis, tightening his grip on his victim's neck. Pain and shock flooded the girl's consciousness, triggering an ingrained flight response as she made one final attempt to escape and survive.

Later, after washing himself in the creek, he burned his clothes. While he waited for the fire to subside enough to be left unattended, he dressed in the clean khakis and collared shirt he had brought with him. He felt much better now, cleansed inside and out, the darkness closed away. It would return again, he knew, and going forward he'd have to be more careful. He had too much to lose now.

CHAPTER TWELVE

Present Day

Opening Parker & Jackson had resulted in a distinct change in the makeup of Allison's law practice. During her decade plus tenure at her previous firm, Johnson & Merritt, Allison had enjoyed the luxury of specializing in one area of the law. Large firms, firms with more than thirty or so lawyers, often assigned partners and associates to various "practice groups" generally dividing the lawyers according to whether they tried lawsuits or whether they fought for their clients with pen and paper in complex commercial or business deals. The larger the firm, the greater the number and variety of practice groups. Thus, in addition to the traditional litigation and transactional groups, Johnson & Merritt had boasted real estate, environmental and governmental affairs practice groups.

As might be expected from a group of individuals second only to physicians in terms of god-complexes, a fierce but unspoken rivalry generally existed between litigators and transactional attorneys, with other specialty practices viewed a distant third by those in the aforementioned "premier" groups. While Allison's specialization of defending employer's from claims of discrimination, wrongful termination or unemployment disputes had slotted her neatly into Johnson & Merritt's litigation group, she had, upon more than one occasion, sat as second chair in several complex transactional cases that had not been resolved by negotiation and settlement.

Most of Allison's corporate clients had followed her to Parker & Jackson, and she continued to handle employment matters for them, but the realities of monthly overhead and salaries for the firm's secretary and paralegal had required Allison to expand her legal practice beyond the narrow confines of employment law. Early on, Allison and David Jackson decided that no matter would be too small for the firm to at least consider, and that only a conflict of interest or ethical concern would justify turning down a prospective client. Legal work was legal work, and at the end of the day, Parker & Jackson had bills and salaries to pay.

Picking up the legal memorandum David Jackson had deposited on her desk earlier that morning, Allison chuckled. *Maybe a Will dispute won't be as boring as the Wills and Estates class was in law school.* As promised, David Jackson had devoted a good bit of time researching Alabama probate and inheritance law after reviewing the documents Jefferson Boudreaux had given him. The legal memorandum he had asked Allison to review was well written, succinct, and concluded that Jefferson Boudreaux had a colorable claim to the estate of his mother Rebecca Fairchild. Allison noted that David had also discussed the likelihood of a vigorous defense by the several charities which had been named the beneficiaries of her estate in Rebecca Fairchild's Will. Because David anticipated an expensive court battle, the memorandum concluded with a statement of the terms under which he, and therefore Parker & Jackson, would agree to accept Jefferson Boudreaux's case: a substantial retainer upfront, and once that was depleted, legal fees billed monthly at a specified rate. In addition, Jefferson Boudreaux would assume any costs and expenses incurred on his behalf. If the firm was successful – either by settlement or trial – Parker & Jackson's final fee would be the larger of the hourly fees expended or 35% of the amount recovered for the client.

Swiveling her chair, Allison reached for the multi-buttoned phone on her desk. A few seconds after she punched in the four digits of her partner's extension, Allison heard David Jackson's laconic hello.

"Nice piece of work." Allison commented as she flipped back through the document in front of her. "Looks like a pretty straight forward claim."

"That's my conclusion, too" David replied. "But I do expect some serious pushback from those charities. A lot of money is at stake here, and I doubt the opposition is just going to roll over and give up a claim to the kind of money we're talking about."

"Well that brings up an interesting point." David's observation caused Allison to reflect on a possibility not addressed in the legal memorandum. "What do you think the odds are that those charities have already spent a portion of the monies they received from the distribution of the Fairchild estate?"

"That's one of the first things I thought about" David answered. "I pulled the probate file in the courthouse. The first distribution is a week from today. If we are going forward with the case I will need to file for an Injunction preventing that action."

"So, are you going to accept the case?" Allison paused, then added "I assume you have reconciled your earlier concerns about Jefferson Boudreaux?"

"Yes, and yes" David replied. "I can't see any reason not to take the case. I guess I was just a bit put off by Boudreaux himself."

"You never did tell me what it was about the man that made you hesitate about representing him." Allison was curious.

"I still can't put my finger on what it is" David admitted. "He is well spoken and clearly intelligent. A bit arrogant, but he'd hardly be the first client I've represented with that character defect."

"But?" Allison questioned.

"It doesn't matter." David sighed. "From everything I have learned, the man is legit and so is his claim. And we aren't in a position to turn down paying work."

"We aren't in the poor house yet" Allison admonished. "If you're not comfortable about taking this case – for whatever reason – then we'll turn it down."

The tick of the wall clock in Allison's office filled the silence as she waited for David's decision.

"No, Allison" David gave a short laugh. "I'm just being paranoid. I'll give Jefferson Boudreaux a call this afternoon and let him know I'll take the case."

"If you need any help along the way, let me know" Allison replied. "I've got some time right now. That is, unless I agree to Frank Martin's request."

"What's up with Frank?" David was glad for a change of subject. He'd have to deal with Jefferson Boudreaux soon enough. Frank Martin was a much more interesting and potentially entertaining topic of discussion.

"Toby Trowbridge has hired Frank as a special investigative assistant for the Sheriff's office." Allison explained. "According to Frank, the girl whose remains were found out on Tom Spenser's farm had a sheet for solicitation in New Orleans. Not to bore you with the details, just suffice it to say that Frank's investigation has pointed at the possibility of a related murder. Frank wants me to help him with the expanded investigation."

"Doing what?" David interjected. "You don't have a P.I. license and so far you haven't described anything remotely like legal work."

"That's exactly what I told Frank last week when he wanted me to ride over to Meridian with him to interview some workers at the Flying J truck stop." Allison continued. "But, I have to admit I am rather intrigued by the idea, so I'm giving some thought as to what, if anything, I can do to assist Frank without violating any professional guidelines."

"Just be careful" David admonished. "The last time you and Frank worked together things got pretty dicey."

"Yep" Allison agreed. "That's exactly what Jim said."

"Listen to your husband, Allison" David replied as he and Allison ended their conversation. "Lady Luck only smiles once on some people."

CHAPTER THIRTEEN

A sharp knock on Toby's office door briefly preceded the tapping of his secretary's square heels as she approached the Sheriff's desk and thrust a sheaf of papers towards the startled head of Calhoun County law enforcement.

"You're jumpy as a cat" Beth observed, seeing her boss reach to cover several pieces of paper laid out on his desk. "Someone who didn't know you might think you were hiding a guilty conscience. What's that you're looking at?"

"Crime scene pictures the Sheriff over in Lauderdale County sent me. Didn't see any need to spoil your appetite right before lunch." Toby pushed back from his desk, then folded his hands across his trim belly. "Pretty nasty scene."

"Tobias Trowbridge, I appreciate your continuing chivalry, but you and I both know nothing shocks me anymore" the white haired woman lectured.

Nodding his acknowledgment to the truth of his secretary's statement, Toby reached for the paperwork still in Beth's outstretched hand. "What's this?"

"Frank Martin dropped it off earlier today. I plum forgot about it 'til now." Shaking her head, Beth mumbled "Don't know where my mind goes some days."

"There's nothing wrong with your mind, Beth" Toby replied glancing through the pages Beth had given over. "If something urgent had come up in Frank's investigation he'd have given me a call, not dropped by a written report."

"Well, it's still worrisome" Beth frowned. "This getting old stuff is for the birds."

Boy is it, Toby thought to himself, reflecting on Beth's old age comment. Toby wasn't that old, just turned fifty, but on rainy mornings the ache in his knees tried to say otherwise. Getting to the gym before sunrise was harder now, but Toby knew if he let up on weightlifting and running the inevitable downhill slide would begin sooner rather than later. *Nope*, he thought, *not going there yet*.

Toby sipped lukewarm coffee from a chipped cup as he perused the report Frank Martin had left for him to review. A life in law enforcement had cemented Toby's original views about coincidences. There weren't any. Even had Frank Martin not held the same skeptical opinion, it would have been hard for either man to ignore the fact that Francine Turner, the murdered woman outside Meridian, Mississippi was the cousin of Toby's dismembered vic Marilee Wingo. Nor, the unlikely 'coincidence' that Francine was murdered within hours of talking to Frank Martin about her cousin. Unfortunately, Frank's report left unanswered more questions than it had answered. Had Marilee Wingo been part of a prostitution ring operating out of interstate truck stops? Or had she simply been at the Flying J because of her cousin Francine? If Marilee Wingo was turning tricks on her own, why had Francine Turner been afraid to talk to Frank at the truckstop? And for that matter, what evidence was there to prove Marilee Wingo was selling her body? Just because she had a solicitation charge in New Orleans a couple of years ago didn't necessarily mean she was still living that lifestyle. Maybe she had hitched a ride with the wrong person.

Toby needed more information. The number for the Lauderdale County, Mississippi Sheriff's office was on the cover letter that had accompanied the Turner crime scene photos.

"Sheriff's Department" a pleasant female voice answered.

"This is Sheriff Trowbridge, Calhoun County, Alabama" Toby responded. "I'd like to speak with Sheriff Gilbert, please."

Hardly had the operator asked Toby to "hold please" than a gruff voice sounded in Toby's ear. "Sheriff Scott Gilbert, here. To what do I owe the pleasure of a call from an Alabama sheriff?"

Sheriffs and police chiefs were territorial animals, this Toby knew for a fact. He, himself, was no exception. Sheriff Scott Gilbert might or might not welcome Toby's intrusion into the Francine Turner murder case.

"Thank you for taking my call" Toby replied deferentially. "I'll try not to take up much of your time, but I think you may be able to help me with a murder investigation we've got over here." Toby hoped being the supplicant would encourage Gilbert to speak frankly.

"This have to do with that P.I. from your neck of the woods? The one who discovered the body of that Flying J employee?" Gilbert sounded peeved.

Sensing a bit of hostility in his counter-part's question, Toby kept his voice even. "Frank Martin is a good man who sometimes forgets he doesn't have a badge. I apologize if he stepped on any toes. If so, that's on me."

"Well, without your man there's no telling when that woman's body would have been discovered" Gilbert allowed. "Guess we can thank him for that."

"Appreciate your understanding" Toby breathed a silent sigh of relief. The last thing he needed was a pissing contest with the Lauderdale County Sheriff. "The main reason I called, though, was to see if you'd be willing to talk to me about Ms. Turner's murder. I think her murder may be related to one in my county, and I'm trying to put together the puzzle pieces. Thought you might be able to help."

"What sort of sick Fuck would do something like that?" Sheriff Gilbert asked after Toby told him about the remains found in Tom Spencer's field.

"That's what I intend to find out. Marilee Wingo's last known address was New Orleans. With no leads as to how she got to Calhoun County, we figured maybe she had been hitchhiking, got picked up by her killer. Frank Martin was showing our vic's picture around truckstops on I-20, seeing if anyone recognized her. When Frank showed Francine Turner our vic's picture she told him the vic was her cousin." Toby stopped to let Gilbert process the information he had just shared.

"Her cousin?" Sheriff Gilbert asked. "There's nothing in my report about that."

"I don't think Ms. Turner was killed because she was Marilee Wingo's cousin" Toby replied. "But I do think she might have been killed because someone saw her talking to Frank Martin, and fingered him for either law enforcement or a private dick. Someone who didn't want Francine Turner talking – maybe about something totally unrelated to our vic's murder, and maybe not."

"Lots of maybes, not many for sures" Gilbert observed.

"Agreed" Toby knew Gilbert's assessment was correct.

"But" Gilbert interjected "I tend to agree with your thinking. Francine Turner had a clean record. No run-ins with the law, no taking up with the wrong kind of people. This is a small community and I'd know."

"Frank said Ms. Turner was supposed to meet him at a diner when she got off her shift" Toby added. "Someone or something made her go home instead. And that got her killed."

Gilbert made no reply, and for a few minutes Toby thought the other sheriff had disconnected the call.

"What do you want to ask that you haven't?" Gilbert inquired quietly.

"I guess the big question is whether your office will work with mine on both murders. Answer questions as they arise." Toby found it difficult to give

Gilbert a coherent response. "I'm not even sure what all the questions are right now. All I know is that my gut tells me there is something important about Ms. Turner's murder that is somehow related to how her cousin ended up in a farmer's abandoned shed in my county waiting for a tornado to rip her to shreds."

CHAPTER FOURTEEN

Dickie Lee Bishop took his job as Judge Jim Kaufman's Bailiff seriously. He had just completed an associate's degree in criminal justice at Ft. Charles Community College when he saw the job posting in the school's job placement office.

"*Applications being received for Bailiff position with Calhoun County Circuit Court. High school graduate or GED, advanced degree with experience in Criminal Justice, Civil Rights or Law Enforcement preferred. Must have good communication skills and work well with others.*"

Dickie Lee had worried over his interview with Judge Kaufman. Would the judge think he was too young? He was pretty sure that the other candidates he had seen waiting to be interviewed had at least ten years on him age-wise. And there was a woman, too. Dickie Lee had heard the judge was married to a woman lawyer. Maybe he'd give the Bailiff job to a female to make his wife happy. By the time Dickie Lee had been called to the Judge's chambers for the interview he had convinced himself he didn't stand a chance.

No one was more surprised than Dickie Lee when Judge Kaufman had called him the next afternoon and offered him the job as his Bailiff. The Judge told Dickie Lee he had been impressed with his eagerness, and he wanted a Bailiff with the kind of energy and motivation Dickie Lee had demonstrated during the interview.

Sometimes Dickie Lee wondered where the past three years had gone, but he had no complaint. Judge Kaufman was a good boss, and even more important to the citizens of Calhoun County, Alabama, he was a fair judge. No one got a raw deal in Judge Kaufman's court, but everyone knew Judge Kaufman's philosophy: if you did the crime, you did the time.

Today, the lawyers in Judge Kaufman's courtroom were trying a criminal case. A simply larceny charge that Dickie Lee thought should have merited a reduced plea instead of a full blown trial. No way the Defendant wasn't going to get convicted, and if the jury returned a guilty verdict Judge Kaufman was sure to impose some jail time. After all, this was the second time this particular defendant had ended up in Judge Kaufman's courtroom. Dickie Lee had quit trying a long time ago to second guess why criminal defense lawyers made the decisions they did. He was just glad it wasn't his ass on the line.

A concerning sound from the bench disturbed the Bailiff's reflection. Turning his head sharply towards his boss, Dickie Lee at first saw nothing amiss. Judge Kaufman was staring intently at the District Attorney who was standing at the podium in the front of the courtroom, giving his closing argument to the jury. Nothing abnormal about that – the Judge was just paying attention. No, something wasn't right. Judge Kaufman seemed distracted, Dickie Lee thought, and he was rubbing his chest with his right hand.

Three things happened simultaneously. As Dickie Lee rose to approach the Judge, his boss fell forward, and a large moan escaped the judge's lips. A stunned silence that lasted only a few seconds, but which seemed like an eternity, engulfed the courtroom freezing lawyers, jurors and spectators into helpless bystanders.

"Quick, Doug" Dickie Lee shouted at the District Attorney as he ran towards the unconscious Judge. "Call 911. Everyone else, stay in your seats."

Judge Kaufman's skin had a bluish cast to it. Offering a prayer of thanks for the CPR training the judge has insisted all courtroom personnel undergo, the Bailiff placed the judge's body on the floor. A quick check of Judge Kaufman's pulse telegraphed the worst possible news to his Bailiff. Desperately, Dickie Lee began compressing the judge's chest trying to restart his heart.

"Don't die on me, Judge" Dickie Lee demanded. "Not like this."

He was still on task when the paramedics arrived.

⚊✛ ✛⚊

Time was her friend right now, at least Allison hoped that was the case. The longer he stayed alive, surely the more likely it was that her husband would be returned to her. Allison and Jim had talked about their fifteen year age difference before they married. Both had recognized the likelihood that Jim would die well before Allison. Even had they been the same age, statistics predicted an earlier demise for males. Well before Charlotte and Mack had been born, Jim Kaufman had set up an estate plan to financially protect both his wife and any children they might have. Over a year earlier, when the Judge had been seriously wounded in a shootout with the man who had ordered his and Allison's execution, Jim and Allison had been forced to have another discussion about what life might be like had Jim not survived.

Sitting in the Cardiac Care waiting room, the memory of that discussion caused Allison an inadvertent shudder. *Please God,* she prayed, *Don't let that be a premonition of what is to come.*

"Ms. Parker?"

Allison whispered a soft *Amen* and opened her eyes.

George Chang, the cardiac specialist she had called in from Atlanta, offered Allison a gentle smile. "I've got good news. As you know, your husband suffered an occlusion in one of the lesser blood vessels in his heart. While that sounds serious, and it's not something to be taken lightly, because of the area affected I anticipate we can address the immediate problem with a couple of stents rather than bypass surgery."

"Thank God." Relief flooded Allison's body. "But, how did we not see this coming?" she asked the doctor. "Jim's had an annual cardiac workup every year since he got that first stent five years ago."

"I've looked at the records from Dr. Bennett's office" Dr. Chang replied, referring to Jim's Ft. Charles cardiologist. "Last year the scans showed your husband had a 40% blockage in one of his arteries. That wouldn't have been enough to warrant surgical intervention, and normally wouldn't be any cause for immediate alarm."

"So, what happened?" Allison demanded.

"The disease process accelerated" the doctor explained. "There's no way to predict something like this. The good news is that your husband's heart has not been significantly damaged."

"When will you do the stents?" Allison asked.

"He's scheduled for 7:00 tomorrow morning" Dr. Change smiled. "You'll have him home by Friday, and he should be back in the office, part time, in a couple of weeks."

Although not scheduled visiting hours for CCU, no one objected when Allison pushed through the double doors of the restricted area. One of the benefits of having Ft. Charles General Hospital as a client Allison mused, nodding to the Charge Nurse at the circular nurses' station in the center of the unit, was that most of the staff knew what her relationship was with the hospital.

"Don't stay too long" was all the uniformed woman cautioned as Allison headed towards the glass cubicle where her husband rested.

The beep of monitors offered a soft accompaniment to the ragged snoring coming from Jim's sleeping face. Trying not to awaken her husband, Allison leaned over the bed railing to plant a kiss on Jim's forehead.

"Hey, there" Jim whispered, opening his eyes and smiling at his wife.

"Hey there, yourself" Allison replied. "I didn't mean to wake you."

"Did Dr. Chang find you?" Jim pressed the bed control to raise himself to a more upright position. Seeing his wife's affirmative nod, he continued "I'm getting another stent. Or two."

"Dr. Chang says you'll be fine. Home in a couple of days, back to work in a couple of weeks." Allison caressed her husband's hand. "And then we are going to take a long, hard look at both of our careers."

"If it will make you happy, we'll do just that" Jim smiled at his wife. "But I'm not ready to leave the bench, and I know you're not ready to quit working."

"I know that" Allison replied. "But I don't want any regrets down the road."

"I'd like to think this is all about my heart attack, but there's more, isn't there?" Jim's raised eyebrows amplified his question.

Allison laughed. "I love you, Jim Kaufman. And, yes, now that I know you aren't going to die on me, this cardiac interlude has simply reminded me take a hard look at our professional and personal lives." Allison moved from her chair to sit on the side of her husband's hospital bed. "I know you're in the right place. I'm just not so sure about myself."

"Frank Martin's request for your help has gotten to you, hasn't it?" Jim inquired.

"You know me too well" Allison responded, shaking her head. "As terrifying as the end of the McNair matter turned out to be last year, I realized how invigorating I found the whole thing to be."

"Allison Parker! Have you turned into an adrenalin junky?" her husband teased.

Ignoring the barb, Allison continued. "Trial work is terrifying in its own way, and I really enjoy doing battle in the courtroom, but there was just something so 'alive' about working with Frank, working through the puzzle and the clues of that investigation. I'm not ready to give up practicing law, but I wonder if there isn't some way I can continue to work with Frank?"

"Well, then" Jim replied. "While I'm convalescing the next couple of weeks, let's see what we can figure out. Don't want my girl to be unhappy."

Ignoring the nurse's admonition not to stay too long, Allison lingered by her husband's bedside until he slipped into a restful sleep. Jim had assured his wife that he would comply with Dr. Chang's discharge instructions, but Allison knew her husband. Twenty years on the bench had accustomed Jim to being the one issuing the orders, not the one obeying them. Jim would pay attention to the instructions that didn't inconvenience him too much, and would ignore the rest. Sometimes, she thought, trying to get her husband to obey someone else was like herding cats. A determined smile crossed Allison's face as she walked to her car. She liked cats.

CHAPTER FIFTEEN

Life had returned to normal. Allison's husband had been discharged from the hospital the day before with light physical restrictions as well as a prescription for cardiac rehab starting in two weeks. Over a breakfast of oatmeal, coffee and juice Jim had assured Allison that he would stay on the couch all day.

"I've asked Becky to bring some files out later this morning." Sensing a retort from his wife, Jim quickly added "There's nothing strenuous about reading, Allison. I'll be fine."

"You have to promise me you'll stay on that couch." Allison was exasperated. "You've been home less than twenty-four hours and you're already trying to get back to work."

"I won't do anything other than read, sleep and eat." Jim assured his wife as he placed his cereal bowl in the dishwasher.

"You're dead meat if I hear otherwise." Allison threatened, adding her empty coffee cup to the assortment of glassware, dishes and cutlery adorning the overloaded dishwasher. "Although I'll make an exception to physical activity if you will unload this dishwasher after it runs."

"Yes, dear" Jim smirked, giving Allison a peck on her cheek as he headed towards the den. "Just let me know what other chores you have in mind that might be an exception to my medical restrictions."

"Smart ass", Allison murmured under her breath as she shepherded her children out the door and into the car. "I'll be checking on you" she called back to Jim, "and you better be behaving."

Two hours later, having deposited Charlotte and Mack at school, dropped two of her suits at the dry cleaners, and returned one of Charlotte's overdue library books to the Ft. Charles Public Library, Allison surveyed the stack of legal files adorning her desk. Dividing the different colored folders by case name, Allison made a quick list of tasks in order of priority. She had two unemployment hearings for one of her corporate clients scheduled for tomorrow. Allison added the number one next to the names of the two employees who had filed with the state unemployment commission seeking benefits for wrongful termination.

Allison didn't think she'd have much trouble defending either hearing – the two employees had engaged in a knock-down, drag-out fist fight at work. One of the terminated employees had ended up in the ER and was now suing the other employee for civil money damages. *Amazing*, Allison thought as she reviewed the incident reports which detailed the destruction of her client's break room where the fight had taken place. *And you can't figure out why you got fired?* All of that evidence and more would weigh heavily against the two in tomorrow's hearing. Allison expected rulings in favor of her client, but she would still need to thoroughly prepare her case. Reaching for her computer keyboard, Allison sent a short email to her secretary, asking Donna to call the witnesses she intended to have testify to remind them of the time and location of the hearing.

Written discovery responses were due in the Shrader case next week. Allison already had her client's responses in draft form. Susan, the firm's paralegal, would take care of preparing the final document and obtaining the client's notarized signature. Checking the calendar, Allison listed the Shrader case as number two on her priority list. A few minutes later, Allison had completed the review of pending matters and listed them in order of importance and need for attention. Assured that nothing had slipped through the cracks, Allison opened the files for the next day's hearing and began to prepare the cross-examination questions she would pose to the two claimants.

At four o'clock Allison pushed back from her desk, satisfied that she was well prepared to defend her client's case. Rotating her head to stretch neck muscles which had cramped from several hours of staring at a computer monitor, Allison's attention was caught by the steadily blinking light on her office phone. As per her custom when preparing for trial or a hearing, Allison had muted the phone while she worked. Phone calls, Allison believed, interrupted the concentration needed to prepare one's case. Removing her phone's sound restriction, Allison punched the message replay button.

"Allison, it's Frank Martin" the P.I.'s voice boomed. "I know you've been busy with the judge's heart attack and all, but Donna said you were back in the office now. Have you had a chance to look at the information I sent over? Give me a call, will you?"

Upon arriving that morning, Allison had tossed her briefcase onto the small sofa she had installed in her office as a comfortable alternative to sitting behind her desk. Laying aside the unemployment case file, Allison moved to the more comfortable locale, retrieved a large manila envelope from her briefcase, and settled herself in a prone position to read Frank's report.

A member of Ft. Charles' legal community, Allison had heard bits and pieces about the woman, or what was left of her, that was found at Tom Spencer's farm. Frank had added more information: the vic's name, Marilee Wingo; her criminal record for solicitation in New Orleans; and her relationship to Francine Turner, the murder victim outside Meridian, Mississippi. Frank had also included a copy of the Turner investigative report from the Lauderdale County Sheriff.

The last item Allison pulled from the manila envelope was a copy of the report Frank had presented to Sheriff Trowbridge. Allison was pretty certain Toby wouldn't approve of her having a copy of what was likely a confidential document. In it, Frank set out the reasons why he thought Francine Turner had been murdered, as well as his suspicion that Marilee Wingo's murder was at least peripherally, but maybe accidently, connected. Frank's report ended with a recommendation that the Calhoun County Sheriff and the Lauderdale County Sheriff set up a joint task force to investigate both murders.

Allison considered the information she had just reviewed. Frank was an excellent private investigator. No doubt about that. But what Frank was suggesting – an organized prostitution ring operating out of interstate truck stops – was a big jump based on the slim evidence and information they had about the Wingo and Turner murders. Plus, any joint task force between the Alabama and Mississippi sheriffs' offices would likely require contact with the F.B.I., an agency currently on Sheriff Trowbridge's black list.

Allison understood Sheriff Trowbridge's feelings. The preceding year, while Allison was knee-deep in the McNair investigation, the F.B.I. had set up a sting operation in Calhoun County on a smuggling case without advising the Sheriff of either the operation or the Fed's presence. Fortunately for Allison, the F.B.I.'s sting operation had uncovered a murder plot against her, her husband and her law partner David Jackson. The Fed's intervention had foiled not only the potential triple homicide - the undercover agent working the sting had gathered concrete evidence of an earlier hit involving the very people who had been the target of Allison's investigation in the McNair case. At the end of a harrowing night where Allison found herself in a starring role, two bad guys were dead, one by his own hand, and a third was in custody.

Toby's office had become involved when the Feds had deposited a guy named Steve Miller in one of the Sheriff's holding cells. The only thing the Federal agents would tell the Sheriff was that his new prisoner had been involved in a shooting at the local Knights of Columbus clubhouse. Because Toby had been kept in the dark about the F.B.I.'s true targets, when Miller started spouting off nonsense about one of Ft. Charles' most prominent residents, Ben Johnson, Toby had picked up the phone and given Ben a call.

Allison thought Frank Martin's suggestion of a joint task force had possibilities. Having the resources available to the F.B.I. would be a definite perk. Whether Sheriff Trowbridge would have the same opinion would rest in large part, Allison believed, on whether the Sheriff still held Agent Wilson Mackey responsible for Ben Johnson's suicide.

"If that son of a bitch had just told me what was going on, I would never have called Ben" the Sheriff had told Allison after the Feds had left town. "We could have arrested Ben quietly instead of being called to an ugly suicide by his poor wife."

Despite Toby's public insistence that the F.B.I.'s silence had caused Ben Johnson's suicide, Allison knew better. Toby blamed himself, even though the facts told another story.

"You can't blame yourself" she had told the Sheriff more than once. "David says Ben never would have allowed himself to be put in prison. Your call just made the inevitable happen sooner rather than later."

Maybe enough time had passed. There was no way to tell without Frank making his pitch to the Sheriff. Or was there another way? Moving to her desk, Allison opened a side drawer and withdrew a stack of small rubber banded cards. A few seconds later Allison exclaimed "Thought I still had that" as she gazed at the business card embossed with the blue and gold seal of the Federal Bureau of Investigation. Jake Cleveland owed her a favor.

CHAPTER SIXTEEN

"It works if you work it" Rice's voice joined several others as the group of prisoners uttered the closing words for the AA meeting that had just ended. Rice had entered rehab in Jackson, Mississippi shortly after he imploded in a drunken rage at his father's funeral. There he had attended daily AA meetings in addition to sessions with a therapist, both individually and as part of a group of other drug addicts and alcoholics. By the time he returned to his home in Sumner, Tennessee to face trial on triple murder charges, Rice had taken the first necessary steps towards recovering his sobriety and his sanity.

Rice never intended to kill his children. His wife Mary Louise had been his sole target. Her and the five million dollar life insurance policy he would claim upon her death. Rice had disabled the brakes on Mary Louise's car the night before she was to leave for a girls' beach trip. The plan had seemed foolproof - but Rice had gotten drunk after he completed his sabotage, and when Mary Louise couldn't rouse him the next morning to take the children to school, she had loaded the children in her car to drop them off on the way out of town. Mary Louise had survived the fiery crash. Rice's children had not.

Initially, Rice had resisted the plea deal his attorney had worked out with the District Attorney. Rice told Jason Brownlow he had nothing to live for, and if Brownlow didn't want to enter a guilty plea for him that Rice would just represent himself. But the time spent at COPAC had done more than separate Rice from drugs and alcohol. When the alcohol infused fog had cleared his brain, and the cravings for drugs had begun to diminish, AA's twelve step program began to make sense to Rice.

Alcoholics Anonymous, Rice was told, offered a simple kit of tools for living. At first, the hokey sayings Rice heard in meetings simply irritated him. "Let Go and Let God". "One Day At A Time". "Easy Does It". Rice considered the slogans nothing more than Pablum for small minds. But, he couldn't ignore the personal stories he heard. Stories told by people who didn't want or need alcohol or drugs anymore. People who could live in the world without a chemical crutch. People who had learned to accept life on life's terms. By the time he was discharged from COPAC, Rice knew that part of accepting responsibility for what he had done was to live with the consequences of his actions. Rice had called Jason Brownlow and told him if the plea deal was still on the table, he would accept it. To many people, three life sentences without the possibility of parole would have been unbearable. To Rice, it was an opportunity to make a living amends.

Kilby offered inmates AA meetings three times a week. The Friday night meeting featured outside speakers who shared their personal recovery stories as part of AA's 12th step directive to 'carry the message to other alcoholics'. The Tuesday and Thursday night meetings were run by the inmates who selected one of the group to chair the meeting and provide a discussion topic relating to AA and recovery. The only difference between AA meetings at Kilby and AA meetings Rice had attended on the outside before his sentencing was the presence of prison guards at the former. Rice thought Kilby's warden was particularly enlightened – most of the guards at the Kilby AA meetings were in recovery themselves.

The strongest and most sacrosanct tenet of AA was anonymity. Every meeting closed with the reminder that 'what you hear here, and who you see here, stays here'. To AA members, violating someone's anonymity was akin to violating the confidentiality of the confessional. In the regular world, the violation of a group member's anonymity might result in the loss of a friendship, or in extreme circumstances even the expulsion of the offending member from the group. At Kilby, the violation of a member's anonymity could result in bodily injury or worse. AA'ers at Kilby might be in recovery from drugs and alcohol, but many of them were still hardened criminals, and a lifetime of bad habits and wrong choices were hard to break.

Rice had heard a lot of harrowing tales in the Kilby AA meetings. To his mind, he and the other inmates attending the meetings were the stark example of hitting a low, low bottom. Likewise, Rice had heard some pretty terrible stories in AA meetings outside the prison's walls. If the people outside Kilby kept on drinking and drugging, odds were they would eventually end up inside Kilby, or a place like Kilby, if they didn't end up planted in a cemetery first.

Breaching someone's anonymity because of what he had heard in a meeting had never occurred to Rice. Until now.

"I've never talked about this a'fore." Rice had to listen hard to hear Del Welch's voice. "Happened a long time ago; I wasn't supposed to see anything." Welch bowed his head, then gave a deep sigh before continuing. "Y'all know my drug of choice…" Del didn't need to name his demon. Everyone in the group knew Del had ended up in Kilby for using and dealing methamphetamine. "I was livin' in Shreveport, out near the airbase, tryin' to pick up odd jobs, get enough cash to stay high." Del paused for a sip of the black tar that passed for coffee in the prison AA meeting. "That damn meth. It didn't take long before I needed more than I had money to buy."

Low murmurs of "yep" and "don't I know" came from several men in the room. Most all gave a nod of understanding. Addicts and alcoholics understood all too well the craving Del was describing. And the lengths an addict would go to satisfy such an unrelenting demand.

"I owed my dealer about fifty big ones" Del continued "and I had zero chance of coming up with the money. So, when one of the guys I smoked with told me he knew of a way to come up with some easy cash, I listened." Small beads of sweat had begun to appear on Del's forehead. It wasn't unusual for AA'ers to become emotional when sharing their drinking and drugging stories with the group, but Del's nervousness had struck Rice as out of the norm. "All I needed to do, Bennie said, was go with him to deliver a package to a place out past Bossier City. Said he just needed a lookout in case things went sideways."

Del's mention of the need for a lookout caught the group's attention. Men who had been examining their fingernails or half dozing now turned expectant faces towards the storyteller.

"Oh, God." A low moan escaped Del's lips as he raised his head to look at the men.

"It's alright" one of the old timers in the group assured the younger man. "You don't have to say anything else."

Rice had not expected Del to continue, but the young convict surprised him. "We got there later than we were supposed to, I guess. Ramshackle house at the end of a gravel lane, probably 20 miles north of Bossier. Maybe when we got there wouldn't have mattered. Shit, I don't even know what was in the package we was delivering to the guy. Bennie told me to wait in the car, and if I saw anyone coming up the drive to blow the horn and be ready to haul ass out of there." Del ran his fingers across his head, a nervous habit Rice recognized as one of his own. "Course, I never was much for obeying orders, so I waited a minute or so and then headed 'round back of the house where Bennie had gone." Del shook his head. "Why the fuck didn't I stay in the car? Sweet mother of God, why? I'll never forget what I saw. Some crazy mother had nailed a naked woman to a cross, except her legs were spread open just like her arms. Her breasts had been cut off, and some kind of long stick was hanging out of her pussy."

No one said a word. Two of the men in the room were convicted killers, and most had lived a brutal life. None were strangers to violence, but the mayhem Del had just described was beyond what even these hardened criminals considered acceptable.

"We left. We just left her hanging there and drove back to Shreveport. Bennie and I agreed it was too dangerous to go to the police. We knew the woman was dead, and frankly, we didn't want to get whoever did that to her going after us. Bennie was afraid it was the guy who had hired him to deliver that package."

"What was in the package?" a convict new to the group asked, violating the group rule against cross-talk.

"Don't know for sure. Bennie never said. All I know is Bennie was hired to pick up a package from one of the hardware stores in Shreveport and drive it out to that place north of Bossier. I didn't want details after what I saw. Too much information can get you kil't." Del looked at the men in the room. "I don't know who done that woman, but I should have at least made a call to the police. No one deserves to die like that." Draining the last bit of coffee from a Styrofoam cup that had seen better days, Del continued "That was 10 years ago. I wonder some-times...is that mother fucker still out there? Would the cops have caught him if I'd made the call? How do I make an amends for that?"

Walking back to his cell Rice reflected on Del's story. It didn't take long for evidence in the outdoors to be eroded. If the woman hadn't been found for days or weeks, would there have been anything of significance recoverable at the crime scene? Did it make a difference now? Maybe the woman had eventually been found and identified. Forensic an-thropologists could determine a whole lot from just a few bones, a fact Rice had learned from another inmate who had earned a twenty to life sentence based on just that sort of expert testimony. *Whatever had happened, it's no concern of yours* Rice told himself. Besides, the story was Del's to tell, not his.

CHAPTER SEVENTEEN

Allison hated driving in Birmingham. Interstate 26 was a nightmare snaking through the downtown corridor. What had the guy who laid out the traffic pattern been thinking when he put the lane exit for I-65 on the far left side of a four lane interstate immediately after a poorly banked curve? Allison cursed as a confused motorist cut over three lanes, barely missing Allison and two other motorists.

Jake Cleveland had agreed to meet Allison while she was in town for a motion hearing on one of her cases. Reluctant to be seen in the F.B.I. offices until she had a deal in place, Allison had suggested she and Jake meet at a coffee shop near the Federal Courthouse an hour before she was due in court. Unfortunately, and typically, Allison had ended up delayed leaving town and was now rushing to make her appointment with the F.B.I. agent. Allison wanted enough time to fully explain her ideas about the joint task force and her inclusion in it. Fifteen minutes later, car parked in the nearest pay lot, Allison hurried into the Starbucks Café on 11th Avenue.

"Allison" a deep voice with a Texas accent tossed a greeting. "Back here."

Ever vigilant, Jake Cleveland had staked out a table at the rear of the coffee shop, positioning himself with his back to the wall so he could see everyone entering the shop.

"You expecting trouble?" Allison teased as she joined Jake at the table.

"You never know" Jake replied laconically. "Better safe than sorry."

Allison certainly wasn't going to argue. Jake Cleveland had saved her husband's life, and she had trusted him with her own. In her line of work, Allison was all too familiar with disgruntled employees and workplace violence. Better safe than sorry was a prudent attitude.

"How's the judge doing?" Jake asked. "I heard he had a heart attack a few weeks ago."

"He's fine, and we're grateful that there was no serious damage to his heart." Allison took a sip of coffee. "Thanks for asking, and thanks for having this coffee waiting for me. Jim's back at work part-time and in cardiac rehab for the next couple of months."

"Well, glad to hear the judge is back on his feet" Jake allowed. "But I know you had a reason for wanting to meet today. What's going on?"

"How hard is it to get a joint task force in place? One that involves the Feds and crosses state lines as well?" Allison hoped the question would pique Jake's interest.

"What sort of joint task force?" Jake replied. "We talking interstate trafficking of some kind? Drugs? Illegals?"

"Murder and prostitution, if Frank Martin is right in his suspicions". Allison knew Jake respected the private investigator who had helped on the McNair case. "We've got two murders – one in Ft. Charles, another over near Meridian, Mississippi. Vics were cousins. Frank thinks the Mississippi victim was murdered to prevent her from talking with him about her cousin."

"Were they both working girls?" Jake used the law enforcement descriptive for prostitutes.

"Our victim, a girl named Marilee Wingo, had a sheet for soliciting from New Orleans. Her cousin, the girl over in Meridian, was working as a clerk at the Flying J truck stop. No priors." Allison pulled a sealed envelope from her briefcase. "Here's Frank's summary. If you're agreeable, I'd like your thoughts on what we've got so far. The Sheriff over in Meridian has agreed to give Sheriff Trowbridge access to any developing leads on his victim, but neither Frank nor I think that's going to be very productive."

"What's Sheriff Trowbridge's position on all of this?" Jake was curious. "It's protocol for a joint task force request to come through official channels."

Allison squirmed a bit in her seat. "Actually, Toby doesn't know I'm meeting with you. That's why I didn't want to meet in your office. Right now this is just a chat between friends. After you look at what's in that envelope, and I hope you will at least agree to review what's there, if you think Frank's suspicions warrant further investigation Frank and I will see if Toby will make a call to your boss."

Jake placed the slim envelope in his coat pocket. "Doesn't feel like there's much in here."

"There's more than you think" Allison's reply held a hint of sadness. "Marilee Wingo died a terrible death. Her cousin Francine Turner had her throat cut. If the same person is responsible for those deaths, he needs to be brought to justice." Allison stood to leave. "Especially if there's the possibility of more victims."

"I'll take a look at Frank's report and maybe give Frank a call. There's likely more he can tell me than what's on this paper. Sex trafficking is a big issue for the agency. If there's enough smoke, I don't think it will be hard to convince Mackey to agree to set up a joint task force." Walking to the door of the coffee shop with Allison, Jake added "Mackey's a company man. Collaring a multi-state sex trafficking ring would look good on his resume."

"Jake" Allison's eyes crinkled with humor. "You know you'd like a piece of this too, just for other reasons."

"You're right about that." Jake's tone was serious as he and Allison parted ways outside the Starbucks. "By the way, what's your involvement in this?"

"Frank's asked me to help out, be sort of a sounding board. That's all." Allison hoped her explanation would be satisfactory. "I offered to call you since I was going to be in Birmingham today."

"Um hum." Jake's raised eyebrows told Allison he wasn't buying her explanation.

"I've got to run" Allison interrupted before Jake could delve any further. "Thanks, again, for agreeing to take a look at this."

CHAPTER EIGHTEEN

I t was late afternoon before Jake Cleveland had a chance to look at Frank Martin's summary. Domestic terrorists were a top agenda item for most F.B.I. offices nowadays, and the Birmingham field office was no exception. It wasn't enough to have to worry about some crazy Ayatollah in Iran inciting Jihad, now the average citizen had to worry about some disillusioned or mentally ill stranger opening fire in the local shopping mall or setting off a bomb made from instructions off the internet. Jake's entire day after meeting with Allison had been consumed with meetings about a new threat near the rocket center in Huntsville, and suspicious internet activity involving a suspected terrorist cell near Foley, Alabama of all places. What was the world coming to, Jake wondered, when you had to worry about being killed in an outlet mall?

Jake pulled a slim sheaf of papers from the manila envelope Allison had given him at Starbucks. Spreading the sheets across his desk, Jake reached first for the Calhoun County Medical Examiner's report. Allison's comment about one of the victims dying a terrible death had caught his attention. Jake knew a lot about terrible death – he'd seen more than his share in Operation Desert Storm before joining the agency – but death in war, no matter how terrible, was something one expected. A terrible death at the hand of some deranged or evil perp was something else.

Andy Dabo had included pictures with his report. *Holy mother of god.* The words slipped unbidden from Jake's lips as he looked at the mayhem captured in 'living' color in the crime scene pictures the M.E.'s staff had taken before bagging and removing what was left of Marilee Wingo from the concrete slab in Tom Spencer's field. Laying aside the gruesome photographs, Jake skimmed the M.E.'s findings. No way to know whether the girl had been dead before the tornado hit, but the M.E. was positive that the storm had done the damage to victim's body. Jake shook his head. What sort of hell had Marilee Wingo suffered before the tornado ripped apart her body? Unfortunately, almost twenty years with the F.B.I.

had acquainted him with more kinds of pain and death than he had ever imagined. He just hoped when death had come for Marilee Wingo that it had been quick.

Reaching next for Frank Martin's report, Jake studied the P.I.'s concise summary of the events that had transpired at the Flying J truck stop outside Meridian, including the subsequent discovery of Francine Turner's body later that evening. Jake knew the Flying J was a cleanly run operation. If Frank Martin was right and a prostitution or sex trafficking ring was being run out of Flying J truck stops, Jake thought it had to be without the knowledge of the company's management – at least its upper management. Flying J was an enormous profit making machine whose owners were billionaires. True, some people could never get enough money, but based on what Jake knew about the owners of the Flying J, he didn't see them adding sex trafficking as an extra source of income.

Frank Martin was convinced that the Wingo murder and the Turner murder were connected. Jake wasn't so sure. What he was fairly confident of, however, was that there was a high probability that Francine Turner was murdered because of something she was going to tell Frank Martin. What that information would have been and why someone would kill over it were the kind of questions Jake tried to answer in most of his cases. At the very least, Jake thought the Turner murder might warrant a closer look by the agency. It wouldn't be much of a stretch to add the Wingo murder to the initial look-see, primarily because of the family relationship between the two victims and Wingo's sheet for solicitation.

Jake was halfway home before he realized what had been picking at the edges of his brain while he had been reading the photos was a close-up of the concrete slab where parts of the victim's remains were found. Four iron manacles protruded from the slab, one in each corner. Based on the location of the gruesome remains, the M.E. had opined that the victim had been restrained in a spread eagle position.

Just like the dead girl who was found in an abandoned cabin outside Houma, Louisiana.

Jake hit the steering wheel with a clenched fist as the memory of the bloodied body of the young Louisiana woman filled his mind. The agency had been called in to consult when the state police had been unable to locate any leads or suspects. New to the Bureau, it had been Jake's first sex crime case, and one he had desperately wanted to close, but the animal who had raped and mutilated his victim had never been found. The M.O. was eerily similar, but that was almost fifteen years ago and a couple of states away from the Wingo murder in

Alabama. Could it be the same perp? Possible, Jake thought, but what were the odds? A copycat maybe? Jake had learned long ago never to ignore the little itch that many times preceded a break or lead in a case. Turning the possibilities over in his mind, Jake knew he'd want to pull the old file on the Louisiana murder.

"Siri, call Wilson Mackey" Jake instructed the teeny woman who lived inside his Iphone. Solving a cold case like the Houma murder, especially if it involved catching a serial killer who was still active, was exactly the kind of publicity the head of the F.B.I.'s Birmingham field office liked. Add to that the possibility of an interstate sex trafficking case. Jake wouldn't have any trouble convincing his boss to investigate the Wingo and Turner murders.

CHAPTER NINETEEN

David Jackson looked over the checklist he had made on the Boudreaux file. The defendants' answers were due tomorrow in the Will contest he had filed on behalf of Jefferson Boudreaux. Rebecca Fairchild's Last Will and Testament had left the entirety of her multi-billion dollar estate to five charities. Instead of generally well-known national charities, Ms. Fairchild had left her fortune to charities David had never heard of.

The Grace Matthews Home for Girls and Women was a domestic abuse shelter outside Waco, Texas. Waveland Dolphin Rescue operated out of several locations along the Mississippi and Alabama Gulf Coast. Records from the North Carolina Secretary of State's office listed Second Chances as a non-profit rehab facility located in Altamahaw, North Carolina. David had to look that one up on google maps. How had a town with 347 residents ended up on Rebecca Fairchild's radar? David figured Second Chances probably employed half of the town's population. There would be a lot of pissed town folk if David was successful for his client. The fourth beneficiary of Rebecca Fairchild's largess was Rat Terrier Rescue in Fair Hope, Alabama. David grinned thinking about Rattie Rescue. His favorite pet as a child had been a brown and white Rattie named Rocky. Secretly David hoped he wouldn't prevail against this particular Will donee.

Interestingly, the fifth charity on David's list of defendants had benefited far more than the other four recipients combined. Rebecca Fairchild had left the bulk of her money to an evangelist by the name of Tommy Ben Vaughn, with the single caveat that the money was to be used exclusively to establish and maintain a television ministry.

Based on the limited investigation he had been able to make so far, David initially thought it unlikely that any of the charities would be able to hire experienced counsel. After all, the Will proceeds were now tied up in court and would not be disbursed until the case was concluded and a decision rendered as to who or what had the rightful claim to Rebecca Fairchild's money. To his surprise, the five charities had combined their limited resources and had retained a reputable Birmingham lawyer to defend all of them against Jefferson Boudreaux's claims. Maybe this Will contest was not going to be as cut and dried as David had originally predicted.

"You got a minute?" Allison's question interrupted David's train of thought.

"Yeh, what's up?" David replied, swiveling his wheeled desk chair to face the doorway where his partner stood.

Entering David's office, Allison perched on the edge of one of the large upholstered chairs facing David's desk. "I just got a call from Jake Cleveland. The F.B.I. is definitely interested in the possibility that Francine Turner's and Marilee Wingo's murder may be related to some sort of trafficking, either sex or drugs. Jake said if Toby and the sheriff over in Lauderdale County make the request, the agency will begin an investigation."

"Have you spoken to Toby yet?" David figured he knew that answer. Allison usually worked the back channels ensuring that the odds were in her favor before making a direct approach.

"I thought I'd leave that task to Frank Martin" Allison replied. "Toby hired Frank to investigate, and if the overture comes as a recommendation from Frank I think Toby will be hard pressed to reject the idea, no matter what his personal feelings about Wilson Mackey may be." *At least I hope that's how it will play* thought Allison.

David leaned back in his chair, placed his cowboy booted feet on his desk and grinned. "And your role will be?"

"I'm not sure yet." A faint frown creased Allison's forehead. "I think bringing in the F.B.I. gives us more assets, on the ground, in cyberspace and with other law enforcement agencies. But, you know the Feds. They don't want civilians messing in their stuff unless it's at their request. Thankfully Jake Cleveland is running the investigation."

"And you think you can convince him to let you in?" David queried.

"I'm betting on it" Allison replied.

David spent the several hours after Allison's visit working the Boudreaux file with an eye towards deciding what sort of written discovery he would need to file as well as what depositions he would need to schedule of officers in the various charities. Based on the law, David knew he would need irrefutable evidence establishing first, that Jefferson Boudreaux really was Rebecca Fairchild's progeny, and second, that the 'adoptions' had not extinguished his client's claim. The information that Boudreaux had provided him, information gathered by others, seemed sufficient, but David did not like to rely on the work of strangers. David reached for the phone on his desk and punched in a number from memory.

"Martin Investigations." The sweet voice of Frank Martin's receptionist filled David's ear.

"Hey, Sonya. It's David Jackson. Is the big man around?"

A slight giggle preceded Sonya's reply. "Yes, Mr. Jackson. Hold on just a minute." David heard another giggle and Sonya's snickered "the big man" as his call was transferred.

"David, good to hear from you" Frank boomed over the line. "How's the family?"

"Fine, fine." David replied. "We need to have you over for a cookout before too long. I know Sarah would like to see you."

"Let me know when and I'll be there. What can I do for you in the meantime?"

"I'm hoping you can find time in your schedule to do a job for me." David explained.

"Depends" Frank didn't mince words. "I'm meeting with Sheriff Trowbridge in the morning to recommend he invite the F.B.I. to become involved in the Wingo and Turner murders. If he says yes, the Feds will take over most of the leg work and I'll have some breathing room. What is it you want me to take a gander at?"

David gave Frank a short run-down on the Boudreaux case, explaining his hesitancy to rely on another investigator's work product. "I think Boudreaux is legit. Can't find anything indicating otherwise, and I think he has a strong claim to Rebecca Fairchild's estate."

"But" Frank spoke as David hesitated. "There's a question in the back of your mind, isn't there?"

"Yes, there is" David admitted. "I've tried to shake it, but it won't go away. And, I want my own investigation into Boudreaux's lineage. I trust your judgment and work, Frank. If there's any way you can take this, I sure would appreciate it."

"I'll let you know after I meet with the Sheriff" Frank replied. "This Boudreaux character sounds interesting. If I can make it work with what else I've got going I'll be glad to take a look-see at Mr. Boudreaux's past."

CHAPTER TWENTY

2008

A satisfied smile moved across the man's thin face
as he fingered the fine linen fabric. *Exquisite*,
he thought, then repeated out loud to the tailor.

"Yes, it's a perfect weight for a summer suit" the
obsequious tailor replied to his client. "And it will
be a nice addition to your wardrobe."

"My wife will need new formal attire. We're going to New York next month and have several black
tie events to attend." The man moved to inspect another piece of fabric. "And I'll need a new dinner
jacket as well."

"Anything you and the Missus need" the tailor
gushed. His client made him nervous for some reason he had never figured out, but he couldn't deny

the man spent money like it was water. "I'll have Linda call your wife and set up an appointment."

"We'll need everything by the tenth. I assume that won't be a problem?" the man asked, the words a statement rather than a question. He was used to people doing as he asked.

"No, no, of course not." The tailor would need to push some other clients back a bit, but it would be worth it, even if he made a few people mad. "Not a problem at all."

Leaving the tailor shop, the new president and CEO of LaPierre Drilling glanced at his reflection in the plate glass window fronting the sidewalk. Tall, slender, well dressed – the epitome of a successful businessman.

An unpleasant memory interrupted the man's self-admiration - no matter how hard the man had worked, any innovation or expanded business plan he had brought to his father-in-law had been rejected.

"Now, son" LaPierre would drawl in the Cajun accent he had never been able to overcome, "I know you mean well, but I built this business and I make the decisions. Just do your job keeping my Cynthia happy. Leave the business to me."

It had taken every bit of will power to still his tongue and play the role his father-in-law had dictated. Someday, he knew, things would be different.

All he had to do was bide his time. Surely the old man would retire when he hit 70.

But he had not. In fact, at the birthday party his daughter and son-in-law had thrown for him ten months ago to celebrate the beginning of his 8th decade, Charles LaPierre had announced he had no intentions of retiring, ever.

"I wouldn't know what to do with my time" the old man said every time the subject was raised. "Y'all haven't given me any grandchildren to play with -I'd be bored out of my mind."

Another frown marred the man's attractive face as he remembered LaPierre's dig at Cynthia's failure to produce offspring. His father-in-law would certainly have been surprised if he had known the real reason for Cynthia's infertility, a botched abortion while she was a LSU.

Whore, the man thought, remembering. *No better than any of the others.* She had hid her transgression from him while they were courting, playing the virgin, acting so innocent. He had almost divorced her when the fertility specialist told him why Cynthia's uterus would never carry his child. But he had always been able to see the end game and thus knew better than to display his revulsion. Her time would come.

As had Charles LaPierre's. The drug the man had researched on the internet worked as planned. The cause of death on LaPierre's death certificate stated "cardiac arrest". Only a forensic autopsy searching for a needle in a haystack would have uncovered the poison that had caused Charles LaPierre's heart to stop. Given his obese father-in-law's medical history - diabetes, high cholesterol and heart disease – the massive heart attack was no surprise to anyone, least of all to the coroner.

Charles LaPierre's Will had left all of his worldly possessions, including 100% ownership of LaPierre Drilling, to his daughter Cynthia. Fortunately, LaPierre's caveman view of women had caused him to place a stipulation in the Will requiring his daughter to install her husband as President and CEO of LaPierre Drilling. His wife was very wealthy, and by association so was he.

Killing her now would draw too much attention. He could wait.

CHAPTER TWENTY-ONE

Present Day

It was only mid-week but the hours Allison had recorded in her day timer since Monday morning told a different tale. Trial work was both exhilarating and exhausting. Non-lawyers, especially people who watched shows like The Good Wife and its ilk, had no inkling of the dreary, sometimes mind-numbing yet necessary back room work that was required before a good lawyer ever uttered the first word in an opening statement. There was no getting around good preparation. More than once Allison had won a difficult case, one she could easily have lost on the merits, simply because she had out-prepared the other side. The overload of work that Allison had plowed through the first three days of the current week were the inevitable backlog of having prepared for, and then successfully litigated, a two week trial for one of her big clients. Another long day, and Allison figured she could come up for air.

"Allison, the Warden over at Kilby is on line one for you" Donna Pevey announced, sticking her head around the corner of Allison's office door. Glancing at the desk phone which had been placed on silent the past several days, Allison noted the blinking red light.

A small shiver brushed Allison's skin as she reached for the phone. Had something happened to Rice?

"Warden" anxiety coated Allison's greeting. "Is Rice alright?"

"Please don't worry, Ms. Parker" came the Warden's quick reply. "I should have told your secretary this was not bad news. Sorry if I scared you."

"No, no." Allison breathed. "No need for an apology. I'm just used to having bad news accompany a call about my brother."

A laugh preceded the Warden's next comment. "Well, I understand that feeling, Ms. Parker, but we've been real pleased here at Kilby with Rice's behavior. He's been a model inmate."

"So, am I to assume this call isn't about my brother?" Allison questioned.

"No, it is about Rice. Or rather, it's a call at his request" the Warden cleared his throat before continuing. "Normally I don't act as the messenger boy for an inmate, but given Rice's relationship to Judge Kaufman, and Rice's insistence that the matter he needed to discuss with you and your husband was of critical importance, I thought I'd make an exception."

What in the world? Was someone threatening Rice? All sorts of terrible scenarios flitted through Allison's imagination. "Did Rice give you any indication about what it was he needed to talk to us about?" she asked the Warden.

"Not a clue, and I asked him point blank if he was in danger" the Warden replied answering Allison's silent question. "He said no, he was fine, that this had something to do with a matter on the outside, something his conscience wouldn't let him ignore."

"Something his conscience wouldn't let him ignore?" Allison didn't like where this thought was taking her.

"I know what you're thinking, Ms. Parker, but I don't believe this is anything Rice has done. I get the distinct feeling this has to do with something he knows. Our inmates hear a lot of jailhouse confessions. My gut tells me Rice has heard something."

"Something that could get him killed if it got around the prison that he had talked, right Warden?"

Allison knew the answer to her question. She was just making sure the Warden knew she was fully aware of her brother's possible predicament.

"Yes, and that is why I think he wants to talk to you and the Judge. No one questions visits from family."

"Thank you for your call, Warden. Jim and I will get up there as soon as we can clear our calendars." Terminating the call with the Warden, Allison pressed the auto dial for her husband's private line.

"Hey, Babe" Jim's deep voice held a caress that Allison never tired hearing. "Is anything wrong?" A call from Allison during business hours was unusual.

"I'm not sure" Allison replied. "I just got off a call with the Warden up at Kilby. He says Rice needs to see the two of us as soon as possible. Something about Rice having something on his conscience that he can only tell you and me." Allison continued her monologue, explaining the Warden's suspicion that whatever Rice knew probably had something to do with another inmate.

The irritating squeak of the support mechanism in her husband's desk chair wafted over the phone line. Allison knew the sound well. In her mind's eye she could see her husband rocking perilously back and forth in the old leather contraption he had inherited from his predecessor, pondering the import of what she had just told him before making any comment. Her husband's proclivity for sober reflection worked well in the courtroom, but sometimes, like now, the habit just drove Allison crazy.

"Jim" Allison interjected. She really didn't see what Jim needed to contemplate. "We need to look at our calendars and decide when we can make the trip to Kilby."

The squeaking stopped. "I agree," Jim replied "but we need to think about the how to handle this visit."

"What do you mean?" Allison asked. "We're Rice's family. There's nothing unusual about family visiting an inmate."

"If what Rice needs to share with us has something to do with another inmate, and the authorities take action involving that inmate shortly after our visit, even the dumbest felon in Kilby is going to put two and two together. We're not ordinary family, Allison. I've put a lot of the inmates at Kilby behind those bars. Inmates hold grudges for a long time." Allison listened as her husband stopped to take a sip of what she assumed was his ever present cup of Joe.

"And if those guys think Rice is a rat, then his life is in danger, if for no other reason than to get back at you." Allison finished Jim's sentence for him.

"Not just to get back at me, although that alone would be a motivator for some of those guys. Unfortunately, Rice would be the main target.

Inmates who rat usually end up permanently maimed, or worse. We need to think about a cover story for our visit" Jim explained. "Something that gives Rice credibility with the other inmates. I'll give the Warden a call later today. I think I may have an idea."

Allison had barely concluded the call with her husband when her office line rang. Glancing at the caller ID pad, Allison noted the familiar number. Better to deal with him now, she concluded. Maybe talking to Frank would help her get her mind off the danger she was afraid her brother was courting.

"Hello, Frank" Allison made an effort to sound cheery. "What's up?"

"I've got good news" Frank's words trampled each other in their attempt to leave his mouth. "Toby's asked the Feds to help on the Wingo case, and he's persuaded the Sheriff over in Lauderdale County to do the same. We're gonna have an honest-to god task force set up right here in Ft. Charles."

"That's great" Allison tried to ignore the frisson of excitement that crossed her body. "I was worried Jake Cleveland had run into red tape when I didn't hear back from him. Maybe this means Sheriff Trowbridge and Special Agent Wilson Mackey have put their differences behind them." At least Allison hoped so. She had never figured out why men had such pissing contests over territory.

"Yeah, I think the prospect of catching a serial killer was the ace that convinced both Sheriffs as well as the Feds that this was a win-win situation for everyone." Frank explained. "But here's the best part. Jake Cleveland is definitely going to be the point man for the task force."

Allison considered that tidbit of information. She and Jake were on good terms. In fact, the F.B.I. wouldn't have even known about this case had she not set up the meeting with Jake in Birmingham and given him Frank Martin's report. Allison didn't see a role for herself in the case so far, but if she did, she thought she could convince Jake to let her on the team.

"You're right, Frank" Allison agreed. Having Jake Cleveland heading up the task force was a good idea. Sheriff Trowbridge likes him, and things ought to work more smoothly than if the sheriff had to deal directly with Mackey."

"Doesn't this tempt you, Allison?" Frank teased, his question holding more truth than he realized.

Allison laughed. "Yes, it does, Frank, but I've got a full caseload right now, plus I've agreed to help David on that Will contest case he has. It's heated up more than we expected. And, Jim and I are going to have to head over to Kilby in the next day or two."

"That boy alright?" Frank asked.

"Oh, I'm sure he's fine" Allison mentally kicked herself for mentioning Rice and the upcoming visit. "We just haven't seen him in a while. Jim had a break come up on his docket and suggested we make a quick trip up and back." *Shut up.* Allison berated herself. *The less people who know about this visit the better.* "Well, I'd better head to the house" Allison tried for a casual retort. "Thanks for calling, Frank. The task force certainly is good news. Let me know if anything interesting develops."

"You betcha'" Frank chuckled as he hung up the phone. "It's just a matter of time before you're right in the middle of this."

CHAPTER TWENTY-TWO

Piles of boxes cluttered the small office that housed the F.B.I.'s joint task force unit. Barely large enough for one person, the space the Calhoun County Sheriff's office had provided Jake and his team was crammed with three desks, as many filing cabinets and the aforementioned boxes containing hardcopy of cold case files with similar MO's to the Wingo crime scene. Thankfully, Jake thought surveying the cramped quarters, the two agents assigned to him would be spending most of their time in the field chasing down any leads that came through the Tip Hot Line that would be set up. *Like sardines in a can* he mused, but nothing that a veteran agent like himself couldn't adjust to. He'd had worse accommodations.

Jake took a sip of colored water from the cracked cup he had snagged from the break room. "This stuff tastes like shit" Jake observed to no one in particular. A Mr. Coffee would be his first purchase tonight on his way to the motel. A man couldn't survive drinking what passed for coffee at the Calhoun County Sheriff's office. *How did Toby drink that stuff?*

An assortment of papers and case files littered the top of Jake's desk. The likelihood of solving the Wingo case, to determining whether Francine Turner's murder was connected, and maybe finding a connection to other cold case sex crimes would be in direct proportion to his team's willingness to pay attention to the smallest detail. Boring, tedious work that might never result in closing the cases unless luck favored them.

Over the years Jake had argued with his fellow agents about the role of luck in solving difficult cases. Many agents, maybe to inflate their own sense of importance, swore that cases could only be solved by expert detective work. While Jake acknowledged the role good, solid detective work played in resolving any case, experience had taught him that some cases would never have been solved absent pure blind luck that often appeared in the strangest ways. The murder-for-hire case that had fallen into his lap was a perfect example. Absent the quirk of fate- or luck – that had intervened during his investigation of a money laundering scheme, Allison Parker, her husband and partner David would be residing in Ft. Charles Memorial Gardens instead of enjoying the daily routine of life in a small Southern town. Picking up the file nearest to him, Jake hoped that same kind of luck would ultimately help solve the cases before him.

The manila jacket read "Case File SC2034: Jane Doe, Houma, LA, 1988". Retrieving several typed pages, Jake began to re-familiarize himself with the first sex crime case he had worked as a new F.B.I. agent. *"Female, approximate age 25 to 30, evidence of vaginal and anal tearing, breast mutilation, puncture wounds in hands and feet. Cause of death, exsanguination due to severe injuries."* Interpretation – the victim had been alive until the very end.

The casefile contained multiple pictures taken at the crime scene, but Jake didn't need to look at those to refresh his recollection. The Houma death scene had imprinted itself in Jake's subconscious, haunting him with horrific nightmares for almost an entire year. The mayhem inflicted on the Houma victim had been so bad that the entire investigative team had been required to undergo counseling by F.B.I. in-house shrinks, and one new agent had resigned.

Jake thought it unlikely that the perp who killed the Houma victim would still be operating. Twenty years, maybe more, was a long time for someone so violent to escape notice. In addition, the amount of violence inflicted on the Houma victim was more likely to occur when a serial killer was mentally decompensating and escalating in terms of actions and proximity in time from crime to crime. Of course, with psychopaths one could never be sure. The perp could have been arrested for something else and been confined for a period of years, he could have gotten better at hiding his victims, he could have stopped for some period for reasons unknown. There were endless possibilities for why this particular crime had remained unsolved. Jake reminded himself to be open to any scenario. Whoever had killed the Houma victim had planned in advance. The kill site was remote, ensuring that the victim's screams would not be heard as well as making the likelihood that the victim would be discovered a random event. But for two hunters who had been chasing wild boar, the Houma victim might never have been found. *Yes*, reflected Jake, *luck had played a role in that case in the beginning. Maybe it would again.*

Most of Marilee Wingo's remains had been destroyed by the tornado that had decimated the shed where she had been chained. Still, Jake mused, there were similarities to the Houma murder. Remote location, arms and legs spread open. Like the Houma victim, Marilee Wingo had been placed in a sexually vulnerable position. Whether she had been mutilated as well would never be known.

Laying aside the Houma casefile, Jake wandered down the hall to Sheriff Trowbridge's office.

"Morning Miz Robinson" Jake nodded to Toby's secretary. "The Sheriff in?"

"Hello Special Agent Cleveland" Beth Robinson replied with a smile. "The Sheriff stepped out for a few minutes. He'll be back right shortly. You're welcome to have a sit and wait." Beth pointed to several straight back chairs lining the wall near her desk. "Don't worry" she laughed. "You won't have to sit in those things too long."

Jake had barely settled into the uncomfortable chair when Toby Trowbridge returned. "Hey, Sheriff" Jake called out. "You got a minute?"

"Sure. Come on in. You want some coffee?" Seeing Jake's expression, Toby added "I brew my own."

The two men engaged in the male version of small talk while waiting for the coffee to be ready, Toby convinced the Atlanta Braves would have a winning season, Jake insisting the Texas Rangers would beat the pants off any team in either league, including that pansy team from Atlanta. By the time the chime on Toby's coffee maker indicated a fresh brew, the Sheriff and the Special Agent had reconciled their differences by agreeing that Peyton Manning was the greatest quarterback ever to play the game of football.

Handing Jake a cup of black coffee, Toby closed the office door. "You and your team set up now?"

"Yes. Scott Miller and Teresa Brown are the two agents that have been assigned to me. They should be here some time tomorrow, but they will work out of the Birmingham office, too, so you won't see them every day."

Toby nodded. "I know your boss thinks there's something to the Wingo and Turner murders. 'Else you wouldn't be here."

"Not just Wilson" Jake placed his empty coffee cup on the front of the Sheriff's desk. "We think the two murders are related, just not how or why. And, beyond that, there are some things about the Wingo case that remind me of an old cold case out of Louisiana."

"What things?" Toby asked, not sure he wanted to know the answer, or the bad news that might eventually follow.

"There was a terrible murder in Houma, Louisiana back in the late '80's." Jake proceeded to give Toby the particulars. "Never had any leads. It's been a cold case for a long, long time."

"Jesus" Toby replied. "What sort of pervert does that to a living person?"

"A sick one" Jake quickly replied, "but a very smart one too. The remote location of the Houma murder, and the positioning of the victim remind me of the Wingo crime scene."

Toby shook his head. "I just don't see how it could be the same guy. Too much time has passed. Even assuming the perp was in his twenties at the time he did the girl in Houma, he'd be in his fifties now, or close to it. Unlikely he'd have evaded capture all these years, no matter how smart he might be."

"Maybe so" Jake allowed. "But whoever killed that girl in Houma, if he's still out there I sure would like to put him down. Someone like that doesn't deserve to be called 'human'."

"That's a fact" Toby agreed. "Other than you thinking there's a similarity between the Houma case and the Wingo case, you got any leads on our current perp?"

"Nada" admitted Jake. "But we will."

Walking back to his office Jake considered why the Sheriff was so certain the Houma perp couldn't be the same guy who killed Marilee Wingo. Intellectually, Jake knew Toby was right. Jake's gut, however, disagreed. Jake knew what that meant. He had more work to do.

CHAPTER
TWENTY-THREE

2012

He didn't like staying in one place too long when he was out hunting. Someone might remember him, give a description to the police, offer some seemingly inconsequential observation that would reveal his identity to the authorities. Fortunately, there was such an abundance of rural and undeveloped land in Texas, Louisiana and Mississippi that he had had his pick of secluded kill spots over the years.

After he married he worried that it would be more difficult to mask the need that periodically drove him to stalk, capture and mutilate the

whores who walked with impunity among the righteous. When God revealed to him his own wife's
whorish past - the promiscuity she had hidden
from him, the botched abortion that meant she
would never bear his child – the man's anger at
the deception had compelled him to hunt without
his usual precautions. Taking the girl in Houma
had been a mistake. Not only had she been a disappointment, his failure to sufficiently plan the
location of the kill site had shown such a reckless
lack of judgment that her body had ultimately
been discovered.

After Houma, the man fell into a despair of sorts.
God had called him to this work, this Holy mission
to punish and purge. Of this he was certain. But
the fear of arrest and incarceration weighed heavily
on his mind, warring with the need to hunt, causing
great internal anguish for the man. He continued
to hunt, but more carefully and less often than in his
earlier years. To assuage the need that arose, unbidden, he had turned his attention to the whore who
shared his bed. *God works in mysterious ways*, he told
himself every time he bound and sexually abused
his wife. A wife must submit to her husband, he told
her. It was God's will. The cancer that had later eat-
en his wife's breasts and uterus had also been God's
will, a fitting end for a whore.

Her death had made him rich, rich enough to finally take revenge on the mother who had abandoned him, rich enough to take back what was rightfully his. Rich enough to be foolish.

CHAPTER TWENTY-FOUR

Present Day

The case management conference set by the court in the Boudreaux case was marked in red on David's calendar. Looking over the notes he had made during his legal research, David felt confident that he would be able to articulate his client's position and support his legal arguments with ample case law.

Jefferson Boudreaux had provided his attorney three separate investigative reports that he had commissioned prior to seeking David's assistance. All three investigators had concluded that at least on paper Jefferson Boudreaux was who he said he was – the only child of Rebecca Fairchild. The investigators had also unanimously concluded that there was no evidence that Rebecca Fairchild had terminated her parental rights. This particular fact gave David a good argument that his client's adoption was null and void. *Should be a slam dunk*, David mused, *even without the Defendants' pending request for genetic testing.*

Picking up the office phone, David punched the numbers for Jefferson Boudreaux's cell phone.

"Yes?" Boudreaux's cultured voice answered.

"Mr. Boudreaux, it's David Jackson. Do you have a minute to discuss a matter that has arisen in your case?" David inquired politely. Dealing with this particular client always made David a tad uneasy although for the life of him he couldn't figure out why.

"Of course" came the quiet reply. "Is there a problem?"

"No, not a problem" David assured his client. "And not an unexpected request given our claim that you are Rebecca Fairchild's son." Clearing his throat David continued. "The Defendants have filed a joint motion for a DNA test. In my opinion, the court will grant the motion. I think it would put your claim in question if you resisted the request."

"I don't understand" Boudreaux interjected. "Haven't you provided the Defendants with copies of the three investigative reports?"

"Yes, we provided copies of those reports as part of our initial discovery disclosures. But nothing is as conclusive as DNA testing" David explained. "The Defendants claim to have genetic material from Rebecca Fairchild, and they want to test yours against hers."

"I find this request overly intrusive" came a haughty reply. "The investigators I hired were tops in their field. There is no reason to require anything further."

"It's your call, Mr. Boudreaux, but I strongly urge you to reconsider. I've researched this particular issue, and I have yet to find a court that has declined to order DNA testing in a case like yours when requested by one of the parties." A small red flag began to wave at the periphery of David's mind. "Is there something you're not telling me Mr. Boudreaux? I don't want to be blindsided if there is something you are withholding."

David's question was met with a silence so lengthy that he wondered if the call had been disconnected. David's "Mr. Boudreaux?" was overridden by his client's terse reply.

"I think the testing is totally unnecessary, but I see your point. Nevertheless, I want you to make a cursory objection to the Defendants' request." Boudreaux ordered. "Acquiescing to your opponents' demands is a sign of weakness."

"Like I said, it's your call" David acknowledged, "but resisting this request is not my recommendation. I will file your objection prior to the case management conference so that the issue will be ripe for the court to decide. But I want your agreement that I can withdraw our opposition to the Defendants' request at the case management conference if, in my professional judgment, I think our position is harming your case."

"Fine" Boudreaux replied sharply. "Let me know what happens."

David drummed his fingers on the top of his desk as he considered the discussion he had just had with his client. DNA testing was a simple procedure. If Jefferson Boudreaux was certain of his lineage, why oppose a test that would solidify his legal claim to the Fairchild estate? David didn't buy the showing weakness argument his client had offered one bit. Swinging his feet from the desktop where they had rested, David headed down the hall for a second opinion.

"You coming to see me?" Exiting the firm's small break room with a cup of coffee and her morning bagel, Allison spied her partner coming down the hallway.

"I thought you were giving up carbs?" David's raised eyebrows underscored his question as he followed Allison into her office.

"Well, maybe not all of them" Allison gave a sheepish grin in reply. "Anyway, I don't want to shock my system all at once."

"Oh yeh" David laughed. "Wouldn't want you to have a sugar meltdown."

"Crap" Allison muttered, throwing the bagel in the trash basket beside her desk. "You sure know how to ruin a good snack."

"You'll thank me later" David replied as he settled into one of the comfortable chairs Allison had for clients who visited her office. "If you've got a minute I want to talk to you some more about the Boudreaux case."

Allison took a long sip of coffee before responding. "What's going on, David? In all the years we've practiced law together I've never known you to have the kind of reservations about a client that you continue to have with Jefferson Boudreaux. I thought this was a fairly open and shut case."

"I thought so, too" David admitted. "And it should be. The investigative reports all say the same thing – Boudreaux's claim is valid, Rebecca Fairchild never severed her parental rights. I knew I'd get a fight from the charities named in her Will, but I felt pretty certain we would ultimately be successful."

"But?" Allison asked.

"The Defendants have asked for a DNA test. They claim to have DNA from Rebecca Fairchild and want to see if Boudreaux is a match." David paused.

"That's no surprise" Allison interjected, "What's the problem?"

"Boudreaux wants to resist the request. He was pretty adamant about it, even when I told him I thought it made his claim look suspect." David began to pace the small area in front of Allison's desk. "He insisted I file a formal opposition to the request. All I could get him to agree was to let me withdraw the opposition motion at the case management conference if I thought our resistance to the testing was hurting us in the judge's eyes."

"Well, some clients are just plain weird" Allison shook her head in sympathy with her partner's frustrations. "As the old saying goes, you can lead a horse to water. You know the rest."

"It's more than that" David's mouth was set in a grim line. "Something isn't right here. I've felt it before, but I just can't put my finger on it."

"You can get out of this case if you want" Allison reminded her partner. "You're still in the early stages of discovery, and I am sure the Court would grant a motion to withdraw if Boudreaux resisted you resigning as his lawyer."

"No, I can't do that" David sighed. "There's a big payday for the firm if we win, and based on everything

I've seen, I think the odds are in our favor. I can't point to any concrete reason I should withdraw from the case. It's just a feeling I have about my client that worries me."

"No case is worth keeping just for the fee" Allison gave her partner a hard look. "But, if you insist on moving forward, I think we ought to ask Frank Martin to take a closer look at Jefferson Boudreaux."

"I've already talked to Frank about this, but I hate to spend the firm's money on what is probably just my imagination" David explained.

"We won't" Allison explained. "Frank owes me some free P.I. time. There's something about this case that keeps worrying you. Maybe it's the client, not the case. I'll give Frank a call this afternoon and let him know this is the freebie he owes me."

"Zachary, good to see you" Jim extended his hand to the redheaded man dressed in a tan colored, military style uniform. "Everything in place?"

"Yes, Judge. Not to worry" the Warden replied. "And how are you Ms. Parker?" he asked nodding at Allison.

Allison looked from one man to the other. "What are you two talking about? Is what in place?"

Directing Jim and Allison away from the prison's security and reception area, the Warden lowered his voice. "Just a small diversion to ensure you can talk to your brother in private without raising suspicion."

Before Allison could ask another question, her husband interjected "I don't know what the Warden has planned, either. Better for us to be as surprised as everyone else."

"Exactly" the Warden agreed. Motioning to a guard waiting nearby, the Warden ordered "Jamison, escort Judge Kaufman and his wife to the cafeteria. They're here for visitation" before turning back towards Jim and Allison to add "We'll see each other before you leave."

Kilby's cafeteria had been built for size and security. The large open space was surrounded on all sides by a high, steel-fenced catwalk. Although the present atmosphere of the cafeteria seemed almost jovial given the presence of families, everyone in attendance was aware of the armed guards stationed above their heads.

The cafeteria proper held 30 or so tables, each with the capacity to seat eight. Given the population of the prison, Allison knew meals would be eaten in shifts. Today, as with all visitation days, each inmate who had visitors scheduled had been assigned a particular table. In order to limit the number of visitors at any given time, inmates were assigned specific visitation days. Allowing open visitation for all inmates on the same day would have been impossible. Allison noted that several of the tables were empty, indicating either an inmate's refusal to see any visitors, or, more likely, evidence that no one on the outside was interested enough to make the long trip to Kilby. A sad commentary either way, Allison thought.

Glancing across the room, Allison saw her brother Rice raise his hand in greeting. "He's lost more weight" Allison remarked to her husband as they moved towards Rice's table.

Rice gave his sister a quick hug, then took his brother-in-law's hand. "Thank you, both, for coming" Rice smiled, holding Jim's hand a bit longer before releasing his grip.

Allison took a seat on the bench next to Rice. "You're too thin, Rice. Are you sure you aren't sick?"

"Oh, I'm fine" Rice replied. "Don't worry about me. How is Mary Louise?"

"No change. The doctors think Mary Louise has reached her maximum improvement. But she is well cared for, and seems content" Allison paused thinking about the physical shell inhabited by what was left of her sister-in-law's consciousness.

"We're not here to talk about Mary Louise" Jim reminded the other two. "Why did you want to see us, Rice?"

A scream of "MOTHER FUCKER, I'M GONNA KILL YOU" assaulted Allison's ears, followed in quick succession by the cacophony of sound created by a table being tossed against one of the cafeteria walls, the combined screams of terrified civilians, and the ratcheting sound of automatic weapons chambering a round of ammunition.

"Get down" Jim yelled, throwing Allison to the ground and covering her with his body. "You too, Rice" he yelled before realizing Rice had already rolled underneath the cafeteria table.

A deafening siren poured its warning from the speakers high on the cafeteria walls as armed guards rushed into the cafeteria. "No one move. Hands on the tables." Compliance was instantaneous as shocked visitors and inmates alike rushed to obey. Peering from her place of safety, Allison watched as two corrections officers restrained the culprit, who now seemed remarkably calm, and removed him from the room.

"Today's visitation has been terminated" the cafeteria's sound system announced. "Please remain at your table until escorted from the premises by a corrections officer."

The sounds of pissed off inmates and disappointed visitors filled the air. "We drove five hours to get here" a gray haired woman complained. "This ain't right" another man complained. "What the fuck?" a disgruntled inmate complained "I don't get another visitation day for a month."

Allison was about to voice her own objection when a young corrections officer appeared at their table. "Judge Kaufman? If you and your group would follow me, please." Noting Jim's quick glance in her direction, Allison gathered her purse and followed the corrections officer as he led her, Jim and Rice out of the cafeteria.

"Where are we going?" Allison whispered to her husband.

"My guess is, somewhere private" Jim replied. "Ten to one that spectacle in the cafeteria was staged."

"To give us an opportunity to be alone with Rice" Allison finished Jim's sentence with a smile.

Stepping between Allison and Jim, Rice added quietly "We won't have much time. I'll be expected back on my block about the same time as everyone else."

"Here we are, Sir" the young corrections officer indicated a nearby door. "Warden Stone said you'd have fifteen minutes. It's the best he can do."

"Thank you, officer" Jim replied. "Stone is it?" he inquired noting the name on the young officer's badge.

"The Warden's my uncle" the officer grinned. "I know how to keep my mouth shut."

As soon as the metal door clicked behind the three, Rice turned to Allison and Jim. "I heard this in a meeting. Breaking someone's anonymity and a confidence shared in a meeting is bad enough in AA, but if this gets back to the wrong people ... well, you get my drift."

"Rice, you don't need to tell us anything" Allison responded. "Nothing can be so important that you would put yourself at risk of being hurt or killed. Nothing."

Rice raised a hand to silence his sister's objection. "That's why I won't identify the source of my information. If he isn't questioned no one will know I've talked."

"I don't like this" Allison ignored Rice's explanation. "We can't guarantee what will happen with the information you plan to share with us. You know that."

Rice shrugged, then opening his arms in a gesture of surrender Allison recognized from their childhood, he began "It happened in Louisiana, near a place by the name of Bossier City."

CHAPTER TWENTY-SIX

A loud moan escaped Frank Martin's lips as he stretched muscles that had spent the last several hours crammed into the passenger side of Jake Cleveland's rental car.

"Why the hell didn't you get something bigger?" Frank complained. "Only a midget could be comfortable in this tin can."

"Uncle Sammy's rules" Jake replied as he exited the driver's side of the Subaru Forester. "I'm lucky to get as nice a ride as this one. Usually it's some piece of crap Chevy."

"Shit" Frank laughed. "Given your history with rental cars, maybe you ought to stick with the cheapest thing they've got."

"It wasn't my fault that ass hat shot up my car" Jake huffed, remembering the shootout that had ended the McNair investigation and had almost ended his life as well. "Wasn't the first time I've been shot at and probably won't be the last." The two men were still exchanging barbs as they entered the front door of the Lauderdale County Sheriff's office.

"Special Agent Jake Cleveland and Investigator Frank Martin here to see Sheriff Gilbert" Jake announced to the receptionist as he flashed his F.B.I. credentials.

"Please have a seat over there." The female deputy indicated a row of chairs which looked exceedingly uncomfortable to Frank. "I'll let the Sheriff know you're here."

Frank examined the proffered seating arrangements, and decided standing was his better option. *Midget car, midget chairs* Frank fumed. All this discomfort added to Frank's irritation about having to make the trip to Meridian to begin with. "Cleveland's running this investigation" Frank had complained to Sheriff Trowbridge. "What am I, his bag boy?" But his Sheriff had insisted, telling Frank "You're my man on the ground, Frank. My eyes and ears. I need to make sure the Bureau doesn't hold out on me. Besides, you're the one whose investigative skills made the possible connection between our murder and the one in Mississippi. You ought to be front and center in this investigation." Frank knew he shouldn't be bothered by the Bureau's role, especially since he was the one who suggested the F.B.I.'s help in the first place. It just boiled down to independence. Frank was a one man operation. Having someone else in charge was not the way Frank liked to conduct business.

"Gentlemen" Frank turned towards the sound of Sheriff Gilbert's greeting. "Thanks for making the trip over." Sheriff Scott Gilbert's fierce handshake and stern visage gave a sharp contrast to his cordial greeting. "I've got a conference room reserved for us." *He's probably as pissed as I am about being ordered about by the Bureau* Frank thought as he followed Jake and the Sheriff down the hall. *This should be interesting.*

The Lauderdale County Sheriff's office was housed in a fairly new building, and as a result the department had been able to avail itself of the bells and whistles associated with newer technology. "Impressive space" Jake complimented the Sheriff as they took their seats around a large table.

"Thanks" Gilbert acknowledged as he reached across the table and pressed several buttons on a black contraption that looked like a mini version of a stealth fighter jet. "Send in Deputy Greene" he ordered the person on the other end of the line. Disconnecting the call, Sheriff Gilbert continued "Deputy Sharon Greene is the department's forensic specialist. I'll let her explain what she's found."

Gilbert had barely finished his explanation when the conference room door was thrust open to admit a tall, raven-haired beauty. "Sheriff, gentlemen" the Amazon acknowledged with a curt nod as she slide into a seat next to Gilbert. Sharon Greene had a white sounding name, but her stunning features telegraphed her strong Native American heritage. Long black hair, caramel colored skin, straight and aristocratic nose – Sharon Greene was likely a member of the local Choctaw tribe.

Eight Native American tribes had once inhabited the area which now constituted the state of Mississippi. Chickasaw, Choctaw, Houma, Biloxi, Natchez, Ofa, Quapaw and Tunica – all that now remained were towns named after the various tribes. With one exception. Taking advantage of their status as an independent nation, the Mississippi Choctaws had embraced the capitalist creed building and successfully running two resort hotels, casinos and an enormous water park outside Philadelphia, Mississippi. Profits from these enterprises were distributed to tribe members, enabling many of them to pursue college and advanced degrees while dramatically improving their overall standard of living.

Frank figured Sharon Greene had been the beneficiary of this largess.

"Sharon, tell these men what you've discovered" Gilbert's directive gave his deputy the go ahead.

The forensic specialist opened the laptop she had placed on the tabletop, and with a rapid click on the computer's keyboard connected to the room's wall screen. "What you're looking at" she told the men "is a list of emails we discovered on Francine Turner's computer, including those that the victim had deleted." Frank nodded. Emails were never truly destroyed or deleted, although most regular users didn't know this. Greene manipulated the computer mouse in her right hand and a new image filled the screen. "In this document we have grouped the victim's emails by sender and recipient, looking for any significant or unusual activity." A clicking sound announced a third image, this one displaying a list of web addresses. "We also collated the web addresses of the sites the victim visited in the past six months. What we've found is quite interesting." Handing Frank and Jake separate manila folders Greene added "I've prepared a summary of the pertinent emails as well as a list of the websites I think may assist us in this case."

Jake laid the folder on the table without opening it. "What are your conclusions, Deputy, based on your forensic investigation?"

"Francine Turner had been researching human trafficking." Greene replied. "There were several emails to journalists who have written on the topic, links to old newspaper articles, even web searches seeking information on task forces and the like. One of the last searches on her computer was for the U. S. Department of Justice in D.C. and Immigrations and Customs Enforcement."

Jake's eyes narrowed. "The Bureau has been looking into human trafficking that is coming out of Mexico, over the Texas and Arizona borders. Have you shared this information?"

"We're sharing it now" Gilbert replied.

"I'll need copies of everything you have on this, electronic file, no summaries." Jake's tone was clear. Addressing his question to the forensic specialist, he asked "You think the vic's interest in human trafficking got her killed?"

"Based on everything we know, that theory fits the best. Francine Turner had no enemies that we have discovered, she was a hard worker, been employed at the truck stop for a couple of years. Nothing in her day-to-day life that would have caused her to be a target. We figure she said something to the wrong person, and that got her killed."

"Like me" Frank interjected. "If your theory is right, someone at that truck stop saw her talking to me the night she was killed. Either that, or she mentioned our conversation to the wrong person. Francine got scared when I told her about her cousin. Wouldn't talk to me any longer at the truck stop. That's why we were meeting down the road at the diner after she got off work." Frank took a sip of cold coffee. "No" he said shaking his head, "someone saw her talking to me and got worried."

"How would anyone have known who you are?" Gilbert asked. "Was anyone near when you were talking to her?"

"The place was pretty busy when I got there. I don't know who was a customer and who wasn't." Frank tried to pull his conversation with Francine into clearer focus in his mind. "I pulled out my P.I. identification when I told her about the Wingo girl. Maybe the wrong person saw it. Damn it, I sure as hell hope I didn't get that nice girl killed."

"No way to know, Frank" Jake Cleveland assured his friend. "Sounds more likely to me that someone knew what the girl was looking into, thought she was too close to something, and decided to eliminate a problem."

"When Deputy Greene showed me what she had uncovered, I knew the task force would want to see the forensic data." Gilbert explained. "That's why I asked y'all to come over today. Unfortunately, I'm not sure this gives us a solid connection to the Wingo murder. It's certainly more than odd that our two victims are related, and we also know Wingo worked as a prostitute in New Orleans. Most victims of human trafficking end up as prostitutes, so Wingo would fit the profile, but we've not uncovered any solid evidence yet that makes the murders of these two women anything other than coincidental."

"I don't believe in coincidences" Jake replied. "Thank you for your time Sheriff, Deputy" Jake nodded in the general direction of his host. "Let's go, Frank. We've got a lot of work ahead of us."

CHAPTER TWENTY-SEVEN

It's too close. Not enough time since the last one. The voice that had always kept him safe sounded loudly in his head. *Not here. Not where you took the last one.*

The man beat his head with closed fists. *Go away, go away* he commanded. *I make the decisions, not you.* He had seen the girl the day he arrived in town. She was walking down the road near the high school, book bag slung carelessly over her shoulder, skirt a bit too short, long slender legs propelling her quickly on her way. He had known not to approach her. It was daytime, and he had other, more important matters to attend to. He had barely been able to hide his look of recognition when he saw her the next morning at the inn where he was staying.

"Mindy, our new guest be staying with us for several weeks" Ed Mitchum explained as he introduced his daughter to the man.

"Pleased to meet you, Sir" the girl had replied shyly before giving her dad a quick kiss and hastily exiting the inn's dining room. "See you after school, Daddy" she called from the front porch, "Love you."

Over a full breakfast of pancakes, eggs, bacon, grits and biscuits, Ed Mitchum had explained how he had come to be a single parent, raising Mindy from the age of six after his wife had died in a car accident. Running a B&B had given Ed Mitchum the ability to be a stay-at-home parent while making a decent income for the two of them. His daughter, the innkeeper boasted, would be Valedictorian this June when she graduated from Ft. Charles High School. She was, he added, his heart and soul.

The girl wasn't like the others. The man had watched her, listened to her conversations with her father and with friends who visited the inn. No boyfriend, either. She would be different, pure, untouched. His penis hardened when he thought of her.

He knew her schedule now. Knew that she often took a short cut home, going through the woods near the high school on the days she stayed late to tutor some of the stupid offspring of the local share-croppers. "I want to do something to help them, Daddy. They aren't lucky like I am" he had heard her explain to her father. "It's only one afternoon a week and I'll be home by 5:30."

The man had spent three afternoons in the woods, making sure there were no homes or barns nearby, calculating how he would take her, where he would conceal her, how he would kill her. The sexual pleasure that his planning brought to him was almost unbearable. How much better it would be when he had her.

Now, he waited for her. *No* the voice insisted, and he almost obeyed. But then he heard her footfall coming down the path.

When he was finished, when she was dead, he masturbated himself as a final pleasure. She had fought him like a wild animal. Who would have thought such a meek and obedient girl would have had that kind of spunk? Fucking her twice had not been enough.

The man removed his clothes and placed them in the bag he had brought with him, replacing his ruined pants and shirt with their identical twins. He would dispose of the bag in the field on the other side of the woods. Glancing at the still form of his victim, the man moved to untie his victim's hands, then thought the better of it. The tableau that was so important to him needed to be just right with this one. Innocent, yet despoiled. He pushed the girl's legs apart and inserted a large stick into her rectum. *A nice touch*, he thought.

Later in the evening, the man was resting quietly in his room when red flashing lights from several law enforcement cruisers cast revolving fingers of flame across the darkened walls.

"No God, No". Ed Mitchum's screams to the Almighty echoed up the inn's stairwell. "Oh, Sweet Jesus, my baby, my poor baby".

The man watched out his window as Ed Mitchum was supported by two uniformed deputies to a waiting car, the sound of the destroyed man's weeping wafting upwards to the man's open window. A cruel smile moved over the man's lips.

The voice tried to reason with the man. *Get out while you can.* The man laughed. No one had ever come close to catching him, not even in Houma. His disguise was perfection.

CHAPTER
TWENTY-EIGHT

Frank Martin rolled up his imaginary sleeves, reached for a fresh cigar, and took a sip of Columbia's finest, home brewed in the French press resting on the side of his office credenza. The last couple of weeks had kept Frank busy, riding sidekick with Agent Cleveland and running down whatever leads looked promising on the Wingo and Turner murders. So far not a lot, but a lot more interesting work than looking into that rich client David Jackson hired him to do a background check on. Even worse, Allison had called him on the free time he owed her, so now not only did he have to spend time on a boring case, he was going to have to do it for free. *Next time*, Frank reminded himself, *keep your damn mouth shut.*

Opening his laptop, Frank began the preliminary fishing expedition that marked the beginning of a Frank Martin investigation. Frank had seen the personal information that Jefferson Boudreaux had provided David Jackson, and based on an initial review, had originally figured his work for Jackson wouldn't consume more than a couple of hours of internet time. But, the closer Frank looked at the documentation the wealthy man had provided his attorney, the more suspicious Frank became. On paper, and even according to some legal documentation that had been provided, Jefferson Boudreaux was squeaky clean. There were good people in the world, Frank knew that. But even the best and most righteous had their flaws. No one was as perfect as Jefferson Boudreaux professed to be.

The L.L. Bean flip clock that Frank kept on his desk showed 8:21 a.m. David Jackson should be at the office by now. Frank pulled his phone out of his pocket and ordered Siri to call David Jackson's office.

"Parker and Jackson" a soft and unfamiliar voice took Frank by surprise.

"Who is this?" he demanded. "Why isn't Donna answering the phone?"

The voice on the other end of the line never missed a beat. "This is the law office of Parker and Jackson. My name is Rose. I am the new receptionist. With whom do you wish to speak and may I say who is calling?"

Frank had begun to identify himself when he heard a call waiting beep on the line. Recognizing the caller I.D, Frank terminated his call to the law firm without answering the sweet voice that belonged to someone named Rose, and clicked over to take the Sheriff's call.

"Frank, it's Jake Cleveland."

"What are you doing on Sheriff Trowbridge's phone"

"I'm at the station. Get down here quick as you can. We've got another murder. Same M.O."

Frank hesitated, then asked "Do we know the vic?"

"Some local high school girl" Cleveland replied. "Got her name here. Uh, Mindy Mitchum, seventeen, father runs a local bed and breakfast. The dad reported her missing when she failed to return home after school. Searchers found her about 10:30 last night."

"Aw, shit" Frank's reply was barely audible.

"What's that?" Cleveland asked. "I couldn't hear what you said."

"I said 'shit'" Frank replied sharply. "I've known that girl since she was a baby. This is gonna' kill Ed. First his wife, and now Mindy." The thought of what must have happened to the young girl was about to make Frank sick to his stomach.

"Toby is handling this right now, but as soon as Birmingham makes the call, our task force will take over. I've asked for more boots on the ground as well."

"He never left the area, did he?" Frank asked.

"Doesn't look like it" Cleveland replied.

"I'll see you in fifteen minutes" Frank assured the F.B.I. agent as he concluded the call. On his way out the door, Frank rang David Jackson's office again. "Rose, this is urgent." Frank stated after identifying himself. "I need to speak with one of your bosses, doesn't matter which."

Less than a minute later, Allison had taken the call. "Frank, what's wrong? Is it Jim?" Although the cardiologist had assured her that her husband's heart was now in good condition, she continued to worry. The urgency of Frank's call had frightened her.

"No, no, Allison. It's not Jim." Frank kicked him-self mentally for not making that distinction when he had classified his call as urgent. "I'm on my way to Toby's office. There's been another homicide.

Same M.O. as the Wingo girl, but this time the vic is local. It's Ed Mitchum's daughter."

"Oh my God" Allison was shocked. "Mindy? She just baby sat for us last Saturday. I can't believe this has happened."

"I don't have any details, just Jake Cleveland's report that it looks like the same guy." Allison heard the sounds of Frank's truck starting. "Tell David I'm going to have to postpone my investigation into that Boudreaux guy for at least the next few days. And, Allison, I really want you to reconsider working with the task force. This is one of our own this freak has killed. You've got a good way of looking at things. We need you."

"Let me move some things around" Allison replied. "I'll try to get down to Toby's in the next hour. Will that be soon enough?"

"Yes." Frank thought briefly about his next request. "You and Jim became close to Ed after his wife died. I think Ed would feel more comfortable if you were there when Jake interviews him. You okay with that?"

"Frank, no one thinks Ed did this to his own child do they?" Allison was horrified by the thought.

"No. But the agency is going to take a hard look at Ed anyway, if for nothing else to see if he had any enemies or was into something that might have resulted in a revenge killing of some sort." Frank thought the latter idea ludicrous, but he knew how the F.B.I. operated.

"Ed didn't have any enemies." Allison was certain. "And there's no way he was into anything illegal or dangerous, either. Whatever Evil killed Mindy, I can't believe it had anything to do with Ed."

"You don't have to convince me" Frank agreed.

A thought entered Allison's mind, causing her to ask "I thought the task force was looking for a connection between the Wingo murder and the murder in Meridian. Something about sex trafficking?"

"That's the current thinking" Frank answered.

"If we've got the same M.O. as the Wingo girl, then something isn't fitting. If I know one thing for certain, Mindy Mitchum wasn't a prostitute. And, she would never have gone anywhere with someone she didn't know."

Frank felt a cold finger run down his back as he considered the implication of Allison's observation. Surely the perp wasn't someone local, but what other conclusion was there?

Allison concluded the conversation, then dialed her partner's extension. Allison recorded everything she knew about the Mitchum murder on her partner's voice mail and advised David that she would be working with the task force as much as she could for the remainder of the week. "I've got a fairly clear calendar, so I think I can juggle half days here and the rest with Frank and Jake" Allison hurried her message before the recording automatically ended. "Oh, and by the way, Frank said to tell you he's had to put the Boudreaux investigation on temporary hold. He'll get back to you on that as soon as he can."

Forty minutes later and with her husband's blessing, Allison walked into the Calhoun County Sheriff's office. She hated the reason she was here – the loss of an innocent life was always tragic, this one even more so because she knew the victim. Allison dreaded seeing the pictures she knew she would be forced to examine, the comparison of M.O.s of this recent murder with the other two the task force was investigating, the intimate details of Ed Mitchum's life that would, of necessity, be shared with her, a rude intrusion into the Mitchum family's life and history. But somewhere there would be a clue. Maybe not to the other murders, but surely something that would bring justice for Mindy's father and retribution for Mindy's death. Mentally girding herself for the task ahead, Allison squared her shoulders and hoped she could hold it together when she saw Ed Mitchum.

CHAPTER TWENTY-NINE

E ngaging in a practice that was as natural to her as breathing, Forensic Specialist Sharon Greene wove the long strands of her jet black hair into one thick braid, flicked the silky rope over her shoulder, and gave her face once last glance in the bathroom mirror. *Acceptable* she thought, turning to search her bedroom closet for appropriate attire. Wearing her Lauderdale County deputy's uniform would not help her get answers where she was going tonight.

Sharon and Sheriff Gilbert had argued about Sharon's suggested foray for days. "It's the only way to get any more information" Sharon had insisted.

"Too dangerous" Gilbert had replied. "You're not trained in undercover operations, and I can't spare anyone for backup."

"I don't need backup from the department. I'll take Tiny." Sharon explained. "No one messes with Tiny."

Gilbert had to admit that his deputy was right about one thing. No person in his right mind would mess with Phillip "Tiny" Whitefeather. Recruited out of high school by Mississippi State, Tiny had played two seasons as a six foot five, 260 pound defensive back before leaving for the pros to make a bigger name for himself. Unfortunately for Tiny, a freak accident off the field had terminated his pro career after just seven years with the Patriots.

Many men would not have adjusted well to such disappointment, but Phillip Whitefeather was not the average man. Thanking the Great Spirit for the opportunities he had been given, and thanking his money manager for suggesting several good investment strategies for his multi-million dollar contract with New England, Tiny had returned to Philadelphia, Mississippi to coach high school football and enjoy a comfortable life.

"What does Tiny think about this?" Gilbert asked.

"I haven't told him yet" Sharon replied, "but he'll be fine with it so long as he can keep an eye on me. He knows I'm not hanging up my badge after we get married, so he can hardly expect me not to do my job now."

Sharon smiled remembering the conversation with her boss. And then she frowned remembering the one with her fiancée.

"Dammit, Sharon. You can't pull this off. You'll be spotted for a cop as soon as you open your mouth."

"Hon, people see what they want to see." Sharon replied. "All those red-neck assholes will see is snatch from the Reservation. It would never cross their pea-brained minds that a squaw would be in law enforcement."

Casting aside a red leather skirt, Sharon selected a leopard mini she had once worn as a Hallowe'en costume. Adding a black lace bra, and cropped blue jean jacket, she scrummaged around the closet floor for the black high heels she was sure she still had. *Please tell me I didn't send those to the Goodwill,* Sharon prayed hopefully. Her petition answered, a few minutes later a woman who only vaguely resembled a law officer exited the house.

The beat up Ford Focus, pulled from the Lauderdale County impound lot as an accessory to the night's charade, coughed into submission as Sharon turned the key in the ignition. A working girl who looked for clients at truck stops wouldn't be able to afford much in the way of wheels, assuming she could afford any kind of ride at all. But, Sheriff Gilbert and Tiny had both insisted that Sharon have a getaway vehicle in the event of dire circumstances.

The piece of junk that Sharon was driving tonight sounded and looked like it was held together with baling wire, just the kind of barely working vehicle someone down on their luck might try to keep running.

There was no guarantee that going to the Flying J where Francine Taylor had worked would reap any sort of intel, but Sharon thought it was the best place to start. There were other truck stops in the general vicinity that hookers might try, but the fact that Frank Martin had talked to the Turner woman at the Flying J just hours before she was murdered argued in favor of making that location Sharon's first stop. If nothing panned out there, she could always try Queen City or Love's. She also remembered an observation Frank Martin had shared with her and Sheriff Gilbert.

"I noticed them when I left" Frank had explained, describing several women he had seen hanging around the trucker entrance at the Flying J when he left to pass the time before meeting Francine Turner after her shift ended. "I started to take a closer look, but Francine had seemed so spooked I figured I'd best make myself scarce. Thought I'd ask her about them later at the diner."

Of course, Frank's opportunity for further discussion had ended with Francine Turner's murder. Tonight, dressed as a girl looking for some business,

Sharon hoped to discover whatever secrets Francine Turner might have taken to the grave.

Sharon glanced quickly at the Flying J's parking lot as she nosed the Ford into a narrow slot close to the trucker entrance. There, across the lot, she thought she caught a glimpse of Tiny's silver F450. Turning her attention to the well-lit doorway marked 'truckers only', Sharon watched as a slim blond sidled up to the doorway, leaned against the building and lit a cigarette. The woman's actions seemed too practiced not to be a calculated move or signal. Sure enough, before the woman took two drags from her cigarette a pair of cowboy boots protruded from the opening door of an 18 wheeler, followed by the rest of the trucker's heavyset body. There was no question in Sharon's mind as to the gist of the conversation which ensued out of her earshot between the trucker and the blond, for in short order the pair had slipped into the driver's cab.

Sharon pulled her phone from her purse, and holding it on her lap where the light from its panel could not be seen by anyone outside her vehicle, punched the favorites tab for Tiny's number.

"You see that?" she asked when Whitefeather answered.

"Yep, though not as clearly as you likely did" her fiancée replied. "Sure looks like we've got a little sales job going on here."

"I'm going to go over there, see what I can turn up" Sharon advised.

"Give me a minute to move my truck to the other side of the lot" Whitefeather ordered. "I want a better shot for the video."

"What video?" Sharon asked.

"Just a little insurance" her fiancée assured her. "A visual is worth a thousand words, or something like that."

Sharon had barely closed the door on her car when she heard soft laughter coming from the direction of the 18 wheeler where the cowboy and the blond had made their rendezvous. The cab door squeaked open, allowing the blond hooker to jump softly to the ground. Lengthening her stride to catch up with the blond woman, Sharon uttered a low "Hey, girl."

The blond glanced at Sharon and kept walking. "What you want, Chickie?"

Moving closer, Sharon replied "I'm need'n some quick cash. Heard this might be the place to make some."

The pair had reached the truck stop's neon lighted side doorway. The blond hooker shook a cigarette loose from a crumpled pack of Winston's she pulled from a purse slung over her shoulder. "Got a light?" she asked.

"Uh, no. Don't smoke" Sharon stuttered a reply.

"Who you workin' for, Chickie?" the hooker asked while she dug through a tattered purse. Her search rewarded by the discovery of a dirty looking book of matches, the hooker lit up a smoke and commented "Ain't seen you 'round here afore."

Sharon glanced around nervously before answering. "This is my first time. My old man kicked me out. I got nowhere to go. Figured I could make enough to get a bus ticket out to Oklahoma. I've got some family out on the Rez there."

"Figured you for Injun, what with that hair and skin color" the hooker sniffed. "Don't matter, none. Nookie sells, whatever the color."

Sharon bit her tongue to keep the sharp retort that rose in her throat. *Play the role* she reminded herself. "I heard this was the best place around."

"Where'd you hear that?" the hooker asked suspiciously. "Who you been talkin' to?"

Sharon hoped the homework she had done around Francine Turner would be sufficient to lend credibility to her cover. Taking a deep breath, Sharon replied "Friend of mine had a cousin 'used to work here. Not in the business, but inside, a clerk or something."

The hooker took a last drag on her cigarette before grinding the butt beneath the toe of her sequined heels. "That cousin have a name?"

Scratching her head, Sharon cast her fishing line. "Um, Frankie, Frances – something like that. No, I remember now. It was Francine. I knew it was something that sounded frenchy."

A sharp hiss escaped from the crimson lips of the hooker. "Who the fuck are you?" she whispered as she backed away from Sharon.

"Someone who can help you" Sharon replied, reaching for the woman's arm. "Please, talk to me."

"The last person who tried to talk got kilt" the hooker jerked her arm from Sharon's grasp. "But you already know that, don't you?"

"I can protect you" Sharon pleaded.

"The law always says that" the hooker sneered. "That's who you are, ain't it?" Seeing Sharon's nod, she continued "This ain't the place to be lookin', Chickie, not less'un you lookin' for trouble." The hooker pulled the ragged pack of smokes from her purse and lit her second cigarette. Old looking eyes in an older looking face gave Sharon a sad look. "Better look close to your own house first, Chickie," the hooker advised as she turned towards the darkened parking lot, "'fore you go lookin' in someone else's business."

CHAPTER THIRTY

A smile creased Allison's face. Charlotte and Mack were at back-to-school sleepovers and wouldn't be home until noon tomorrow. As much as she adored her children, Allison understood the need for couple time. The steaks had thawed and marinated, twice baked potatoes were ready to pop in the oven, and the ingredients for one of Allison's famous Caesar salads awaited on the kitchen island.

"Jim, grab the good bottle of Cabernet from the cabinet would you, please?" she called out. "The one we got in New York last year."

"Are we celebrating something special" her husband asked, walking into the kitchen. "That cab wasn't cheap."

"Just celebrating the fact that this is the first time we've had an entire 18 hours to ourselves in I can't remember when" Allison replied.

Jim retrieved the expensive wine from its resting place, expertly removed the cork and poured the dark red liquid into two Waterford goblets. "Here's to us" he toasted as he handed Allison a crystal wine-glass. "And to the next 18 hours" he added with a wicked grin.

From the day they had first met, Allison had felt a primal, sexual attraction to the man who was now her husband. Shocked at what she had originally thought too vast an age difference, not to mention a potentially difficult professional conflict, Allison had tried to ignore Judge Jim Kaufman's overtures and to quash the x-rated thoughts she kept having about him. But the judge had been persistent, and Allison had not been able to ignore her increasing feelings. Twelve plus years and two children later, Allison's desire for her husband, and his for her, had only increased.

"You sure you want to eat right now?" Jim's question brushed Allison's ear as his lips sought the back of her neck. "I'm not that hungry. For food" he added.

Allison felt the flutter in her stomach as a warm, familiar flush filled the lower part of her body. Her breath hitched as she turned to meet her husband's embrace. "Me neither" she replied as she reached underneath Jim's grey t-shirt to stroke the still taut muscles of his abdomen.

Jim's response was automatic. Deft hands unbuttoned Allison's shirt, then caressed nipples which had become erect and hard. "My God, I love you" he uttered before placing his mouth on Allison's left breast and sucking gently.

Their breathing was quick, their hands frantic on each other's clothing, pulling and tearing the obstructions to each other's flesh. Reaching beneath her bare buttocks, Jim lifted Allison to the edge of the kitchen island, then spreading her open, drank fully of the nectar that she carried there.

Allison's climax was almost instantaneous. "Now, Now" she beseeched her husband, pushing him back and sliding her body forward to straddle her husband's erection. Rocking back and forth, mouths pressed together, the age old action of lovers trying to consume one another, Allison and Jim consummated a fiery love that the years had done nothing to diminish.

Several hours later, a smug Jim observed "Not bad for an old man."

"All my friends would be jealous" Allison agreed, laying her head on her husband's chest. Taking advantage of the child-free hours, Allison and Jim had moved their lovemaking from the kitchen to the den and then finally to their bedroom. "Three times in three different places in one evening. Is that a record?"

"I just hope it's not my last hurrah" he laughed. "I won't be able to move tomorrow."

The sounds of the den's grandfather clock wafted down the hallway. "It's midnight" Allison observed, counting the bongs from the antique time keeper. "And I'm actually hungry. How about a midnight snack?"

"Flapjacks and blueberry syrup" Jim agreed, pulling on a bathrobe and heading towards the kitchen. "While I'm cooking you can fill me in on what you learned today about Mindy Mitchum's murder. We got sidetracked earlier…"

"There really isn't much to tell." Allison began as they entered the kitchen. "Looks like the same M.O. as the girl found out in Tom Spencer's field. If it's the same guy, then he's probably local. The task force doesn't want to look at that possibility too hard 'cause that works against their theory that the first murder and the Meridian murder are related." Allison opened the refrigerator door, pulled out a carton of orange juice and poured a tall glass. "Want some juice?" she asked her husband.

Jim shook his head, declining Allison's offer. "The fact that the same perp did two murders here doesn't necessarily mean there's no connection to the Meridian case. Didn't you tell me the first victim here and the victim in Meridian were related?"

"Yes, cousins. Jake Cleveland thinks it can't just be a coincidence, especially given the proximity in time that the two murders occurred."

Jim flipped a fat pancake in the air, then satisfied of its perfection, slid it onto a plate containing three of its brethren. "Here you go. Butter and syrup's on the table. What do you think? You agree with Jake's assessment?"

"It seems weird to me that cousins would both be murdered within a few days of each other" Allison paused to lick syrup from her fingers. "But, stranger things have happened. And I don't think we can ignore the fact that two very similar murders have occurred right here in Calhoun County within a couple of weeks of each other." Allison wiped her mouth with a checkered napkin, drank the last of her juice and added "Our priority has to be the local cases. That's why Frank and Sheriff Trowbridge asked me to help. The more eyes working this case, the greater the likelihood that we'll find the clue that will lead us to our perp."

Jim gazed at the woman sitting before him. Stubborn, beautiful, smart. After the McNair case he had vowed never to allow Allison to get involved with anything that would put her life at risk. Who was he kidding? Allison was her own woman. If she wanted to be involved in something, all he could do was voice an opinion and a concern. "Just promise me you will be careful" he asked his wife.

"Jim" Allison replied with a hint of exasperation. "This is not McNair. No one is after me, I am not a target. Sheriff Trowbridge just wants me to attend Ed Mitchum's interview and to review some of the investigative reports and old case files. I'll be fine."

"Yeh, poor Ed." Jim shook his head. "I can't imagine there's much left for Ed to live for now. How can life be so cruel to one person?"

"How can someone bind and mutilate a young girl like Mindy" Allison asked. "If I can play any role in apprehending the animal who killed Mindy, my time will be well spent helping the task force."

Jim's outstretched hand grasped Allison's small one. "I'm sorry I asked about any of this. Let's go to bed. We could both use some sleep."

Allison placed her arm around her husband's waist as they walked down the hall to their bedroom. She was indeed, a blessed woman, she thought. Silently, Allison offered a prayer for Ed and Mindy Mitchum. Tomorrow would come soon enough, and she would have work to do.

CHAPTER THIRTY-ONE

"Good News" David Jackson told his client over the phone. "The DNA results are back. There's no doubt you are Rebecca Fairchild's offspring."

"Of course there isn't" Jefferson Boudreaux huffed. "The testing was an insult to my integrity."

"Look, Mr. Boudreaux," exasperation tinged David's reply. "No one was insulting your integrity. As I tried to explain to you when the Defendants first asked the Court to order DNA testing, their only defense to your claim was to prove you weren't Rebecca Fairchild's offspring. The testing results make your claim pretty much a slam dunk at this point."

"Well" came a mollified response "I still think the testing was an unnecessary intrusion. The investigative reports I provided you from independent sources clearly established my lineage."

"I understand your position" David told his client "but those reports were subject to attack for a variety of reasons, especially since you were the person who paid for them. The DNA results are not."

"Then can I conclude that my case will now be quickly resolved?" Boudreaux asked.

"Quickly will depend on how soon I can get a motion for summary judgement in front of the court, and how quickly we can get a ruling. The law is on our side now that we have established your lineage. Unless the Defendants can provide evidence that your mother disinherited you, evidence which I believe does not exist, the court should rule in your favor and set aside the bequests left to the Defendants in your mother's Will."

"My investigators turned over every rock and looked in every cranny. I was never disinherited." David thought Boudreaux sounded agitated. Maybe the man wasn't used to people disputing his word.

"Yes, I've read their reports" David assured his client. "But in litigation one can never be too assured of a result until the verdict is rendered. It's to our benefit that this is a bench trial. The judge will follow the law as long as the facts of the case support it, which in your case they do."

After assuring his client that he would have the motion for summary judgement filed within the next two weeks, David was able to terminate what had become an increasingly distasteful conversation. In all the years of practicing law, David had never had a client that he had come to detest the way he did Jefferson Boudreaux. It wasn't the case itself – Boudreaux had a valid claim to Rebecca Fairchild's money, and as his attorney, David had an obligation to press the claim. David really couldn't figure out what it was about his client that caused such an increasingly visceral dislike of the man. Allison would tell him his 'red flags were up, a phrase his partner used when her intuition warned her something wasn't right. Whether red flags or gut intuition, something wasn't right about Jefferson Boudreaux. Time to press Frank Martin to get his background check finished.

"Martin Investigations". Frank's receptionist answered David's call.

David identified himself and had barely settled back in his desk chair, feet on his desk, before Frank's booming voice answered.

"I know why you're calling" Frank began, "and I promise I'll get you that report in the next couple of days. I've been tied up on those murders."

"I know, Frank, that's why I haven't pushed you, but I really need your investigative skills, and I need them now." David was insistent.

"Why?" Frank was curious. "I thought this was just a double check on the information you already had on your client."

"The information I've got deals solely with my client's birthright claim. You know, who he is, who his mama was, has he been disinherited, any facts that would bar him from making a claim to set aside Rebecca Fairchild's Will."

"And?" Frank questioned.

"I'm satisfied he is who he claims to be. The DNA testing ordered by the court came back with a positive match for him and Rebecca Fairchild." David answered. "If there is evidence of disinheritance, I think Boudreaux's investigators would have found it."

"So what do you need me for?" Frank asked. "Sounds pretty cut and dried to me."

"Something isn't right. I can't put my finger on it, but I can't shake my feelings either. At first I thought I just didn't like the guy's pretentious behavior – and let me tell you Jefferson Boudreaux is a real piece of work."

"I'm sure he's not the first asshole you've represented" Frank laughed,"and probably not the last either."

"This isn't a joke, Frank" David admonished the investigator. "I'm telling you, something isn't right about this guy."

"Ok, ok" Frank cajoled. "I believe you. Is there anything in particular that you can think of that I ought to be looking at?"

"Actually, there is" David replied as a thought crystalized in his mind. "What's really bugging me, and I just now realized it, is why Boudreaux fought so hard to prevent DNA testing."

"Explain" Frank ordered.

"Boudreaux was adamant that I oppose the Defendants' request for testing. Claimed it was an insult to his integrity, that his investigators had proved beyond a shadow of a doubt that Rebecca Fairchild was his mother. Even after I explained to him that DNA testing could win the case for him he wanted me to resist the request."

"You got those DNA result" Frank asked.

"A copy of them. UAB's Medical Genetics Lab in Birmingham has the sample" David explained.

"Send me a copy of the results and the contact info of the person you dealt with at the lab. In fact," Frank added "give the lab a call and make sure I can have access to that sample if need be."

"What are you thinking?" David asked the investigator.

"I'm thinking your instincts may be right" Frank replied. "This case has just gotten a hell of a lot more interesting." Frank Martin chewed the end of his cigar and processed the information he had just heard from David Jackson. When David had first retained him to do the background check on Jefferson Boudreaux Frank had taken a quick look at Rebecca Fairchild's estate and Will. The eccentric billionaire had left quite a fortune - commercial real estate in Chicago, New York, L.A. and London, plus a jewelry collection that likely rivaled the one Elizabeth Taylor had collected over the years, not to mention millions of dollars in blue chip stocks. If Jefferson Boudreaux could prove he was the legitimate heir of Rebecca Fairchild, he would instantaneously make the list of the world's wealthiest individuals. DNA testing was the one sure way to prove his claim. Why would a man as intelligent as Jefferson Boudreaux appeared to be resist such a simple, non-intrusive test? It didn't make sense.

The email flag on Frank's computer announced the arrival of a new message. Clicking the computer mouse, Frank opened David Jackson's missive and reviewed the attached DNA report. Tossing the now demolished cigar towards the overflowing trash can next to his desk, Frank decided to take advantage of his most current contacts.

"Task Force" Jake Cleveland's gruff voice asserted.

"Jake, old man. I need a favor" Frank stated rather than asked. "Got a DNA profile I'd like to run through the system. Can I send the report to you?"

"This have anything to do with our cases?" Jake figured he had a 50-50 chance of getting a straight answer from Frank.

"Uh, maybe" Frank fudged. "Got a tip from a local that I'd like to pursue."

"How'd you get a DNA report?" Jake knew he had to ask.

"It's on the up and up" Frank assured the F.B.I. agent, hoping Cleveland would not probe further. "Doubt anything will come of it, but.."

"But, you want to use government resources to scratch that little itch you've got, that it, Frank?" Cleveland asked.

"Just this once" Frank replied. "If I get a hit who knows where it might lead." Privately Frank thought it highly unlikely Jefferson Boudreaux's DNA would be in the system, but the man's resistance to the testing seemed suspicious to Frank.

"Whose DNA is it?" Cleveland needed some justification for running the request.

"A client of David Jackson's." Frank hated giving up this information. "David asked me to take a deeper look at the guy. Got some concerns, especially since the guy resisted giving a DNA sample in a Will contest case."

"This sample taken legally?" Cleveland wasn't about to bend the rules on an illegally obtained sample.

"Pursuant to a court order, UAB's genetics lab did the testing. Everything's on the up and up" Frank replied, declining to add that the aforementioned court order restricted the use of Boudreaux's DNA to a comparison with a sample from Rebecca Fairchild. Frank didn't believe in giving out unnecessary information.

Jake Cleveland considered Frank's request. He'd worked with the investigator long enough to know Frank wouldn't make a request to use the F.B.I.'s resources if he didn't have a good reason. "Send me what you have" he told Frank. "I'll make the request. Let you know what comes back."

"Thanks, Jake" Frank replied. "It's probably nothing and I'll be apologizing for wasting the Bureau's time."

The conversation with Cleveland concluded, Frank considered his next move. If Boudreaux's DNA was out there, the F.B.I.'s system would eventually get a hit. However, unless the DNA was connected with a crime, a match wouldn't necessarily give Frank the depth of intel he liked to have when researching a target. Sifting through the pile of documents and files covering his desk, Frank retrieved the investigative reports David Jackson had sent over a couple of weeks earlier. Boudreaux had commissioned two reports purportedly to establish his entitlement to the Fairchild money. Flipping quickly

through the typed pages of each report Frank high-
lighted the dates and locations where Boudreaux
had lived. He would double check that information
this afternoon. If the information was legit, Frank's
next move would be to dig a little deeper at each
location. David Jackson was right. No one was as
squeaky clean as Jefferson Boudreaux appeared on
paper.

CHAPTER THIRTY-TWO

F t. Charles buried Mindy Mitchum on a sunny morning in early May. Filled to capacity, overflow mourners having to sit in the Fellowship Hall listening to the service via intercom, First Baptist Church offered little comfort to the members of the small town who wondered how such a horrific crime could have happened to one of their own.

Allison hated funerals. It was bad enough when the deceased was old, or had been sick, but to have to bury a young child or teen – well, it was just about too much for Allison to handle. Listening to the Pastor intone about God's mercy and His inscrutable will, Allison's thoughts had turned unbidden to memories of Rice's children and the funeral of her niece and nephews just two years earlier. Life was cruel, and Allison knew no amount of talking about God's mercy was going to change that fact or give Ed Mitchum any comfort.

Out of respect for his long-time friend, Sheriff Trowbridge had decided to wait until a week after the funeral to interview Ed Mitchum. A few days' delay wouldn't bring back Mindy Mitchum, nor would it, in Toby's mind, make any difference in apprehending the killer. The Sheriff had called Allison yesterday, reminding her to be at the Sheriff's department for today's 2:00 meeting.

"Ed, I know this is hard for you" Toby began as soon as he, Ed and Allison were seated around the conference room table, "but memory fades quickly, especially memory for details, so it's really important to do this now, even though you are still hurting."

Ed Mitchum wiped a tear from the corner of his eye. "I know, Toby" he acknowledged, "it's just so damn hard. I keep thinking about what my baby went through."

Allison reached across the table, taking Ed's hand. "Those are painful thoughts, Ed. I had them for a long time, too, remembering Rice's children and how their lives were ended. It's a natural part of the grieving process."

Ed's hollow eyes sought Allison's own. "Will it go away?" he asked.

"No" Allison shook her head, "but it won't hurt as bad after a while, and eventually it won't be the first thing you think about each morning."

The three sat silently for a few minutes, then the grieving father turned to the Sheriff. "I'm ready to do what I can to help. Can't imagine it's much, can't understand why any of this happened. Ask me anything and I'll do my best to give you an answer."

"Mind if I record this?" Toby asked. "It's easier than taking notes, and we won't miss anything later."

"You going to read me my rights?" Ed asked with a sad smile.

"Actually, yes" Toby apologized. "It's standard procedure, Ed. Nothing personal. Nobody thinks you killed your child."

Miranda warning completed, accompanied by Ed Mitchum's waiver of counsel, Toby began the interview with a series of expected who, what, when and where questions. To each question, Ed Mitchum gave a negative reply or simply stated "I don't know." Forty-five minutes into the interview, Toby had as much information as he had prior to asking the first question – absolutely zero.

"I'm sorry, Toby, Allison" Ed looked around the table. "There's just no explanation for what happened to Mindy. We kept to ourselves, we paid our bills, had some close friends, just lived a regular, quiet life. Mindy was a good kid. Made good grades, no trouble in school or with other kids in town. I've wracked my brain trying to figure out who would want to do this, and the only thing I can figure is a stranger. Except Mindy wouldn't have gone off with someone she didn't know."

"Had she made any new friends?" Allison asked. "Or talked about someone out of her normal circle?"

"She had started doing some tutoring after school for some of the sharecropper kids" Ed replied. "I hadn't thought of that. Maybe one of those kids did this."

"We'll look into that" Toby made a quick note on the legal pad in front of him. "Did Mindy mention any names?"

"No" Ed shook his head. "I don't even know whether they were boys or girls, or how old they were. Why didn't I ask about that?" Ed's question hung in the air.

"What about you, Ed?" Toby asked. "Any new friends or acquaintances?"

"Between being there for Mindy, and running the Inn seven days a week, I haven't had time for a social life in years." Ed replied. "I hardly have time to know my guests, as far as that goes. 'Cept the guy who's been staying at the Inn the past couple of weeks. Jefferson Boudreaux." Ed glanced at Allison. "Your law partner is handling a Will dispute for him."

"I haven't met Mr. Boudreaux" Allison commented "but I know who you are talking about. He's the apparent heir to the Rebecca Fairchild fortune."

"What do you know about Mr. Boudreaux?" Toby asked.

"Not much, really" Ed allowed. "He's a business man from Louisiana. Polite, polished, keeps to himself. Nice guy."

"Did Mr. Boudreaux have any interaction with Mindy?" Toby dismissed Ed's description of Boudreaux as a 'nice guy'. Some of the most successful criminals had evaded capture because they had seemed so normal, Ted Bundy being a prime example.

"No more than any other guest" Ed replied. "Boudreaux doesn't go out much, so he'd be at the house most afternoons when Mindy got home from school, and they'd have breakfast together just because that's the way I run the Inn. I imagine they got to know each other a bit, but nothing more than passing conversation would be my guess."

"We'll have a chat with Mr. Boudreaux as well." Toby turned to Allison "Would you ask David Jackson to give his client a call and tell him we'd like to talk to him?"

"Do you think he had something to do with Mindy's murder" Ed was clearly shaken by the thought.

"Doubtful" Toby replied. No need to worry Ed Mitchum at this point with what might well turn out to be a dead end. "I am more interested in anything he might have picked up on in his conversations with Mindy."

The remainder of the interview yielded no additional information of note. After his daughter's murder, friends had urged Ed to shut down the Inn, at least temporarily, but Ed had refused. "I need to keep busy" he had explained. When Toby and Allison ran out of questions, Ed Mitchum headed back to the Inn to receive new guests.

After Ed left, Allison shared her partner's earlier conversation with the Sheriff. "I didn't want to say anything in front of Ed, but David has some reservations about Jefferson Boudreaux and he's hired Frank Martin to do a background check on the man."

"What kind of reservations?" Toby asked as he escorted Allison to her car.

"It's nothing David can really put his finger on" Allison explained. "David thinks the legal claim to the Fairchild estate is well-founded. He says the DNA evidence proves Jefferson Boudreaux is Rebecca Fairchild's bastard, and there is no evidence that she ever disinherited him."

"So, what's the problem?" Toby interrupted.

Allison dug in her purse for her car keys, then leaned against the side of her SUV before answering. "The Defendants had a DNA sample from

Rebecca Fairchild and they asked the court to order Boudreaux to give a sample for comparison. David became concerned when Boudreaux tried to avoid the testing, even after David explained that a match would prove Boudreaux's claim."

"That seems rather slim to me" Toby observed. "That's all?"

"I trust David's instincts. He thought there was something off about Boudreaux from day one, but there was never any one thing that David could point to that justified his feelings or caused him to decline the legal work. This business with the DNA brought David's concerns back to the forefront, and he gave Frank a call." Allison explained. "I've never known David Jackson to investigate one of his clients. The fact that he asked Frank Martin to take a closer look has significance"

"It certainly can't hurt to take a look at the guy" Toby replied. "Other than the sharecropper kids, this is the only lead we have, and while I think both are probably a waste of time and resources, we've got to take a look."

"I'll talk to David tonight about setting up an interview with Mr. Boudreaux" Allison informed the Sheriff. "And I'll ask David to put a fire under Frank. If anyone can find dirt on someone, it's Frank."

CHAPTER
THIRTY-THREE

R ice had ignored his symptoms for as long as he could. His appetite wasn't much, and he'd been losing weight for a while now, but Rice had chalked up the loss of appetite and subsequent weight loss to his dislike of most of what passed as food in the prison cafeteria. Nothing tasted or looked good anymore, and when he ate he felt so bloated most of the time that he ate less and less of what was served.

The pain in Rice's gut had started a couple of weeks back. Not all the time, just intermittent, and just infrequent enough for Rice to ignore as anything really serious. Probably just heartburn from the shitty food he thought. But last night the pain was so bad that Rice thought he might die. As much as he hated to go to the prison infirmary, Rice knew he had no choice.

"We'll need to run some tests" the prison doctor stated after listening to Rice's description of his symptoms and making a cursory exam.

"What kind of tests?" Rice asked.

"I'd like to schedule you for an endoscopy as soon as possible, along with a stomach CT" the doctor replied. "We'll need to schedule this off-site. I'll start the paperwork today."

"What are you looking for?" Rice asked as he buttoned up his prison shirt.

"Your symptoms could be caused by any number of things" the doctor stopped entering data on his laptop and turned to face his patient. "Could be as innocuous as an ulcer, but the combination of your symptoms makes me want to take a closer look."

"A closer look for what exactly?" Rice pressed.

"It would be unusual in a man your age" the doctor began "but not unheard of."

"And?" Rice encouraged.

The doctor considered the patient before him. He knew Rice Parker's history, knew why he was in prison, knew who his family was. He also knew his patient had been a model prisoner who was active in the prison's AA program and literacy program. Rice Parker had come a long way since his conviction and incarceration. As strange as it sounded, this inmate had become an asset to the prison population at Kilby. The doctor hoped he was wrong about what he thought was the most likely diagnosis for Rice Parker's symptoms.

"Stomach cancer, Rice" the doctor reluctantly admitted. "I hope I'm wrong, but ...."

"Don't apologize" Rice interrupted the doctor. "I figured it was something bad, that's why I'm here."

"Let's not jump to conclusions before we get the results of the tests" the doctor cautioned. "Like I said, it could be something as simple as an ulcer. I just want to make sure it's not something more serious."

Two hours had passed since Rice left the prison's medical clinic. The information Rice had pulled up about stomach cancer on the prison library's computer wasn't as bad as he thought. As long as he wasn't at Stage IV where the cancer had spread to other organs he had a good chance of beating the big C or at least slowing its progress. The stunned feeling that had overtaken Rice when the doctor had first mentioned the word "cancer" had slowly mitigated as Rice had researched his odds and remembered the teachings he had learned in AA. Yes, he reminded himself, he would live in the present and see what the test results showed. The future would be here soon enough. Whatever the outcome, Rice was determined that he would accept the path before him.

CHAPTER THIRTY-FOUR

"Lying to your boss is a bad idea" Phillip Whitefeather reminded his fiancée. "It's a good way to get fired."

"I haven't lied to Sheriff Gilbert" Deputy Sharon Greene explained. "I just haven't told him everything I heard."

Whitefeather laughed. "Right. You've only declined to share with him the most important piece of information that girl gave you."

"It's not solid intel" Sharon hedged. "All she said was I ought to look in my own house. For all I know she was messin' with me when she said that."

"Or, she could have been giving you a serious warning" her fiancée replied. "Are you worried that Sheriff Gilbert might be dirty?"

Sharon never hesitated in her reply. "No way Scott Gilbert is dirty. That man is as squeaky clean as they come, boy scout clean."

"Then why the hesitation in telling him what you were told?" Whitefeather was curious.

"I want to nose around a bit more, go back to the truck stop and see what else I can turn up. All I have right now is that cryptic comment from one hooker. I want something more concrete, maybe some corroboration from another girl" Sharon explained. "You up for a return visit tonight?"

"Let's work it a bit different this time." Whitefeather had an idea. "You be the backup. I'll be the John."

Sharon considered the proffered scenario. She liked it. "I can't wait to see what you wear" Sharon grinned.

Sharon spent the rest of that Saturday afternoon cleaning her apartment and grabbing a catnap. The night trade didn't get started until almost midnight, even in truck stops. Sharon was an early riser. Being alert and on her toes at the witching hour required either a few hours of sleep in the afternoon or early evening. By the time she heard the knock on her door at 10:00 p.m., a lengthy nap and two espressos had Sharon wide awake and ready for work.

Mississippi, especially the area around Meridian, was largely rural and agricultural. Industry, such as it were, congregated on the Gulf coast with pockets of commerce sprinkled across a few inland cities. Jackson, the state capitol, still hosted a large rodeo each February. First time visitors to the capitol during the two weeks of the Dixie National often wondered if they had somehow landed in Texas instead of the Magnolia state. The Texas cowboy influence had infiltrated Mississippi decades earlier and showed no signs of going back where it came from. Phillip Whitefeather's attire of cowboy boots, jeans and Western shirt wouldn't raise an eyebrow at the truck stop. Only the fully loaded, new model F-450 pickup he was driving would show him for a potential mark in the early hours of the morning.

"If you aren't a sight" Sharon laughed. Her fiancée was more of a khaki's and Izod man. "Where did you find that shirt?"

"Salvation Army. You wouldn't believe the stuff they've got in the store in Jackson. The price tag was still on it. Guess money comes so easy to some people they can just throw out their clothes." Whitefeather shook his head thinking about the waste.

"Yeh, I know" Sharon replied. "But duty calls. You ready?"

Twenty minutes later Whitefeather pulled his truck into the commercial end of the Flying J truck-stop outside Meridian. He and Sharon had agreed he would go in the facility first, look around and act a little nervous, then exit through the trucker's entrance and walk slowly back to his truck. "Play the nervous John" Sharon had advised. Whitefeather promised to do his best.

This time the pair had decided to rely on better technology than a cellphone video. Although not authorized, Sharon had absconded from the Sheriff's department with some basic surveillance equipment. Whitefeather was wired for sound and his conversations would be recorded remotely by the unit that Sharon had in her car. Sharon's visual surveillance would be limited. She couldn't afford to be recognized by anyone who might have seen her when she was posing as a hooker. Instead, she would rely on what she could hear from Phillip's wire.

"Hey Baby" came a soft voice that sounded familiar. "What you lookin' for?"

Sharon heard Whitefeather clear his throat. *Good*, she thought, *act like this is something you've never done before.* "Uh, I'm not sure" Whitefeather stuttered. "Maybe I've made a mistake."

"We wouldn't want that, would we, big boy" the voice cooed. "Maybe I can help you remember what you came here for."

Sharon heard footsteps approaching Whitefeather and the unidentified woman. "Do I know you?" a harsh male voice asked. "You look familiar to me."

"Uh, no. Can't say as I've ever met you before" Whitefeather lapsed into a drawl. "Just passin' through headin' over to Monroe."

Sharon opened and then quietly closed the door of her car. Moving as quickly as possible, she was glad she had decided to wear black leggings and a black, long sleeve tee. Hopefully no one would see the dark shadow moving towards the lighted trucker's entrance. Twenty feet from Whitefeather and the two strangers, Sharon crouched beside the engine of a parked 18-wheeler and pulled out her service revolver.

If she hadn't been worried about her fiancee's safety, Sharon would have laughed out loud. The man to whom the harsh voice belonged was a grossly exaggerated caricature of a New York pimp. Skin tight black pants, pointy leather shoes, blue silk shirt unbuttoned halfway down his chest, Sharon was surprised some local boy hadn't beaten the crap out of the guy just for looking the way he did. The 20x magnification of the field glasses Sharon had brought caused a sharp intake of breath. *Shit. He's got a blade. And I bet he knows how to use it.*

"Look man" Whitefeather showed the open palms of his hands to the pair. "I'm not lookin' for trouble. Truth is, I was just hopin' I might find a little fun to break up my drive."

The woman stepped towards Whitefeather. "Honey, this might be your lucky day." Motioning back towards the pimp she continued. "Rich here gets antsy sometimes. He's not used to you big Southern boys."

"How much?" Whitefeather asked, pulling a wad of bills from his shirt pocket. Sharon returned her revolver to the shoulder harness she wore across her chest. It had just been a false alarm. The evening was back on track. She would stay in the shadows until Tiny and the hooker moved to his truck.

Sharon never heard her attacker, only the whispered words before everything went black. "You should have left well enough alone."

CHAPTER THIRTY-FIVE

Why did I ever agree to do this for free? Frank grumbled. He had exhausted all of the internet leads and informational phone calls that he could think of. No way around it, he was going to have to do boots on the ground, old fashioned P.I. work to get to the next layer on the Boudreaux investigation. Frank didn't believe in the supernatural, ESP or any of that other new age crap all the young people were into nowadays. But, he had to admit, there was something he couldn't explain that many times happened when he lay aside the modern way of investigating and returned to his roots. A stray comment here, an old newspaper article there, a person he never knew existed – some weird "something" would happen that would crack a case wide open. Mapping out his route to several small towns in Louisiana where Boudreaux had lived, Frank knew he would need just that sort of extra help on this case.

Frank dialed Allison's office number. In short order Rose – he really needed to meet the woman behind that voice, Frank reminded himself – put his call through and Allison's hello came over the line.

"Allison, it's Frank" he announced.

"I know. Caller ID and Rose pegged you right away."

"Didn't your mama tell you to identify yourself when you call someone?" Frank asked.

"Yes, Frank, she did, but that was a long time ago" Allison laughed in reply. "What's up?"

"I'm heading over to Louisiana to take a closer look at Jefferson Boudreaux's past. Figure I'll be gone maybe a week, give or take a day or two."

"Ok" Allison replied, not sure why Frank was telling her this instead of giving this information to David Jackson. The Boudreaux investigation belonged to her partner. "Do I need to pass this on to David?"

"No, he already knows. This is a request that involves your work with the Task Force" Frank explained. "You know the court ordered Boudreaux to submit to a DNA test?"

"Yes, David told me." Allison replied.

"Well, Jake Cleveland is running Boudreaux's DNA through the F.B.I. database for me, and"

"Frank" Allison interrupted, "the court order in David's case applied only for that case. Surely David didn't give you access to Boudreaux's DNA information?"

Frank considered his answer, or rather considered which answer he should give, then decided to go with the truth. "I asked for the sample and David gave it to me. He and I both know what that means."

"I can't believe Jake Cleveland would be a party to this" Allison huffed.

"Jake doesn't have all the facts. All I told him was that the sample was obtained pursuant to a court order. And it was. He knows it belongs to one of David's clients, just not that we don't have permission to run the sample nationwide."

"I know you walk close to the line sometimes" Allison admitted, "but you could lose your license over this, and so could David. What in the world were the two of you thinking?"

"Something's not right about Jefferson Boudreaux. I know it. David knows it." Frank figured Allison knew it, too.

"That's not enough of a reason." Allison was getting angry. "David's actions have jeopardized the integrity of this firm. I insist that you stop this investigation and you ask Jake to withdraw the DNA tracking request. As soon as this conversation is finished David Jackson and I are having a 'come to Jesus meeting'. I will not tolerate this kind of deception involving a client's private information."

"Too late" Frank's reply was answered with a low buzz. Allison had terminated the call. Frank hoped David Jackson was out for the afternoon. Maybe that would give Allison some time to reconsider. Parker & Jackson was a good firm. He'd hate to see David and Allison split ways over a slick character like Jefferson Boudreaux. The best way to avoid that kind of outcome would be to prove David and himself right with regard to their target. Gathering miscellaneous files and notes, Frank headed for his truck.

Night had long since fallen when Frank turned off I-10 and headed towards Morgan City. According to the information Frank had reviewed, both what David had given him and what Frank had confirmed himself, Jefferson Boudreaux appeared to be a true rags-to-riches story. Poor boy educates self, works hard, marries the boss's daughter, and inherits big time when the boss and daughter die. *The ultimate payoff*, Frank thought, listening to the bitch-in-the-box direct him to the Motel 6 he intended to make his headquarters for the next few days. But, people could look good on paper and still have a lot to hide. Most people in small towns were afraid of those who held power, and Jefferson Boudreaux certainly fit into that category. His company, LaPierre Drilling, employed a good number of the town's residents. Finding someone who might carry a tale against as wealthy a man as Boudreaux might prove difficult. Difficult, but not impossible. A lead was out there somewhere, and Frank would find it.

CHAPTER THIRTY-SIX

A loud belch announced the settling of the Huddle House breakfast special in Frank's abundant stomach as he eased his truck into the parking lot of LaPierre Drilling. Frank wasn't sure what to make of the building that was set to the left of the paved area. Off shore drilling was big business, and an expensive one. As a result, the largest oil companies had the lock on most of the off shore sites. The few smaller companies like LaPierre Drilling which were privately owned usually spent hard earned profits on equipment rather than company headquarters. Most were housed in modest, sometimes ramshackle structures, not a penny wasted on non-productive buildings. To Frank's surprise, the sleek, one story structure displaying the

LaPierre Drilling name and logo across the front looked brand new.

The lobby of LaPierre Drilling was empty save for a woman of indeterminate age who was sitting at a dark wood desk to the left and center of the front door. A stylish sofa and several chairs composed a seating area on the other side of the room. Two large portraits near the back wall of the lobby caught Frank's attention. One was Jefferson Boudreaux. The other, Frank figured, had to be Charles LaPierre.

"Hello Ma'am" Frank introduced himself. "Is Mr. Boudreaux here?"

"No," the woman answered curtly. "And he only sees people by appointment." Returning to her perusal of a People magazine that Frank had interrupted, the receptionist's actions telegraphed Frank's dismissal.

"Ms. Skinner, is it?" Frank read the nameplate on the front corner of the receptionist's desk. "Perhaps you can be of help?"

Suspicious eyes gave Frank the once-over. "I've told you, Mr. Boudreaux only sees people by appointment. He makes the appointments, not me. You'll have to call ahead next time."

"I'm on a tight schedule" Frank explained, relying on his regular cover as a roving reporter. "My editor wants the story by this coming Friday. I guess

I'll just have to leave Mr. Boudreaux and LaPierre Drilling out of the article."

"What article?" Curiosity got the better of Ms. Skinner, just as Frank had anticipated.

"The newspaper I work for is doing a series of articles on self-made, successful business men" Frank lied. "The editor met Mr. Boudreaux a couple of years back and thought his story would be of interest to our readers." Frank hoped the receptionist wouldn't press for details. "If you've been with the company for a while, maybe I could interview you instead, get the perspective of someone who's been close to Mr. Boudreaux and the company's day-to-day affairs. I'd mention you as the source in my article, of course."

The suggestion of media exposure usually got the attention of even the most reticent individual. Fortunately for Frank, Ms. Skinner was no exception. Everyone wanted their fifteen minutes of fame.

"Well, I *have* been with LaPierre Drilling for many years" the receptionist began, a trace of Cajun lineage accenting her words. "Mr. Charles hired me after my husband died on one of the offshore rigs. Widowed with two young'uns to raise. Mr. Charles was good to me, took care of me and my baybeez."

"I understand Mr. Boudreaux married into the LaPierre family, is that right?" Frank offered the receptionist an easy opening into the LaPierre family dynamics.

A slow nod preceded the receptionist's reply. "Yes. He married Miss Cynthia." Before Frank could pose his next question she added "Poor, poor Miss Cynthia."

"Why do you say that?" Frank asked.

"That girl was the apple of her daddy's eye." A slight smile passed over the receptionist's face before fading quickly. "Things would have been different if Mr. Charles had known what went on between his daughter and her husband."

Frank cautioned himself. *Slowly, now. This is good stuff.* "Well, sometimes things between a husband and wife aren't what they seem, good or bad" he replied."

"Miss Cynthia was only a few years younger than me. I had just started working for Mr. Charles when Miss Cynthia married Mr. Boudreaux. I know it sounds strange, that someone like Miss Cynthia would be a friend to someone like me, but we just hit it off right away." The receptionist paused, then reached for the Pepsi bottle sitting on her desk. Taking a sip she seemed to be gathering her thoughts. Frank thought perhaps she would tell him nothing further. In fact, he was rather surprised that the woman was being so forthright to begin with. What had gotten her started?

"I ain't never told anyone what I'm getting ready to tell you. Couldn't take the risk while my babies was still young, then I had grands to take care of, too. But they's all on their own now, and I've got enough saved up that it don't matter none if I lose my job." The receptionist's expression was grim. "And it's not right for Mr. Boudreaux to get the credit for what Mr. Charles built with his own two hands."

Frank made a calculated move. "Do you mind if I record what you're about to tell me? I'll give you the tape when I leave if you change your mind about me having it."

Becky Skinner shook her head. "No, no reason to hide the truth any longer. All the people that could be hurt by it's dead. Ain't nothing gonna' hurt Mr. Boudreaux. That man's too mean."

Frank worked hard to keep the surprise he felt from showing on his face. "What is it you need to tell me, Ms. Skinner?"

"He beat her. Beat her and made her do unnatural things, sexual things. Things no Christian woman should even know about. Said if she told anybody he'd kill her daddy first, then come after her. Told her he'd killed his share of whores, and he'd do her, too." A tear rolled down the receptionist's cheek.

"How do you know this?" Frank asked quietly.

"She ran away once, after he'd made her do something unspeakable – I can't even repeat it now all these years later. He'd beaten her pretty bad that time, bad enough she thought maybe a rib was broken. I told her she needed to tell Mr. Charles, or to call the police, but she begged me to keep quiet. I bandaged her best I could, but by the next morning she had gone back to him." The woman began to sob. "Miss Cynthia never said another word to me, but the light was gone out of her eyes and I knew whatever he was doing to her, it hadn't stopped. When the cancer took her it was a blessing."

"Why are you still working here, Ms. Skinner? Your friend is gone, and as you say, you have enough put by now." Frank wondered.

"I don't know" the receptionist replied. "Maybe the good Lord knew you was gonna' come one day, and He was waitin' to give me this chance to do right by Miss Cynthia."

When Frank left an hour later, he knew David Jackson's gut had been right. Given what Becky Skinner had ultimately shared with him, Jefferson Boudreaux was a sexual sadist. Hardly ever was someone with Boudreaux's affliction satisfied with just one victim. Had he killed others like Cynthia LaPierre had told Becky Skinner? It seemed likely, but where, how and when? Referring to one of the reports David Jackson had given him, Frank began to plot his next step.

CHAPTER THIRTY-SEVEN

The storm that was currently pounding the daylights out of Ft. Charles could barely be heard in the windowless room that housed the F.B.I. task force in the Calhoun County Sheriff's Department. Leaning back in her chair, Allison tried to work out the kinks that had taken up residence in her back. When stretching her arms and rolling her shoulders produced only a modicum of relief, Allison gave a sigh and reached in her purse for an Aleve. Maybe if she moved everything to the floor she could change her position enough to stick it out for another hour.

"I didn't know you were coming in today" Jake Cleveland announced as he walked into the small space. "Why do you have all those files on the floor? Something wrong with the table?"

"I got here about 1:00" Allison replied glancing at her wristwatch. "Three hours sitting at that table was all I could handle."

"Yep, it's not the best accommodations, but I appreciate you helping." Jake looked at the yellow legal pad by Allison's side. "Find anything interesting?"

"The files you had pulled from the agency's cold case locker have been enough to give me nightmares. All the NRA needs to do is publicize some of these unsolved murders and let the public know the perps have never been caught. That'd be the end of this foolishness over gun control" Allison predicted.

"Never underestimate the far left and the fairy land they inhabit" Jake laughed. "It's always the gun's fault, no matter what the facts say."

"Don't you know it" Allison agreed shaking her head. "Anyway, I've divided the unsolved murders into two categories. One with sexual mutilations or overtones and one without. Andy Dabo wasn't able to determine the condition of Marilee Wingo's body prior to death, so she may or may not have been killed by the same person who killed Mindy, and she may or may not have been a victim of sexual mutilation. That puts the Mitchum case in the mutilation column and the Wingo case in the simple murder column." Reflecting on what she had just said, Allison wondered if there was anything such as simple murder. "I focused only on cold cases from Texas to Alabama. Expanding the geographical scope was too burdensome, at least for just one person. I told Scott Miller what I was doing when he called in yesterday. He and Teresa will take a look at the cases in Georgia and the Carolinas if we get any hits from our list."

"Alabama and Mississippi cases make sense" Jake agreed "but what made you look at Louisiana and Texas?"

"Well, we've got the two here in Ft. Charles, we've got the Turner murder over near Meridian – which I don't think fits in the sexual mutilation column – and then there is that case my brother Rice told me about over in Louisiana."

"What case? What are you talking about?" Jake asked.

"I meant to tell you about that after Jim and I got back from Kilby. One of the guys in Rice's AA group told a pretty gruesome tale about a murder the guy had come upon outside Bossier City back maybe ten or fifteen years ago. Rice couldn't get the visual out of his head. He was so disturbed about it that he risked carrying a prison tale just to make sure someone on the outside knew about it. The murder was in Lousiana, and the injuries to that victim were almost identical to some of what was done to Mindy Mitchum."

"And you forgot to tell me?" Jake's face had begun turn red. "This is exactly the type of M.O. that you and the others are supposed to be looking for."

"Don't get your damn panties in a wad" Allison retorted. "You've been in Birmingham and I was busy looking through the Louisiana cold cases." Rifling through a stack of manila files on the table nearest to her, Allison grabbed a folder and thrust it towards Cleveland. "I found the Bossier City case and another one, too, that I think you will find particularly interesting. Take a look."

Jake Cleveland stared at the folder in his hands. It was the case from Houma, the one he had tried so hard to solve so many years ago. "Mother-fucker" he whispered, "it can't be."

Allison gave the agent a hard look. "Thought that might get your attention. Your name was on the jacket as junior investigator. When were *you* going to tell *me* about this case?" she asked, biting her tongue to keep from adding "asshole" to the end of her question.

"I didn't think it could be the same guy" Jake smacked the table with his fist, knocking several files to the floor. "I remembered it after our meeting in Birmingham, and it's what prodded me to call Wilson Mackey and ask for the task force. But the more I thought about the Houma case, the more I became convinced that it couldn't be the same guy as our killer. And I still think it's long shot" he said, more to convince himself than Allison. "Even if the Houma and Bossier City killings are related, there's simply too much time between those murders and the ones here in Ft. Charles."

"It would be unusual" Allison agreed, "but not unheard of. Look at the Grim Sleeper."

Jake knew all about the Grim Sleeper case. The Grim Sleeper was a nickname given a fifty-seven year old garbage man in Los Angeles who was indicted on ten counts of murder in 2010. Media dubbed the suspect "the grim sleeper" because he had allegedly taken a fourteen year hiatus from 1988 to 2002 before resuming his crimes.

"What I've discovered is, I think, significant." Allison continued. "In the last twenty-five years there have been eight unsolved murders of young women who had been raped and then sexually mutilated, either pre or post mortem. The first three were in Texas between 1975 and 1980. The other five were in Louisiana between 1981 and 1998, including the Houma and Bossier City cases."

"Nothing after that?" Jake asked. "In any of the four states you looked at?"

"Murders, yes" Allison acknowledged. "Sexual mutilations, zero. Until Mindy Mitchum's murder here."

"And maybe Marilee Wingo, given the fact that she had been chained to the floor of that out building." Jake added.

Allison gathered the files that had fallen to the floor after Jake's attack on the table. If they were dealing with one killer, and the eight cases in Texas and Louisiana were his handiwork – she had to think the killer was a man – where had he been between 1989 and the present? Were there other cases they hadn't connected? Had he simply quit for a while? There were still too many holes, too many unanswered question to form a working theory.

"You know what?" A thought crossed Allison's mind. "Frank Martin is in Louisiana right now doing some work for David Jackson. If it's ok with you" she asked Cleveland "I'm going to give Frank a call and get him to do some leg work for us."

"Good idea" Jake nodded. "Give him the names and locations of the Louisiana victims. See what he can find from talking to the locals. People in small towns don't forget crimes like these, no matter how much time has passed."

CHAPTER THIRTY-EIGHT

I t hurt to move. *Shit*, Sharon Greene thought as she took in her surroundings. *Shit, shit and double shit.* As her eyes adjusted to the deep darkness around her, Sharon realized she wasn't bound. That wasn't necessarily a good thing. If her captors had worried about her being able to escape she would surely have been as trussed up as a turkey waiting to be someone's holiday dinner. Definitely a bad sign that she could move unhindered.

A soft moaning sound reached her ears from the darkness beyond. Cocking her head, Sharon listened intently. *There, not too far away* she thought, as she heard the sound again. Feeling the rough ground with her hands, Sharon crawled towards the moaning.

"Tiny" she gasped, recognizing her fiancee's voice. "Tiny, can you hear me?"

A raspy "yes" answered her. "Over here."

Before she could reply, a small light illuminated Phillip Whitefeather's battered face. "Oh, my God. How bad are you hurt?" she asked, crawling rapidly towards her fiancée.

"'bout the same as that time I took that bad hit in the Seahawks game. 'Cept I was a good bit younger and in a lot better shape." A slight smile creased Whitefeather's face.

"Where are we?" Sharon asked. If Tiny was able to joke he was going to be alright. "Where did you get that light?"

"I had my phone down my boot for safekeeping. Glad Steve Jobs thought of that flashlight app. The guys who ambushed us took my keys and ID and frisked me after they got me on the ground, but they didn't check my boots" he explained. "Amateurs. I should'a put a piece down my boot. They'd have never found it either."

"What happened? The last thing I remember is someone telling me I should have left well enough alone" Sharon's head was beginning to pound.

"I was chatting up that working girl when her pimp showed up, pissed" Whitefeather began to explain.

"Yes, I saw that. It's what made me get out of my car and move closer to you" Sharon interrupted. "I guess that was my mistake."

"I think they had already made me by then. It's as if they knew we were coming" Whitefeather explained. "Are you sure you didn't let any of this slip at work? Say anything to anybody in the Sheriff's office?"

Sharon considered the question for a few minutes, then replied "No, I didn't talk to anyone at work because I knew if it got back to Sheriff Gilbert he'd have my ass."

"Someone had to know" Whitefeather insisted. "There's no other explanation. The guys who hit us were too prepared, and wherever we are, I think that was planned ahead of time, too. We aren't tied up, and they obviously didn't kill us. That means they don't figure on us getting out of here. Ever."

"Well, I plan on proving them wrong on that count" Sharon wasn't a quitter and she knew her fiancée wasn't either. "Can you move?"

"It'll take more than a couple of redneck white boys to keep me down" Whitefeather replied. "If they put us in here, then there is a way out. We'll back up until we reach a solid wall and then reconnoiter clockwise. I charged my phone before we left Meridian. We ought'a have seven or eight hours of light. We'll find our way out of here by then."

Their progress was slow. They had no idea how large a space they were in, or how long it would take to make their planned circuit. They couldn't afford to miss whatever might offer them an escape from the dark prison that contained them. Two hours had passed according to Sharon's wristwatch when her hand touched rough wood.

"Tiny, here. Feel this" she commanded. "Is this what I hope it is?"

The narrow band of light from Whitefeather's phone moved across a rectangular piece of rough hewn lumber which was wedged into the wall of their enclosure. "There's no latch" he observed. "Let me see if I can move it." Whitefeather placed his shoulder against the wood impediment and pushed. Nothing. Adjusting his stance, Whitefeather attacked the wooden object again, harder this time and with more prolonged force.

"I think it moved" Sharon whispered.

"It did" Whitefeather grunted as he redoubled his efforts.

With a loud crack, the wooden planking gave way revealing a narrow corridor, a hint of pale grayish light barely visible some distance down the passage.

"Let's go." Whitefeather grabbed Sharon's hand and headed down the open tunnel. "I think we're in an old mine shaft" he observed feeling the slight breeze that now wafted towards them.

"Liberty Mining did some work over in Kemper County back in the 90's" Sharon told her fiancée. "Just thirty or so miles north east of Meridian. Those mines have been abandoned for several years."

"It'd be a good dumping place" Whitefeather observed as they limped towards the light ahead of them. "Ten to one that's where we are."

Their escape was slow and painful. Sharon was worried. Whitefeather's breathing sounded labored, but every time she suggested they rest he insisted they press forward. "We'll still be in the middle of nowhere once we get out of this mine, if that's where we are. We've got to get in touch with Sheriff Gilbert as soon as possible."

The sun was setting when Sharon and White-feather stumbled from the rock cliff which hid the mine's emergency exit. They had been trapped for almost twenty-four hours. Holding his phone towards the sky, Whitefeather exclaimed "Three bars. Thank you, Jesus."

Later, Sharon would wonder if Tiny's reference to the Son of the Almighty was the key that unlocked that crucial memory. She *had* mentioned the sting to someone, just not someone who ought to be passing information.

CHAPTER THIRTY-NINE

W as life in prison not enough? The news that
had arrived in the morning mail had rocked
Allison to her core.

"Dear Sis,
Writing this letter is the chicken's way
out for me. As bad as this news is, I couldn't
tell you over the phone, and I didn't think I
could handle telling you in person. Writing
gives me enough distance, and time, to think
about what I want to say.
I've got cancer. Stomach cancer. I've
known something wasn't right for a while, but
I figured whatever it was would work itself out
and go away. Wishful thinking. At any rate, I

had gotten to feeling so bad that a couple of weeks ago I went to see the prison doc. I got put through a bunch of unpleasant tests, and then got the bad news.

Actually, it could be worse news. If the cancer is still contained within my stomach – and they think it's only in something called the subserosa layer and a few lymph nodes – then I've got a decent shot at living for several more years. The three year survival rate for Stage Three stomach cancer is forty-eight to fifty percent. With a little luck I'll be on the high end of the bell curve and get more time than that. Won't know for sure how bad it is 'til they do the surgery to remove part of my stomach, but so long as it hasn't broken through into other organs I've got a fighting chance. I'll do chemo and radiation, too.

Kilby has a surgical hospital here on the grounds. By the time you get this letter I'll be heading into surgery. I don't want you here while they're cutting on me. The surgeon knows to contact you if there are any complications. Otherwise, I want you to wait until you hear from the Warden before you come up here. I won't feel too good for a while, and there's nothing you can do for me here that can't be handled by one of the staff nurses.

Don't cry for me either. There's nothing that can happen to me in this life that is as bad as what I did to my wife and kids. God grant me the serenity to accept the things I can't change.

I love you.

Rice"

Tears began to roll down Allison's face as the full impact of Rice's words hit home. Over the past year and a half Allison's relationship with her brother had improved dramatically, from one of almost complete estrangement to one with the promise of true closeness. The price Rice had paid had been high, no doubt about it, but recovery and AA had banished most of Rice's demons, or at least given him a way to deal with them. Allison couldn't bear to think that having finally found her brother, in a manner of speaking, she would now lose him.

Wiping her face with the back of her hand, Allison opened a new browser window on her computer and typed in *stomach cancer.* Looking again at Rice's letter, Allison clicked on the link for the Mayo Clinic. The first thing Allison noticed was that stomach cancer was uncommon in the United States, with most cases being found in China and Japan. *Figures,* she thought, *only Rice would have that kind of bad luck.* But, if Rice was right about the stage of his cancer and it was still contained in his stomach, according to what she was reading her brother could expect to live maybe as much as four or five years. It wasn't much, but it was better than an instantaneous death sentence. Everything would depend on what the surgeons discovered.

Allison reached for her phone. She wasn't about to wait for a call from Warden Stone. After identifying herself to the prison's operator, and again to the Warden's secretary, Allison waited only a few seconds before Zachary Stone took her call.

"Ms. Parker, I know why you're calling. I told Rice I'd hear from you the minute you got his letter."

"Warden, I should be furious at you for not contacting me yourself" Allison replied, "but being pissed at you is low on my list of concerns right now."

"I understand, but you have to realize without Rice's permission my hands were tied. HIPAA and all that stuff, you know."

"Yes, I know." Allison did know. The Health Insurance Portability and Accountability Act, known as HIPAA, was a pain in most people's derrieres. Intended to set national standards for protecting an individual's private health information, adherence to the federal law had caused a mountain of unnecessary paperwork. Now, almost ten years later, most patients who were given written HIPAA notices tossed them unread into the trash. Keeping a person's medical information private was, Allison often thought, a no-brainer. Passing a lot of bureaucratic rules and regulations was overkill. "I also know that Rice gave written permission for me to access his medical information when he was processed into the system at Kilby" Allison reminded the Warden. "HIPAA doesn't apply."

A short silence followed before the Warden spoke. "Guilty as charged, Ms. Parker. I should have contacted you. Won't happen again."

Mollified, Allison accepted the Warden's apology. "That's water under the bridge. My main concern is Rice. Is he out of surgery? When will I be able to speak with him?" As an afterthought she added "Who is the surgeon? I want to speak with him as soon as possible."

"Rice is in the recovery room. Dr. Jim Brantley did the surgery. He's a surgeon from Montgomery. He has your phone number and I'm sure you'll get a call from him in the next hour or so. As for Rice, I'd wait until tomorrow to try to talk to him."

"I'm coming up there first thing in the morning" Allison replied. "And I'm not waiting for Dr. Brantley to call. What's his number?"

"Here's Brantley's on call number" the Warden stated, "but don't bother to come up here tomorrow. Rice was adamant that he wanted no visitors, including family, until he knew the extent of the cancer and had a chance to process the news with his doctor. If you come up here you won't be admitted."

"We'll see about that" Allison threatened as she terminated the conversation. "We'll just see." But Allison knew she would adhere to her brother's wishes. When he was ready to see her, whenever that was, she would drive to Kilby. Until then, all she could do was pray.

CHAPTER FORTY

Houma, Louisiana, Frank had learned, was the parish, or county as everyone else in the country called it, seat for Terrebonne Parish. The 2010 census had pegged the population at a hair over 32,000, but you could never be sure just how accurate those numbers were. People, like politicians, lied when it worked to their benefit. Like much of North America, Houma had been settled originally by Native Americans before their land was stolen by European invaders around 1834. In short order the only vestige remaining of the original inhabitants was the name of the town.

Wealth had bypassed Houma. Almost twenty percent of the population lived below the poverty level, with an average annual income of less than

$35,000.00. Steeped in Cajun culture, many residents continued to earn a living the way their ancestors had – as fishermen, shrimpers, lobstermen or hunters. Only recently had some men been enticed to work in the oil or shipbuilding industries.

Much of Terrebonne Parish where Houma was located was populated by abundant wildlife, including alligators, bald eagles, heron and other swamp dwelling creatures. Tourist activity, such as it were, included swamp and marsh tours for the adventurists and the Bayou Terrebonne Waterlife Museum for those wanting more sedate exposure to the area's native inhabitants.

Frank knew from reading the case summary that Allison had emailed him on the Houma murder victim that the body had been discovered by two local hunters, Alcide Baligant and Emile Gautier. Noting the ages given by each man during his police interview, Frank calculated that the men would now be in their early 40's. With luck they would still be living in or around Houma and Frank would be able to interview them.

Tossing the remains of his cigar to his truck's passenger side floor, where it rested comfortably with multiple empty McDonald's bags and discarded Styrofoam coffee cups, Frank considered the tasks before him. When he got Allison's call he was already on the road to Houma to check out a lead on

Jefferson Boudreaux. Once Becky Skinner had gotten started dishing out dirt on her current boss she
had been a treasure trove of information. Not only
was Boudreaux an alleged wife beater and sex pervert, Skinner had been suspicious of Boudreaux's
out-of-town travel. "Weren't no reason for him to be
going over to those towns all by himself. LaPierre
Drilling didn't have any business over that way, and
I know he and Miss Cynthia didn't have no social acquaintances over yonder neither." Stopping to make
the sign of the cross, the receptionist had added
"Up to no good, I tell you. That man was the devil's
spawn."

Houma had been one of the towns named by
Becky Skinner. With Allison's official request from
the Task Force asking him to extend his trip to
Houma and Bossier City, Frank figured he'd kill the
proverbial two birds with one stone. Checking the
Tripadvisor app on his phone, Frank chuckled to see
the Howard Johnson Motel listed as a four star ac-
commodation. *God only knows what a two star looks
like if Ho-Jo's gets four stars* he thought. *Maybe this one
has an attached restaurant.* Using the website link for
the motel's number, Frank made a two-night reservation, reserving it with his credit card for a late
arrival. No telling what the afternoon would bring
and Frank didn't want to be burdened with an arbi-
trary check-in time.

Frank's first stop would be local law enforcement. His Task Force I.D. ought to get him cooperation that otherwise might not be there. Grateful that the Terrebonne Parish Sheriff's Department was easy to find, Frank parked two blocks down on Main Street and ambled over to the Courthouse Annex.

A young woman behind a glass window took Frank's name and told him to wait while she contacted the Sheriff. While he waited Frank perused the wanted posters adorning the reception area walls. In addition to those wanted by the local constabulary, the F.B.I.'s ten most wanted stared grimly from black and white photos. Of the ten alleged criminals peering down from their perches, Frank counted only two women.

Frank's reverie was interrupted by a hearty "hello".

"I'm Sheriff Claude Chabaud" said a large, dark-haired man. "I was expecting you – got a call earlier this afternoon from Special Agent Jake Cleveland. The Terrebonne Parish Sheriff's Office is always glad to help brother law enforcement."

"Great" Frank replied. "I didn't realize Jake was going to call. I guess you know then why I'm here?"

"Partly" Chabaud nodded. "I know you want to talk about that terrible murder back in '98. I've pulled our file on that case. She's still a Jane Doe, never did get an identity on her. The Agent told me you might have another matter as well, but he said you'd fill me in on that."

"We think your Jane Doe may be related to several recent murders in Mississippi and Alabama" Frank explained. "Lots of time's passed between your murder case and our current ones, but the M.O.'s are too similar to ignore. What I'm really interested in is talking to whoever handled the investigation, if he's still around, and looking at any evidence you might have kept."

"I handled the investigation" Chabaud replied. "I'd been Sheriff for a couple of years when we got that case. Not much to tell you. A call came in through 911 from one of the Gauthier boys, Emile I think it was. He and a friend had found that girl's body while they were out hunting wild pigs. Emile stays out by Terrebonne Bayou. I'll give you directions to his place if you want to see what he remembers."

"Is the M.E. who did the autopsy still around?" Frank asked.

"Nope" Chabaud shook his head. "Doc passed away a few years ago."

"Any chance y'all still have the girl's clothing in the evidence locker?" An idea formed in Frank's head.

"I looked after I got the agent's call. The case never went anywhere, and per our protocol, we just boxed up everything and sent it to secure storage. We've got her clothing, shoes and a hair band."

"I'd like to take that back with me, if possible" Frank requested.

"Figured you would" the Sheriff acknowledged. "We'll just need to take care of the paperwork so we can track chain of custody. Probably won't ever matter, but you never know."

Forty-five minutes later, Jane Doe's sealed evidence box riding shotgun, Frank headed out East Tunnel Boulevard following the directions Sheriff Chabaud had given him. Chabaud hadn't been any help on Frank's other investigation. "Can't recall hearing the name Jefferson Boudreaux" the Sheriff had told him, and a look through the Department's data base had turned up a big fat zero. Maybe he'd have better luck with the Gauthier man.

CHAPTER FORTY-ONE

Jefferson Boudreaux was not a happy man. It wasn't the upcoming police interview that bothered him. Dealing with a backwoods sheriff like Trowbridge might actually be entertaining. The years Boudreaux had spent leading a double life had sculpted him into a superior actor, at least in his own mind. He knew, also, that he wasn't really a suspect. As David Jackson had explained, the Sheriff just wanted to see if Boudreaux remembered anything Mindy Mitchum might have mentioned or let drop in a casual conversation in the afternoons when she returned to the Inn.

What irritated Boudreaux was his own irresponsible behavior. If he had hunted further away from Ft. Charles, overridden his urge to take the Mitchum girl, just listened to the voice that told him not to hunt so soon and so close to the girl the storm had taken – the morons who passed as law enforcement in Calhoun County would have eventually lost interest in the whore he had picked up in Meridian. His mistake had been taking one of their own.

The local paper had run a big story on the creation of the F.B.I. Task Force working in conjunction with the local sheriff and the sheriff over in Lauderdale County. When David Jackson had contacted him about today's interview Boudreaux had taken the opportunity to gather information from his lawyer.

"I can't imagine what I could tell the Sheriff that would be of use" Boudreaux began by complaining. "I hardly saw the girl."

"It's just part of the investigation" David had attempted to placate his client. "The Sheriff is talking to anyone who might have come in contact with Mindy in the weeks before she was murdered. Since you've been staying at the Inn for the past several weeks you're on the list of interviewees."

"I read something in the paper last week about a task force being set up. Are these interviews connected with that?" If the Feds were going to be involved in his interview Boudreaux wanted to know upfront.

"I don't think so" David had replied. "I just got a call from the Sheriff's secretary asking me to get in touch with you about coming into the office."

Further conversation with his lawyer had proved unproductive. Boudreaux had not wanted to sound too interested in the details of the investigation nor too worried. When David Jackson asked if his client wanted him to be present at the interview, Boudreaux had declined. "That won't be necessary. I can't imagine this will take long. No need to waste your time and my money."

Boudreaux arrived at the Sheriff's office a few minutes before the time scheduled for his interview and was promptly ushered into a small, windowless conference room. Measuring no more than twelve by fifteen, Boudreaux noted with some unease that video equipment had been set up at the end of the room's single table. Of further concern was the fact that one wall consisted entirely of mirrored glass. Boudreaux wondered who would be watching his interview on the other side of the one-way vantage point. *No matter,* he thought basking in the assurance of his superiority. *Let them look.*

"Mr. Boudreaux" a tall man entered the room and extended his hand. "I'm Sheriff Trowbridge."

Boudreaux remained seated, reaching across the table to give the Sheriff's hand a quick shake. "And who is this?" he asked inclining his head towards the slim and well-dressed woman who had followed the Sheriff into the room.

"I'm sorry" Toby replied. "I thought you and Ms. Parker had already met. Allison and David Jackson are law partners."

"Why is she here?" Indignation coated Boudreaux's question. "I told Jackson I had no need for counsel at this meeting."

"I'm not here to represent you, Mr. Boudreaux" Allison smiled as she took a seat across from her partner's client. "I am doing some liaison work between the Sheriff's department and the F.B.I. Task Force. The Task Force is looking into possible connections between the Mitchum murder and some other cases the Agency is looking into."

Boudreaux frowned. "Isn't that some conflict of interest? Your firm represents me and you are here in some sort of adversarial capacity?"

Toby and Allison shared a glance. The hostility evident in Jefferson Boudreaux's voice filled the conference room.

"This is simply an information gathering interview" Toby hoped the interview wasn't going to be stopped before it even started. "Ed Mitchum said you were usually at the Inn when Mindy came home from school each day. We're just hoping you will remember something that might help us."

"I don't see my presence in this interview as a conflict of interest" Allison interjected. "However, if you feel otherwise, I will certainly recuse myself and have someone else take my place."

Boudreaux considered Allison's offer. Asking her to leave might look suspicious. Better to let her stay and just watch what he said. "No, it's fine." Boudreaux placed a relaxed smile on his face. "I've just watched too many lawyer shows. I'm glad to do anything I can to help find that poor child's murderer. Ask away."

Toby began by informing Boudreaux that the interview would be videotaped. "Standard procedure" he assured Boudreaux. "Saves having to take notes." No mention was made of who, if anyone, might be watching or taking notes behind the mirrored wall. Boudreaux decided not to ask.

The first fifteen minutes passed quickly as Boudreaux answered the softball questions he had anticipated from the Sheriff. "I never had much of a conversation with the girl", "I only saw her at breakfast most days", "No, she never mentioned a boyfriend". *Piece of cake,* he thought satisfied with his performance.

"Mr. Boudreaux, I have a few questions for you as well" Allison stated after Toby indicated that his portion of the interview was concluded.

The strained look on Boudreaux's face belied his calm voice. "I believe the Sheriff just stated we were finished."

"Oh, he is" Allison replied. "It's my turn now. As I explained before we got started, the Task Force is also investigating Mindy Mitchum's murder." Allison made a show of shuffling through several typed pages in front of her before continuing. "I have a few questions that the Task Force has asked me to pose. Let's start with the reason for your presence in Ft. Charles."

"You already know the reason for my presence in this town" Boudreaux spat. "To claim my inheritance."

Allison nodded, ignoring Boudreaux's tone. "When did you first arrive in Ft. Charles?"

"You know that too." Boudreaux gave a more civil reply. *Careful*, he cautioned himself. "Same day I checked into Ed Mitchum's B&B."

"I believe that would have been the day after the tornado came through town, is that right?" Allison inquired.

Boudreaux pretended to give the question some thought. "Yes, I guess it was. Tornadoes are a way of life in Louisiana where I live. I just don't remark on them much anymore."

"Mr. Boudreaux, I'm curious as to why you are staying here in Ft. Charles. Don't you have a business to run in Morgan City?" Allison was particularly interested in the answer to this question. She knew from talking to her partner that the court had yet to set a trial date on Boudreaux's Will contest.

"Actually I am planning on returning to Louisiana within the next few days. After the tragedy with the Mitchum girl I thought my presence at the B&B might be of some small help to her father." Boudreaux fidgeted with his necktie. "Someone needed to be there with the man, and I understood him to be without other family."

After a few additional but inconsequential questions, the Sheriff thanked Boudreaux for his cooperation, apologized for inconveniencing him, and escorted him to the lobby. Toby wanted to process the interview with Jake Cleveland who had been watching through the one-way mirror. By the time Toby returned to the conference room an argument between Allison and Cleveland was in full swing.

"Why in the Hell did you bring up the tornado" Cleveland yelled. "What were you thinking?"

"Get a grip" Allison retorted. "I'm not hard of hearing and yelling is unprofessional."

"Don't fucking lecture me" Cleveland retorted, but at a much lower decibel. "I just wish you hadn't played that card."

"I made a spur of the moment decision" Allison explained. "Based on some of what Frank Martin has uncovered, Boudreaux was into some weird sex stuff with his wife. It's not too far a stretch to think he branched out at some point."

"That is the wildest speculation" Trowbridge interrupted. "You don't have anything other than a statement from a possibly disgruntled employee to support that kind of accusation. And so what if he and his wife were into kinky sex? That doesn't make the guy a murderer."

"And, it doesn't merit giving him a head's up on our own suspicions if he is involved" Cleveland added. "We already know he was here around the time the tornado hit. There was no need to spotlight that bit of info."

"I guess you're both right" Allison admitted. "I just thought the question might take him off his guard, thought I might get some sort of reaction. The guy's like stone most of the time."

"You did get a reaction" Cleveland observed. "Just not to the tornado question."

"Really?" Allison asked. "Which one?"

"When you asked him when he planned to leave town. I thought his answer was pretty damn lame, and he started messin' with his tie while he was answering" Jake replied. "First and only show of emotion during the entire interview."

"Yeh, I thought his answer was fake" Trowbridge agreed. "Like he just grabbed it out of the air. Jefferson Boudreaux doesn't strike me as the kind of person with love for his fellow man. Can't see him putting himself out for anyone but himself."

"And there is no reason for him to hang around on account of the case David is handling for him" Allison added. "We're missing something, I just don't know what. Maybe Frank will have some answers for us."

CHAPTER FORTY-TWO

Sheriff Scott Gilbert frowned at the two miscreants before him, one of whom was his own deputy. "I'm waiting for an explanation, and it damn well better be a good one, Greene."

Sharon Greene swallowed hard. "Chief, I know it was a stupid move, but I was afraid you wouldn't approve the undercover work, and I was sure I was on to something. What happened to Tiny and me proves I was right."

"And it could have just as easily proved you dead" Gilbert bellowed moving around the side of the hospital bed to face a prone Phillip Whitefeather. "And, you" he continued, poking a finger in Whitefeather's face, "I can't believe you let her talk you into, into...

Hell, I don't even know what kind of name to put on the sort of danger you and Sharon got into."

Trapped by the I.V. line snaking out of his arm and the heart monitor restricting him to what passed for a bed in the emergency room at Rush Memorial, Whitefeather glowered. "I don't need a lecture from you. Already got one from Sharon's dad."

"This isn't a lecture. It's a statement of fact" Gilbert began before Sharon Greene interrupted.

"Y'all stop it" she demanded, then realized who she was talking to. "Sorry, Chief, but I don't think you and Tiny arguing is going to help. Someone who knew I was a deputy made plans to take me out, and Tiny with me. Something bad is going on at that truck stop, and it's big enough that at least two people were willing to risk a murder charge to hide it. Tiny and I weren't supposed to get out of that mine alive."

Chagrined by his fiancee's reprimand, Whitefeather addressed the Sheriff. "I'm sorry about the whole thing, Sheriff. And I'm grateful that Sharon and I are alive."

Gilbert nodded. "Did you get a good look at any of them?"

"No" Whitefeather replied. "They came up behind me, knocked me down, and trussed me up good. There were two of them, both hooded and wearing gloves. Can't tell you if they were white, black or purple."

"What about you, Sharon?" Gilbert asked turning to his deputy.

"I just heard a voice, and then the lights went out" Sharon paused, "but the voice was familiar. I've been racking my brain since we got to the hospital trying to remember where I've heard it." That last statement wasn't exactly true, but surely the person who had hit her wasn't who the voice sounded like it belonged to.

"Man or woman?" Gilbert pressed.

"Man. Definitely a man" Sharon replied, "He told me I should have left well enough alone."

"So that means whoever hit you knew you were going to be at the Flying J that night" Gilbert deduced. "Who knew about your plans?"

"That's my thinking, too" Whitefeather added. Turning his head towards his fiancée, Whitefeather asked "Want to tell the Sheriff what you told me after we got out of that mine?"

Sharon sighed. "I just can't believe he would have anything to do with this."

"Who?" Gilbert asked.

"Father Anuncio. In confession last week I asked forgiveness for lying to my boss." Sharon gave a sheepish smile. "Father asked me what I had lied about and I told him. Thinking back on it, he asked me a lot of questions, but at the time I thought he was just trying to figure out how bad my sin had been so he could give me the proper penance."

"Are you telling me that the voice you heard before you were knocked unconscious belonged to a priest?" Gilbert frowned.

"I guess I am" Sharon replied. "I just can't believe it."

"Believe it" Gilbert replied. "Murder isn't that far removed from pedophilia. No telling what sort of man hides behind those black robes."

"Father Anuncio is not a child molester" Sharon retorted.

"Not saying he is" Gilbert replied, "just pointing out that a priest's robes don't bestow goodness on the wearer."

The trio's conversation was halted by the entrance of the ER doctor who had examined Whitefeather when he and Sharon had arrived at Rush. "Your tests results are negative, Mr. Whitefeather. I imagine you'll have a pretty good headache for the next few days, but your electrolites are back in balance so there's no need to admit you. The nurse will be in to unhook you and give you your discharge papers shortly."

"I told you I didn't need to be here" Whitefeather complained to Sharon. "We've got work to do figuring out who did this."

"Neither of you are doing anything" Gilbert admonished the pair. "Greene, you're on administrative leave until I tell you otherwise. Tiny, you're a civilian. Stay out of this or I'll lock your ass up just to keep you out of more trouble. I'm going to call Bishop Kopacz over in Jackson" Gilbert added referring to the Catholic Bishop in charge of the church in Mississippi. "I want to know more about Father Anuncio."

⊷⊶

"Catholic Diocese of Jackson" a pleasant voice answered Gilbert's call.

Gilbert identified himself, pronounced his call to be on official business, and asked to be connected with Bishop Kopacz.

"Scott" Bishop Kopacz addressed the Sheriff warmly. "Our receptionist said this was official business. I was hoping you were calling to tell me you were returning to the church."

"Your Excellency, I need some background information on one of the priests in your Diocese" Scott replied ignoring the Bishop's comment about the state of his church attendance. "Confidentially, of course."

"We are always glad to assist law enforcement when we can" the Bishop began, "but only when to do so does not cause conflict with our sacred duties."

"I'm not asking you to breach the confessional" Gilbert explained. "Just looking for background on Father Anuncio over in Meridian. How long has he been a priest? Where is home for him? How many parishes has he served before coming to Meridian?"

"Why do you want this information, my son?" Kopacz wanted to know.

"One of my deputies thinks he may be peripherally involved in a matter she is investigating" Scott fudged. "Nothing serious. I just don't know much about him."

"And if you had returned to the Church, you wouldn't have to ask me all these questions about your own priest, would you?" Kopacz gently reprimanded. "Father Anuncio is from Colombia, as in the country. His family escaped the drug cartels when he was a teenager. Father Anuncio's calling is strong. I find it hard to believe – no, impossible to believe – that he would be involved in any criminal behavior." The Bishop paused, then asked "That's what you suspect, isn't it? That he is involved in something illegal?"

"I'm not at liberty to share that sort of information, Your Excellency" Scott replied, "but perhaps you are right. Maybe it's time for me to return to the Church. I am sure Father Anuncio would hear my confession."

"Scott, don't use the church for improper purposes" Bishop Kopacz reprimanded the Sheriff. "If Father Anuncio is doing something he shouldn't, tell me and let the church handle it."

"Like the church handled the crimes against my brother?" Scott retorted. "Not a chance. And by the way, don't give the good Father a head's up, either. That would be interfering with a criminal investigation. I'm sure you'd agree the Church doesn't need any more bad press."

Sheriff Gilbert hoped the Bishop would heed his warning about not contacting Father Anuncio. Better not to take any chances. Looking up St. Patrick's webpage, Gilbert scanned for the days and times of confessional. *Saturdays 4:00 to 4:30 or upon request.* Gilbert was certain that the request of a lapsed Catholic for reconciliation would be readily granted any time he wanted.

CHAPTER FORTY-THREE

Emile Gauthier lived in a shack. A big shack, but a shack nevertheless. A long, narrow porch piled with rusted crab pots, a bale of barbed wire, and assorted unidentifiable trash ran across the front of the barely standing wooden structure. A door adorned by peeling gray paint was flanked by a pair of double windows, one of which sported a large crack down the left side of the glass. There might be curtains, but it was hard for Frank to tell given the dirt caking the windows themselves.

An old pickup truck, probably a 70's something model, sat tireless on four cinderblocks a few feet from the porch. Underneath, a tired looking hound lounged, or maybe was dead. It never moved as

Frank drove onto a dirt patch that once might have been a grassy front lawn.

Frank cut his engine and took in the discordant view behind the shack. Twenty or so yards beyond the decrepit hovel, Frank was amazed to see a shiny, multi-hull Boston Whaler fishing boat perched on a large trailer. Fishing had never been Frank's thing, but he knew about Boston Whalers from a friend who was a fishing nut. Starting around thirty-eight thousand, a new Whaler could top out at over fifty grand. The beauty sitting behind Emile Gautier's place looked brand, spanking new.

Well, everyone has their own priorities Frank mused as he climbed the sagging front porch steps. "Anybody home?" he called.

The door edged open allowing the double barrel of a shotgun to respond to Frank's inquiry. "Who are you and what do you want?" the rough voice demanded a quick answer.

"Sheriff Chabaud told me you might could give me some help" Frank invoked the Sheriff's name for any protection it could provide. "Don't mean you any harm" he added.

"Cain't be too safe nowadays" answered a trim, overall clad man who emerged from the house. "And you ain't any kind of watch dog" he hollered at the still sleeping dog lying under the jacked up truck.

"Worthless" the man added as he gave Frank a on-ceover before lowering the shotgun. Frank wasn't sure whether the man meant him or the dog.

"I'm Frank Martin" Frank offered his hand. "Are you Emile Gautier?"

"That be me" the man nodded. "How's old Chabaud doing? He ought to be retired by now." Gauthier brushed a pile of rags off a rocker and motioned for Frank to take a seat. "What is it that the Sheriff thought I could help with?"

"I need to give you some background, first" Frank stated, then explained the Wingo and Mitchum murders, added the question about Francine Turner, and ended with the creation of the Task Force. "We think we may have a serial killer. The Task Force took a look at some of the older cold cases across the South, and that girl you and Alcide Baligant found came up."

Emile Gauthier pulled a pack of crumpled Camels from one of his pockets, shook out a cigarette, and paused to light up. "Nasty business, that was. Nasty."

"Indeed" Frank agreed. "Chabaud told me he handled the investigation, and he told me everything he could remember. But I thought maybe you might remember something different since you found the body."

"They never did find out who that poor thing was." Gauthier sucked in a lungful of poison. "Now you tellin' me they never caught the evil that hurt her like that, neither, that right?"

"If he's been caught, it was for something else" Frank replied. "1998 was a long time ago, but the murders we've got in Alabama look a lot like the work of the same guy."

Emile Gauthier took a last drag, then ground the half smoked cigarette under the heel of his leather boot. The old hound dog slowly drug its body up the short stairs to the porch, whined for attention or food, collapsed at Gauthier's feet and commenced to snore. Frank waited. He was pretty certain Gauthier had more to share. Whether he would or not remained to be seen.

"This is a beautiful place, here on the bayou" Gauthier commented. "Beautiful and cruel, it's true, but cruel only because nature dictates that some must die to feed others." Gauthier reached for the shotgun he had laid by the porch railing and sighted it towards the nearby woods. "It was early fall. A 'corse you know that or you wouldn't be here asking me questions. Back then, Alcide and I had a little drug business we was runnin'. Didn't pay too careful attention to who we sold to, just lookin' to make a little extra cash. Young and stupid, figured we were too smart to get caught. I tell you that to explain why we'd sell weed to a total stranger – but we did." Gauthier lowered the shotgun to his side, keeping his finger on the trigger. "Anyway, about ten that morning Alcide got a call from one of his contacts, said a guy was looking to make a buy. Alcide set up a meet and sold a couple of ounces to the guy who showed. Late in the afternoon, same day, Alcide and I head out hunting. First time I had hunted with this gun" Gauthier turned the shotgun towards Frank, but with the double barrels lowered. Frank shifted uneasily, noting that Gauthier's finger had not moved from the trigger.

"We hadn't been out long when Alcide found her. I heard him screaming, thought he'd been stuck by one of those old boars we was huntin' – they's mean mothers what can kill a man in less'un five minutes." A shadow seemed to pass over Gauthier's face. "By the time I got there Alcide had puked all over himself, and I could see why. What was layin' inside that cabin barely resembled a human, 'cept her face was unmarked."

"I've seen the pictures" Frank interrupted. "I'm sure it was a shock for both of you."

Laying aside the shotgun, Gauthier lit up another cigarette. "Alcide and I both did time in Somalia. We've seen that or worse. That wasn't what made Alcide puke."

"What, then?" Frank asked.

"Alcide had seen that woman a couple of hours earlier. She was in the car with the guy he sold the weed to." Gauthier explained. "Alcide figured he'd sold weed to a killer."

Frank was stunned. "There isn't anything about this in the case file. Did you tell Sheriff Chabaud?"

"We argued 'bout what to tell, but Alcide was frightened out of his wits. Don't know what he was more afraid of – going to jail for dealing or having that killer come after him for ratting." Gauthier scuffed the toe of his boot in the dusty porch floor. "I know it was wrong. But we were young, and there wasn't anything we could say to bring that poor thing back to life. And neither Alcide nor I wanted someone crazy enough to do what was done to that woman coming after us."

Berating Emile Gauthier was pointless. This Frank knew, but maybe something could yet be salvaged. "Do you think Alcide would remember what the man he sold the weed to looked like?"

"You can ask him yourself" Gauthier walked to the porch's screened door and called inside "Alcide, it's OK. You ain't gonna' be arrested."

Once again, the door to the house creaked open. The skeleton who shambled out looked decades older than Alcide Baligant's thirty-nine years. The yellow caste of his skin and shaking of his hands telegraphed Baligant's problem before the smell of whiskey hit Frank's nose. "My sister works in Chabaud's office. We knew you was coming. Jest had to make sure why" Alcide offered in a raspy voice.

"I'm not aiming to cause you any trouble, Mr. Baligant" Frank began. "Not you or Mr. Gauthier. Nobody's going to come after you for dealing pot or not telling Sheriff Chabaud about what you saw. It's like I told Mr. Gauthier, there's a possibility, albeit a slim one, that the murderer is still active. Now that I know you saw the man who likely killed that girl here, it would be mighty helpful if you could tell me what you remember about him. Anything at all."

Baligant slowly lowered himself to the porch steps. The hound dog which had been snoring only a few minutes earlier trotted over to the seated man and put its head in Baligant's lap. "Good dog" Baligant whispered as he scratched the hound behind its ears. "Good dog."

"What do you remember about the guy who bought the weed?" Frank prodded. "What kind of car was he driving? Was his hair long or short? What color was it? How about skin color?" Frank reached for the case file he had retrieved from his truck. "Give me a minute to pull out something to write on" he told Baligant.

True to form, the case file Frank had hastily put together after arriving in Houma was stuffed to overflowing with information from the Wingo and Mitchum murders as well as the independent investigative reports David Jackson had sent to him on Boudreaux. "I know I've got a legal pad in here somewhere" Frank muttered as he began pulling various papers from the folder and tossing them on the porch floor.

"Why you lyin' to me?" Frank heard cold anger in Alcide Baligant's voice. "You already know what he look like."

A black and white photo was clutched tightly in Alcide Baligant's hand. The investigative report to which it had been attached lay discarded nearby. "He's older now. But the devil is still in his eyes."

CHAPTER FORTY-FOUR

A llison studied the large crime board that hung on the wall beside her desk at the firm. Across the top she had written "Mitchum", "Wingo", "Turner", and "Cold Cases". Using different colored markers, Allison had listed manner of death, cause of death, age, identifying characteristics in each column, adding date of death as a subcategory under "Cold Cases". Actually, the "Cold Cases" column had been expanded, like a tree branch on Ancestry. com, to list the three cold cases from the F.B.I. files that most closely resembled the M.O. used in the Mitchum, and probably Wingo, murders.

The damage done to the Jane Doe in Houma, Louisiana in 1998 most closely resembled the damage done to Mindy Mitchum. Andy Dabo's

ME Report opined that Mindy had been alive when the cutting was inflicted, but dead when her rectum was puntured, horrific facts which Dabo and the Sheriff had decided to withhold from Ed Mitchum. Dabo attributed the cause of death to manual strangulation based on the petichiea evident in Mindy's eyes, and that was the only information the M.E had shared with the victim's father.

Allison knew there were sick people walking the planet. Her husband Jim had seen his share of them in his courtroom, but none whose crimes reached the malevolent magnitude of what Allison had read about in the F.B.I. cold case files. The Houma murder and Mindy's murder weren't the only cases where the victim had been sliced or sodomized. Allison's gaze returned to the two other cold cases she had placed on her board. These were simply the ones that had remained unsolved in four Southern states. How many were there in the rest of the country? Frank Martin's call had come just an hour earlier. His written report would follow, but he had wanted Allison to know about Alcide Baligant's reaction to Jefferson Boudreaux's picture as well as what Sheriff Chabaud had told him about the crime scene.

"It wasn't in the police report" Frank's voice crackled from a bad cell connection.

"What wasn't in the report?" Allison asked. "I'm having trouble hearing you. Are you on the interstate yet?"

"Ten miles out from I-90" Frank replied. "Must be between cell towers. Can you hear me now?"

"Yes, that's better" Allison replied. Frank's voice was clearer. "What wasn't in the report?"

"There was a rose left with the victim in Houma" Frank responded. "Store bought, long stemmed. A calling card."

"I'm surprised a detail like that wasn't in the original report" Allison mused. "A calling card is a significant clue. But I don't remember seeing anything like that in the Mitchum crime scene report."

"Look again" Frank suggested. "I didn't remember anything either until I pulled out the copies of the crime scene photos I have with me."

"Give me a second" Allison placed Frank's call on speaker, retrieved a file marked "Crime Scene Photographs, Mitchum Murder" and pulled out several color photos. Spreading them across her desk, Allison asked "Which picture, Frank?"

"It's in two of them. The ones taken from behind the body. You can see the flower off to the left of the lower part of the picture" Frank instructed.

Allison reached for a small magnifying class she kept on her desk in lieu of readers. Slowly, she examined the first picture. "Damn" she whispered. "I see it. But it's not a rose. Looks like a lily of some sort. Could just be a coincidence."

"There's more" Excitement tinged Frank's tone. "Alcide Baligant identified a picture of Jefferson Boudreaux as the guy he saw with the Houma victim the day she was killed."

"How could he identify someone he only saw once, and twenty years later to boot?" Allison wondered about Baligant's credibility. "That's pretty slim."

"He was certain" Frank replied, "but I've saved the best for last."

"Which is?"

"I've got the Houma victim's clothes. For some unknown reason, they never ran a DNA test. The stuff has been boxed and sealed in the Sheriff's evidence room for years." Frank's words tumbled out of his mouth. "If we can get DNA off of the vic's clothes.."

"We can match it against Boudreaux's" Allison finished for him. "Frank, get back here as fast as you can. Forget going to Bossier City. If you're right, we're about to solve two murders, and maybe more."

"I'm driving straight through" Frank informed Allison before terminating the call. "Should be back around seven or eight tonight."

The white sheen of the crime board glistened under the office's fluorescent ceiling lights. Frank's call had confirmed her earlier suspicions. Taking up a black marker, Allison placed a line through all of the listed cold cases save one. She would focus on Houma.

Allison faced a dilemma. Did she have a professional responsibility to her partner to advise him about his client's possible, no probable, history as a murderer? She knew David had hired Frank Martin to investigate Boudreaux, but Frank had not said anything to her about sharing the new information with David. Maybe she should call Jake Cleveland first. After all, if DNA from the Houma victim's clothes matched Boudreaux's DNA, Jake's oldest cold case would be solved. And that calling card? What was that the significance of the flower near Mindy Mitchum's body? Maybe nothing, and what did that prove? Nothing concrete, and likely not enough to arrest Jefferson Boudreaux for Mindy Mitchum's murder.

Pacing her office, Allison knew she was getting ahead of herself. If Andy Dabo couldn't pull DNA from the Houma victim's belongings, all they had was the word of a backwoods, drug-dealing, Cajun alcoholic claiming that he had seen Jefferson Boudreaux with the victim. A good defense attorney would shred Alcide Baligant to pieces. Even with a DNA match, they would still have only a circumstantial case. No one witnessed the Houma murder and Allison didn't peg Jefferson Boudreaux as the confessing type.

All of her options weighed and considered, Allison headed down the hallway to David Jackson's office. Jefferson Boudreaux needed a little push.

CHAPTER FORTY-FIVE

The sanctuary of St. Patrick's Church was large, yet intimate. A small confessional booth was tucked into the back of the left transept, its placement intended to transmit a sense of privacy to the congregant seeking absolution. Muted strains of late afternoon light filtered through the stained glass windows of the sacristy, crowning the large crucified Christ which hung below with a golden halo.

The small sign hanging beside the confessional's door indicated that the box of contrition was currently in use. Earlier that morning, when Sheriff Gilbert had called the Parish office to schedule a private confession, Father Auncio's assistant informed the Sheriff that a 4:30 appointment would be available that very afternoon. Now, looking around the sanctuary, the Sheriff saw no other parishioners. After the penitent currently inhabiting the confessional left, it would just be the Sheriff and Father Anuncio.

Taking a seat in one of the pews near the altar rail, Sheriff Gilbert closed his eyes. Surrounded by the faint yet lingering scent of incense and burning candles, Gilbert reviewed what he had discovered about Father Anuncio. The preceding evening, the Sheriff had spent several hours attempting to get a handle on who the priest might be. A search of the Meridian Star's archives had produced a short article in the paper's religion section when the good Father had been assigned to St. Patrick's. Not much in the article, nothing that Bishop Kopacz hadn't already shared. What had surprised the Sheriff was the discovery that the priest had a Facebook page. Gilbert never had been able to understand why anyone would want to post personal information on the internet. He had to admit, though, that being able to peruse suspects' public postings was something he found helpful on more than one occasion. Gilbert chuckled quietly remembering how a local car thief had been arrested – the moron had posted a picture of himself and the stolen vehicle on something called Instagram.

Most of Father Anuncio's Facebook postings were about church events or charity fundraisers. Gilbert had been about to disconnect from the priest's page when he decided to look at Anuncio's family connections. Bishop Kopacz said Anuncio's family had immigrated to the U.S. when the priest was a youth. Gilbert had assumed that meant all of the family had become U.S. citizens and had remained in this country.

Gilbert had been partially correct. Anuncio, his parents and his three sisters had all become naturalized citizens, but one of the sisters, Isabella, had later returned to Colombia. A post from last year on the priest's Facebook page showed Isabella with an Amnesty International co-worker in Medellin. Colombia was a dangerous country, and Medellin an even more dangerous city. True, the drug cartel had been dismantled to a degree with the death of Pablo Escobar, but drug running and the crimes that accompanied that profession made living in Medellin a risky choice. Gilbert intended to ask Anuncio about his sister.

The soft click of a door closing caught his attention. Gilbert watched as an elderly woman moved away from the confessional booth, made her way up the aisle, and then settled into a pew near the back of the church to begin saying her assigned penance. *Time for a little chat, Father* Gilbert thought as he moved to the confessional to confront the priest.

The inside of the confessional booth was dimly lit. Memories from his youth flooded to the surface, temporarily distracting Gilbert from his mission. Once, the church and her sacraments had given his life a comforting rhythm. Gilbert was surprised that the simple act of entering the solitude of the confessional booth had triggered a longing for that connection.

No time for that now, he thought as he knocked on the slatted window to let the priest know he was ready.

"Forgive me Father for I have sinned" Gilbert remarked after the priest opened the partial divide between the two.

"What is the nature of this sin?" Father Anuncio asked.

Satisfied that his target was present, Gilbert replied "I have numerous sins, Father. It's been decades since my last confession, but that's not why I am here."

"Why are you here my son?" The priest's voice was gentle and inquisitive. "Are you in spiritual pain?"

"I should be asking you the same question" Gilbert replied. "Or maybe you should be seeking absolution yourself."

"Who is this?" the priest demanded. "This is the house of the Lord, not some place for pranks."

"I'm Sheriff Scott Gilbert, Father. And I'm doing you a favor by having this conversation privately."

"What do you mean, doing me a favor?" Anuncio lowered his voice.

"One of my deputies and her 'partner' were assaulted a few days ago while on an undercover assignment. I believe you know the deputy, Sharon Greene. She's a devout Catholic; in fact, I understand you hear her confession on a regular basis." Gilbert let that comment rest in the priest's ears before continuing. "I'm certain you would recognize her voice and she yours."

"I know Sharon" the priest's voice was barely a whisper. "Is she alright?"

"Funny you should ask, Father" Gilbert sneered. "Sharon said the last voice she heard before she was knocked unconscious was yours." The Sheriff waited silently for the priest's reply. Not hearing a sound from the other side of the partition, Gilbert began to think the priest had slipped away.

"May God forgive me" Anuncio began. "They wanted me to kill her, the one with her, too. Leaving them in the mine was the only thing I could think of. I hoped they would escape, but if they didn't, I told myself their death wouldn't be on my hands."

"Who is 'they'?" Gilbert interrupted. He couldn't imagine anyone ordering the priest to commit one of the seven deadly sins. "And what were you doing at that truck stop?" If the priest wasn't denying his involvement Gilbert wanted to get as much information as possible. He might regret not Mirandizing the priest later, but Gilbert was willing to take the risk.

"Cartel" Anuncio breathed the name. "They have my sister. I've probably signed her death warrant by talking to you, but I can't let anyone else get killed."

"What are you involved in, Father?" Gilbert asked, this time more softly.

"Drugs never were the Cartel's only business" the priest replied. "Drugs made the most money, but the sex trade and other kinds of smuggling turned a profit for the Colombian bosses as well. Six months ago a man approached me after Mass and handed me an envelope. He told me my sister's life depended on my cooperation. Before I had a chance to recover from my shock he had disappeared into the Sunday crowd leaving the church."

"Was he talking about Isabella?" Gilbert asked. "The one working in Colombia?"

"Yes. We knew she was missing. We'd gotten a call from Amnesty International and our State Department. The family was asked to be patient, to let the authorities handle the kidnapping." Anuncio laughed bitterly. "I knew what that meant. We'd never see Isabella alive again. And then I got the video. My baby sister was alive. Beaten, but alive. If

I wanted her to stay that way I would have to do as I was told."

"You should have gone to the authorities" Gilbert replied.

"No. Going to the authorities would have meant my sister's certain death." The priest's reply left no room for argument.

"If Sharon hadn't recognized your voice, we wouldn't even be having this conversation would we, Father?" Gilbert thought he knew the answer to that question.

The sound of soft weeping filled the silence of the confessional. "I couldn't let anyone else be killed" the priest repeated, his answer a seeming non sequitur to Gilbert's question.

"Was someone else killed, Father?" The priest's answer had placed the Sheriff's instincts on full alert.

"She was innocent." The priest continued to weep. "An example to show me they were serious."

"Who, Father?" Gilbert asked again.

"Francine" the priest choked out the name. "Francine Turner."

CHAPTER FORTY-SIX

Heart palpitations and night sweats accompanied by an overwhelming sense of dread had initially led Jefferson Boudreaux to believe he might be having a heart attack. Anxiety was an emotion foreign to the man who had always believed himself superior to those around him, a man in complete control of his destiny, unaffected by those lesser beings with whom he was forced to interact. His visit to the Ft. Charles Hospital ER had been an embarrassing admission of weakness, a trait Boudreaux despised. The condescension shown to him by the ER doctor had been almost unbearable.

"You're fine, Mr. Boudreaux" the young doctor crooned. "EKG's normal, blood enzymes are not elevated. There's no evidence of a cardiac event."

Laying aside Boudreaux's medical chart the doctor had continued. "Lots of patients confuse an anxiety attack with a heart attack. Similar symptoms, but nothing alarming." It had taken all of Boudreaux's willpower not to hit the doctor when he patted Boudreaux on the arm, adding "My recommendation is for you to take it easy for a few days."

The liquid sparkled deep amber as Boudreaux poured the Scotch whiskey into the iceless glass. Settling himself in the overstuffed armchair by his bedroom window at the Inn, Boudreaux considered his options. Logic dictated several reasons for him to leave Ft. Charles. First of all, his presence wasn't currently needed in his legal case. In fact, if David Jackson was successful with the motion for summary judgment he intended to file next week, there wouldn't even be a trial. If the court ruled against Boudreaux on the motion, it would be months before the case was litigated. It might be an entire year before the matter of his inheritance was finally settled.

Secondly, Boudreaux needed to get back to LaPierre Drilling. He had competent men working for him, but leaving the shop unattended for too long was problematic. The call he had received this morning bore out his concern, and upon reflection Boudreaux surmised that the conversation with his lackey had been the precipitator of his anxiety attack.

"Mr. Boudreaux, Sir, I hate to bother you while you are out of town" the obsequious voice of Randy Melton, one of Boudreaux's office snitches, dripped across the phone line, "but I think you ought to know about this.."

"If you have something to say, say it" Boudreaux ordered. "Otherwise you're wasting my time."

"Well, uh.." Melton stammered. "I thought you'd want to know some paper is doing a story on you."

"What are you talking about?" Boudreaux wondered if his employee had been smoking something other than cigarettes.

"Some guy was chattin' up Miz Becky, wanted to know all about you. He was here more'un an hour. I couldn't hear too much, didn't want the old bag to know I was listenin'" Randy offered up the lame excuse for his lack of complete knowledge. "After he was gone I quizzed Miz Becky 'bout who that guy was, what he wanted. All she would say was that some newspaper was doing an article on you."

"Did she tell you what newspaper? Or the name of this reporter?" Boudreaux asked.

"Uh, she said the guy never told her who he worked for" Randy replied.

"What about a name" Boudreaux repeated. "Did she say a name?"

"Yes, Sir, I didn't make a note of it, but I well remember it because of that old TV show. His last name was 'Martian'". The snitch snorted "you think he was from outer space?"

Boudreaux replayed the conversation in his mind while he finished his drink. As soon as he got back, Becky Skinner would be the first to go, and that idiot Randy right after her. Boudreaux didn't know who had come asking after him, but he knew for damn sure it wasn't a Martian.

Although LaPierre Drilling was a successful privately owned operation, the likelihood of one of the trade papers doing a feature on him was remote. Over the years Charles LaPierre had taken the credit for each of Boudreaux's profitable ideas. When the old man died the rumor mill was rife with questions about Jefferson Boudreaux's ability to run the company. No, there was no way any of the trade journals would do a story on him. Those vultures were waiting to pick his bones when LaPierre Drilling ultimately failed.

The more Boudreaux had tried to figure out why someone would be asking questions about him, the more nervous he had become, convinced that the snooping stranger had an ulterior motive in mind. By the time Boudreaux had driven himself to the emergency room he could hardly breathe.

He was calmer now. Whatever the stranger thought he would discover by talking to LaPierre employees, Boudreaux reassured himself that the conversations would be of no real consequence. He knew Becky Skinner didn't like him, but he doubted the woman had any knowledge of his extracurricular activities. Becky Skinner could be made to look like the disgruntled employee she was.

Despite his internal reassurances, the voice that he had ignored when he took the Mitchum girl continued to nag him. *Something is not right. What have you forgotten?* And then the ultimate question. *Why are you still here?* Boudreaux was pondering these questions when his cell phone rang.

"Mr. Boudreaux, this is Donna Pevey, David Jackson's secretary. He asked me to give you a call." "Yes?" Boudreaux replied. *What now?*

"Mr. Jackson received a call from the Task Force that is investigating the recent killings. One of their investigators would like to ask you a few more questions. Can you come in tomorrow afternoon, say around 2:00, for another interview?"

The voice in Jefferson Boudreaux's head was screaming, but with an enormous effort he replied calmly "Well, certainly. As I told the Sheriff, anything I can do to be of help I'm glad to do. By way, who is conducting the interview?"

"I'm not sure" Donna Pevey replied. "All I know is Ms. Parker asked me to reserve our conference room for tomorrow's meeting."

"Allison Parker, Mr. Jackson's law partner?" Boudreaux asked.

"Yes, Ms. Parker is working with the Task Force on the local murders" Donna explained, unaware that Boudreaux was already acquainted with Allison's role in the investigations. "I'll let David and Allison know you will be available tomorrow at 2:00."

Jefferson Boudreaux poured himself another shot of liquid fortitude. The Parker woman was trouble. He'd sensed it when she interrogated him in the Sheriff's office. Sipping the expensive Scotch, Boudreaux felt a tinge of anger spark deep inside his belly. *That bitch deliberately tried to distract you,* the Voice whispered. *She's a whore, just like the others.* A familiar heat filled Boudreaux's loins. Yes, she had flaunted her body, he remembered, Boudreaux's imagination providing a characterized version of Allison with breasts exposed leaning over the conference room table to cross-examine him. Boudreaux unzipped his pants. A few hard strokes, and he was finished, his fantasy now firmly established in his mind.

A part of him, the sane part, knew the action Boudreaux contemplated could not end well, that this time there would be no escape. But the Voice was too loud, and the urge too strong.

CHAPTER FORTY-SEVEN

"Sheriff Gilbert, Lauderdale County, Mississippi calling for Sheriff Trowbridge" Scott Gilbert informed Beth Robinson. "Is he in yet?"

"Of course he is" sniffed Trowbridge's secretary. "It's after 8:00. Hold on and I'll see if the Sheriff has time to take your call." Beth Robinson thought the Mississippi sheriff sounded a tad too big for his britches. She'd let him wait a minute or so before putting the call through to her boss.

"Who is it, Beth" Toby called from his office. He could see the blinking 'hold button' on his desk unit. "Are you actually screening my calls?"

"It's that upstart young sheriff over in Meridian" Beth yelled back, not bothering to leave her desk. "Won't hurt him to be on hold for a while."

"Beth" Sheriff Trowbridge cautioned, "you can't keep doing this. If I'm not on the phone when I get a call, put it through immediately." Toby knew his reprimand would go unheeded. His secretary considered herself the guardian of the gate, bless her heart, and no amount of ordering, cajoling or begging had changed her behavior. Reaching for his phone, Toby depressed the red blinking light and answered "Sheriff Gilbert, to what do I owe the pleasure of a call so early in the day?"

"I've got a lead on the Turner murder. And I don't think it's connected to the two in your county" Amending his answer, Gilbert added "No, I am certain it's not connected to those murders."

"First things first" Toby replied. "What's the lead?"

Scott Gilbert looked at the statement Father Anuncio had given as he answered Trowbridge's question. "One of the local priests is involved. He's in protective custody, although under arrest. A copy of his statement should be coming in on your fax machine as we speak."

"Beth" Toby covered the phone's mouthpiece and yelled for his secretary. "Check the fax machine. Important document coming in from Lauderdale County." Returning his attention to the Mississippi Sheriff, Toby replied "Beth will bring the fax as soon as it arrives. In the meantime, give me the highlights, starting with how a priest is involved in a murder."

"It's hard to believe" Gilbert observed, launching into a detailed narrative of the priest's confession and the tie to one of the Colombian cartels. "I wanted you to be the first to hear about this before I called that F.B.I. agent Cleveland. I know I've got to kick this upstairs. We don't have the manpower or experience to deal with those folks."

"What I don't understand is the priest's connection to the sex trafficking" Trowbridge interjected. "Why was he of interest to the cartel?"

"There's a large transient Hispanic population in Mississippi. It's been a problem for a while now, especially where they've come in illegally" Gilbert replied. "According to Father Anuncio, the cartel was using the hope of a new life in this country as a lure to smuggle young women from Mexico and South America into Texas and New Mexico and then force them into the trade with threats. A few months ago the cartel moved its operation into Mississippi. The cartel told Father Anuncio his sister's life depended on his cooperation. His job was to report any information he received in confession or otherwise that might expose the cartel's activities."

"A terrible choice" Toby reflected, "but I really don't see how a local priest would get enough information to be of any use to the cartel. I doubt any members of your team talking in confession."

"That's where you'd be wrong" Gilbert advised as he launched into an explanation of Sharon Greene's confession that almost got her killed. "Father Anuncio passed Sharon's undercover plan to his Cartel contact, and you know the rest. Sharon and Tiny Whitefeather are lucky to be alive."

"Sounds like that's the only mitigating factor I see in the good Father's actions" Toby observed. "If you believe the priest, throwing the two of them in that old mine is the only thing that kept them from being executed."

"I think his conscience finally got to him" Gilbert replied. "That and guilt over Francine Turner's death."

"Whatever it was, and I'm inclined to give the credit to good police work on the part of your deputy, this is a great collar for your office. I appreciate getting a personal call on this, and ahead of the F.B.I. to boot" Toby thanked his counterpart. "You want me to transfer this call to Jake Cleveland? He's in the Task Force office as we speak."

"Actually" Gilbert replied, "why don't you do the honors? Remind the Feds that us country boys can solve crimes just fine on our own."

"Did Cleveland rub you the wrong way when he and Frank Martin met with you?" Trowbridge knew some state law enforcement officers carried a chip on their shoulders when it came to working with Federal agencies.

"Nah, he's okay" Gilbert admitted. "Better than most. I just know as soon as the F.B.I. gets my report, Francine Turner's murder is going to take a fat back seat to the Cartel's sex trafficking crimes. Francine Turner deserves better and I'd like to keep her case as long as I can."

"I understand" Toby replied. "I'll pass on your report and Anuncio's statement to Jake Cleveland as soon as we hang up. And I'll mention your request to sever the Turner murder for separate prosecution."

Toby Trowbridge took a few minutes to study the fax report that Beth had laid on his desk during his telephone call with Scott Gilbert. The Cartel connection would be a coup for Jake Cleveland and the Task Force, but it didn't answer the question of who murdered Marilee Wingo and Mindy Mitchum.

"I'm going over to Jake Cleveland's office" Toby advised his secretary as he exited his office and turned down the hallway towards the east end of the building.

"Wait" Beth Robinson ordered her boss. "Frank Martin dropped this off last night with the after-hours clerk. Sandy brought it by while you were on the phone this morning with Sheriff Gilbert." Toby looked briefly at the sealed manila envelope. "It'll have to wait" he commented as he returned the envelope to his secretary. "Put it on my desk and I'll take a look when I'm finished with Cleveland. If it was important Frank would have called."

"He did" Beth Robinson hollered after her unheeding boss. "That man needs a hearing aid" the secretary complained, laying the unopened envelope on the Sheriff's desk. "One of these days he's going to miss something."

CHAPTER FORTY-EIGHT

"I thought we agreed your only involvement would be reviewing case files" Jim Kaufman reminded his wife. "Is this why you asked Cindy to make the carpool run for you this morning? So we could talk?"

"I didn't want to get into this last night" Allison responded, pouring herself another cup of coffee "because I knew you would take this the wrong way. All I am doing is interviewing Jefferson Boudreaux a second time."

"Damn it, Allison" Jim exclaimed. "That's not all you're doing and you know it. You promised me you wouldn't put yourself in harm's way again."

Allison reached across the oak table and covered her husband's hand with her own. "And I intend to keep that promise. I'm conducting the interview in our conference room. David will be in the room with me, and Frank Martin will be waiting in my office. Nothing is going to happen to me."

"Does Jake Cleveland know about this?" Jim asked. "I can't believe he'd go along with this cockamammy scheme."

"Jake knows about the possible Houma connection" Allison replied, avoiding the direct question. "Frank is delivering the evidence box to Jake this morning. I wanted him to take everything to Andy Dabo for DNA testing, but Frank said the F.B.I. lab could get it done faster."

"If Boudreaux is the Houma killer, this is 100% Task Force business" Jim replied. "There's no need for your involvement or for a second interview. What am I missing?"

"Well, we have a small evidentiary issue." Allison gave her husband a rueful look. "Technically, the Court order allowing Boudreaux's DNA testing was limited to establishing whether he was Rebecca Fairchild's offspring. Even if we get a match on the Houma victim's clothes, or on Mindy Mitchum's clothing and remains, we're caught in a legal catch-22. No court is going to allow us to introduce the DNA evidence in the murder cases. Fruit of the poisonous tree and all that."

"And your plan is?" Jim Kaufman figured better to hear it now than to be surprised later.

"Frank and I are going to work up some questions that we hope will make Boudreaux nervous. We'll make up some information about what has been uncovered in Mindy's murder, maybe a question about M.O.'s, enough to get Boudreaux's attention" Allison explained.

"Surely you don't expect a confession?" Jim asked.

"Of course not" Allison replied, "but maybe enough of a slip to lead us to some evidence we can use."

"What do you have, legally obtained or otherwise" Jim asked making the mental switch from spouse to judge, "and what do you have that is pure speculation?"

A small built in desk was nestled into the end of one of the kitchen's long granite countertops. Pushing back from the kitchen table, Allison moved quickly to the desk and retrieved a yellow legal pad and pencil from one of the drawers. "Here" she replied seating herself at the large kitchen table, "I'll list the strengths and weaknesses of our 'case' and you can decide."

Following his wife's lead, Jim retrieved a second legal pad and began making notes as his wife dictated.

"I think we have a lot in the plus column" Allison started. "Regardless of how it was obtained, if Boudreaux's DNA is a match for any of the victims, we know who our murderer is. We might not be able to use the DNA in the murder cases, but we could focus our energies in gathering admissible evidence proving his involvement. Second, we have a witness who can place Boudreaux with the Houma victim. That fact alone should get us a court order to legitimately test Boudreaux's DNA for a match on the Houma victim. Third, the M.O. in the Houma case is very close to the M.O. in Mindy's case, enough for reasonable cause to test his DNA against that found at Mindy's crime scene." Laying aside her pencil, Allison addressed her husband. "What am I missing?" Before Jim could reply, Allison added "Oh, and we have a witness who can testify that Boudreaux sexually abused his wife for years."

"I doubt the court will allow you to put on evidence about what went on between Boudreaux and his wife. She's dead, and any third party testimony about what the wife may have spoken about is rank hearsay" Jim pointed out. "Since you would be using the witness' testimony to prove the truth of the utterance – that Boudreaux was a sex pervert who abused his wife – I can't think of any of the evidentiary exceptions to the hearsay rule that would allow the testimony."

"Yeh, I couldn't think of one either" Allison admitted, "but there's no reason I can't put that bit of information in front of Boudreaux during the interview."

"Further" Jim continued, "you still have a problem being able to use Boudreaux's DNA in a criminal prosecution even if you match his to the Houma victim."

"Unless we can get the case before the Grand Jury, either here or in Louisiana, and get Alcide Baligant to testify that he saw Boudreaux with the Houma victim before she died" Allison replied. "With a Grand Jury indictment, I feel confident we could get an order for Boudreaux's DNA."

"Be careful, Allison" Jim cautioned. "If Boudreaux is who you think he is, he has been smart enough to evade capture for decades. He won't be easy to fool, and odds are he is extremely dangerous."

Allison's reply was interrupted by the sound of an incoming text message on her phone. Laying aside her legal pad, Allison retrieved the buzzing phone from her briefcase. *Ed Mitchum here. Mr. Boudreaux asked if you could pick him up for this afternoon's meeting. Said he didn't know how to contact you. Anything I need to know?* Allison considered the request. It was an odd one, but she couldn't see any harm in offering her suspect a ride from the Inn to the law office. Typing in a quick reply, Allison told Ed she would be at the

Inn around 1:45. *Thanks, I'll let him know* came Ed's response.

"What was that all about?" Jim asked.

"Oh, nothing" Allison replied. "Just something Ed Mitchum wanted me to look into." No way was she going to tell her husband she would be alone in a car with a murder suspect. "Well, I'd better get going." Allison gave her husband a peck on the cheek, gathered her briefcase and purse, and headed towards the kitchen door. "Quit worrying. It's just an interview."

CHAPTER FORTY-NINE

"Donna, I'm running over to Ed Mitchum's to pick up Mr. Boudreaux for his interview" Allison stopped at her secretary's desk on her way out of the office.

"I'll be glad to do that for you" Donna Pevey replied. "I thought you wanted to meet with Frank before Boudreaux's interview? He'll be here in about fifteen minutes."

"Frank and I spoke this morning" Allison explained. "I've got my questions prepared, and Frank will be listening in via the conference room intercom. If something pops he'll let you know and you can come in with a note."

"I think it's weird that Mr. Boudreaux didn't ask David to pick him up. After all, David's his lawyer, not you." Donna observed. Hearing no reply from her boss, Donna continued "That man gives me the creeps. I think you ought'a call him a cab."

Allison smiled. After the McNair case, her secretary had become suspicious to a fault, especially so when the target of her suspicion was a wealthy white man with bad manners. "I agree that asking me to give him a ride is rather strange" Allison replied, "but I'm hoping to use it to my advantage."

"Good luck with that" Donna scoffed. "Betcha' lunch tomorrow he doesn't say a word to you on the ride over."

"Taking that bet would be totally unfair to you" Allison laughed as she exited the office building. "Tell David and Frank we'll get started as soon as I get back with our target."

Ft. Charles, Alabama was a relatively small Southern town and without the presence of Manship College, Ft. Charles, would likely have met the fate so many other towns of its size had encountered. Fortunately for its residents, the Methodist Church had decided that Ft. Charles was a perfect locale for one of the co-ed institutions of higher learning that the church had been called to establish across the South in the late 1800's. The town and the college had embraced one another, and by the time the college's 100th anniversary had rolled around, Ft. Charles had gained a reputation on par with Oxford, Mississippi as a premier college town.

Passing by the Calhoun County Courthouse where her husband ran a tight ship, Allison let her mind wander as she made the turn onto the state highway towards the Ft. Charles Inn. *Donna was right. Why would Jefferson Boudreaux ask her to give him a ride to his interview? Did he intend to try to intimidate her before the interview began?* Reaching into the center console's glove compartment, Allison pulled out the .38 handgun she kept concealed there and stuffed it inside her purse. *Don't be paranoid* she chided herself. But she made no move to return the gun to its original location.

Ed Mitchum's B&B was located a few miles from town. When Ed had opened the Inn ten years earlier, many town folks thought he had lost his mind. "Who would want to stay way out there?" they asked themselves. But Ed had proved them wrong. The Ft. Charles Inn with its gardens and quiet tenor had proved attractive to travelers and business people alike. When the county school board built a new high school two miles away four years later, retail businesses had moved in Ed's direction. The Ft. Charles Inn was still 'in the country' but the small nearby city was close approaching. However, according to her partner, Jefferson Boudreaux had chosen the Inn not for its beauty and solitude but solely for its proximity to the Fairchild property further down the highway.

A scalloped white sign with black lettering announced the location of the Ft. Charles Inn to the left of the highway and down a narrow, paved road. The isolation that attracted many of the Inn's guests now caused an inadvertent shiver up Allison's back. The Inn seemed deserted, not a single car in the parking lot. Glancing at the dashboard clock, Allison confirmed that she was right on time. Where was Boudreaux? Allison's hand depressed the car horn at the same time she heard the passenger door behind her open.

"So nice of you to come" Jefferson Boudreaux said as he pressed the cold metal end of a gun against the back of Allison's neck. "Turn the car around and head north on the highway, Ms. Parker. I've decided to move our meeting to a new location."

⇒≺⊢ ⊣≻⇐

It wasn't until 2:00 in the afternoon during a court recess that Judge Kaufman realized what had been bothering him since his conversation that morning with his wife. Ed Mitchum didn't text. Jim had teased his friend multiple times about being technically impaired, but Ed Mitchum's reply had always been the same "If you can't take the time to make the call, what you have to say can't be important." Either Allison had lied to him about who sent the text, or someone other than Ed Mitchum had typed the message. Neither option offered a good outcome.

Judge Kaufman donned his black robe and headed from his office towards the courtroom. "Dickie Lee" he called to his Baliff, "As soon as I reconvene Court I want you to place a call to Ed Mitchum. Find out if he's talked to my wife today, or sent her a text" the judge ordered. "Let me know as soon as you talk to him."

"Yes, Your Honor" the Baliff replied. "Everything okay with Ms. Parker?"

"Just call the courtroom to order" the judge replied ignoring his Baliff's question. "then get on the horn to Ed Mitchum."

The defendant's expert witness had just begun her testimony when the Baliff slipped back into the courtroom. "Mr. Mitchum said he hasn't seen or talked to your wife since last week. Said he sure didn't send her a text" the Baliff whispered to his boss. "And you just got a call from your wife's secretary. She said Ms. Parker was due back at the firm an hour ago with some guy named Boudreaux. The secretary's called Sheriff Trowbridge, too."

Jim Kaufman rose from his seat, immediately gaining the attention of the inhabitants of the courtroom, his face drained of color. "An emergency has arisen" the judge informed the surprised crowd. "Court will be adjourned until further notice. Jurors, you are not to discuss this case with anyone. Counsel, I apologize for the interruption, but my wife's life may be in danger." Before the stunned lawyers could make a reply, Judge Kaufman had fled the courtroom for his chambers, leaving twelve bewildered jurors still in their seats.

"Dickie Lee, call Sheriff Trowbridge" the judge ordered as he shed his judicial robes and grabbed his car keys from his desk. "Tell him I'm on the way. And call Ed Mitchum back. Have him meet me at the Sheriff's office."

Ten minutes later, tires screeching, Jim Kaufman slide his car into a vacant slot in front of the Sheriff's office, cut the engine and ran for the entrance to Toby Trowbridge's domain. *Please God*, Jim petitioned an Entity he wasn't sure existed. *Don't let that bastard hurt her.*

CHAPTER FIFTY

Her captor was agitated. If that had been her only worry, Allison might have had hope for a better outcome. To her dismay, Jefferson Boudreaux's disjointed and angry conversations with an unseen third party convinced Allison that whatever sanity Boudreaux might once have possessed, the behavior before her was fueled by pure, unadulterated, off the deep end, insanity.

The gun which Allison had tucked into her purse lay scattered across the floor with the rest of her purse's contents. Lipstick, hairbrush, wallet, checkbook – Allison didn't see her cell phone but was pretty sure she had put it in her purse before she left to drive out to Ed Mitchum's place. Even if she could get loose, Allison thought getting to her gun ahead of Boudreaux would be a long shot.

"I hate to sound like a cliche', but you know you can't get away with kidnapping me and whatever else you have planned." Allison was grateful her voice didn't sound as terrified as she felt. Tied to a chair in what must have once been a sitting room in the Fairchild mansion, Allison knew her only weapon was time. "The F.B.I. has matched your DNA to the murder you committed in Houma" she fibbed. "I bet it's a match for the trace evidence found on Mindy Mitchum's clothing."

"Shut up" Jefferson Boudreaux yelled, slapping Allison across the face. "You don't have anything on me, Bitch."

Ignoring the pain, Allison spit out blood that oozed from her split lip. "We have an eye witness to the Houma murder." "I told you to shut up" her tormentor yelled, striking Allison again.

Undeterred, Allison continued. "The guy who sold you some weed I.D.'ed you from a current photo. The F.B.I. has more than enough to put you away."

Jefferson Boudreaux paced. The plan he had concocted the day before to kidnap the Parker woman now revealed itself as both ill-conceived and completely futile. A question wavered in the distance of his mind: how had he allowed himself such a gross error in judgment? Sweat beaded on Boudreaux's forehead as he struggled to see a way out of the trap he had created for himself.

"People are already looking for us" Allison hoped she was correct. Giving Boudreaux too much information was a risk, but given the odds of her survival, she felt her options were few. "The F.B.I., the Sheriff's Department, my partner, and especially my husband. It won't matter what happens to me. You're already a dead man." Allison paused. "Unless you give yourself up."

The bitch is right, you stupid fuck the Voice commanded Boudreaux's attention. *All this for what? Because the cunt wanted to question you again?* A narrow boning knife lay on a small table, its blade glistening under the light from a nearby lamp. *This is all her fault* the Voice rendered its judgment. *Punish her.* Sliding his finger gently along knife's sharp edge, Boudreaux smiled at Allison. "Since it won't matter what happens to you, I might as well enjoy myself."

━╋ ╋━

"She was going to pick up Jefferson Boudreaux for his interview" Donna Pevey explained to the men crowded into Toby Trowbridge's office. "I've tried calling her cell but it's going to voicemail."

"Time isn't our friend" Jake Cleveland interjected. "I got a call from the lab in Birmingham on my way over here. We've got a match on Boudreaux's DNA with Mindy Mitchum's clothing. We know he's killed at least once. It won't be a stretch for him to do it a second time."

"Where could he take her that he wouldn't be seen?" Allison's husband asked. "Have you put out an APB on Allison's car?" Jim directed his second question to Toby. "We can't just sit here."

"Yes, but there haven't been any hits" the Sheriff replied.

"Shit" Frank Martin exclaimed, remembering a crime story he had watched the night before, "I should have thought of this earlier. What about pinging her cell phone?" Turning to the F.B.I. agent, Frank asked "Jake, can't your guys do that?"

Cursing silently for not being the one to think of Frank's suggestion, the F.B.I. agent pulled out his phone, punched in a ten digit number, listened to a prompt, entered a four digit code and then asked Jim for Allison's cell number which he quickly entered. Completing his task, Cleveland answered Martin's question. "Yes, and done. Coordinates on any hit will be sent immediately to my cell."

"I can't sit here any longer" Jim Kaufman informed the group. "She's out there somewhere. I'm going to look for her."

"I'm coming with you, Judge" Dickie Lee Bishop told his boss.

"When did you get here?" a surprised Jim Kaufman asked his Baliff.

"Came right after I called Mr. Mitchum" the Baliff explained. "Come on, Your Honor. I'll drive."

"Call me if you get a fix on Allison's phone" her husband ordered Jake Cleveland. "Don't leave me out of this."

"Understood" Jake Cleveland acknowledged. He knew what Jim Kaufman was capable of. The judge would be welcome when they went after Jefferson Boudreaux.

CHAPTER FIFTY-ONE

The blow to her head had knocked her out. At least that's what she thought must have happened given the pounding going on inside her skull. As awareness slowly returned, Allison realized she was no longer tied to a chair. Craning her neck, Allison saw with horror that her arms were tied above her head to the posts of a large bed. Only secondarily did she realize that her legs had been tied, apart, to each of the bed's bottom corner posts. Allison fought the tears that seeped from her eyes. This was the Houma murderer's M.O. She had been right. Jefferson Boudreaux was a killer.

With great effort, Allison raised her head and examined her torso. Her clothing lay in shreds around her, clinging wetly to parts of her naked body. A small trickle of blood ran from the center of her belly to her left side but she felt no pain. Focusing herself, Allison tried to determine what other injuries or insults her body might have suffered while she was unconscious. Other than the small cut on her stomach, which she now believed happened when her clothing had been removed, Allison didn't sense any other bodily assault.

Escape was paramount. Allison struggled with the cords that bound her arms and legs to the bedposts. Was there some give in the one that held her right hand? If she could just get one hand free... Allison twisted her wrist back and forth, pulling it towards her, then pushing it away, ignoring the blood and pain that began running from the cuts inflicted by the rawhide binding. Footsteps reached Allison's ears. Frantically she increased her efforts to free her hand.

"You're wasting your time" Jefferson Boudreaux laughed. "They all tried to escape. You won't be any different."

"Why are you doing this?" Get him talking, Allison told herself. "Hurting me will just make matters worse for you. Let me go and I promise I'll do everything in my power to help you."

Boudreaux sat beside Allison on the bed and began stroking the inside of her thigh. "You're much prettier without your clothes. And in much better shape than I expected.

Allison forced herself to look directly at her tormentor. "Jefferson, you don't want to do this" she insisted in a voice she forced to be gentle. "You're a good man who's been misdirected. It's not too late for you." Maybe a different tactic would work in her favor.

Boudreaux moved his hands upward, dragging his fingers across Allison's stomach. "Such a shame to destroy" he whispered, cruelly squeezing Allison's breasts.

"You don't have to destroy anything" Allison pleaded with the man she was certain would end her life. "I have children – two small children. You know what it is like to be orphaned." Tears ran down Allison's face. "Please, don't make my children orphans."

"They'll be better off without you." Jefferson Boudreaux reached for the knife he had placed beside Allison. Smiling, Jefferson Boudreaux stood, unbuckled his belt and let his pants drop to the floor. "The ones that fight are always the best" he smirked. Picking up the knife, Boudreaux straddled his victim and pressed the knife tip into the hollow at the base of Allison's neck. "Don't give up on me now" he ordered.

A scream escaped from Allison's lips as Boudreaux carved a shallow line from Allison's sternum to her pubic bone. Despite the pain, Allison fought against the straps that held her captive. He had thought to toy with her, maybe to skin her – he'd never done that to any of the other whores. But the Voice intruded. *She will bring your end. Punish her.* Raising the knife over his head with one hand, and stroking his erect penis with the other, Jefferson Boudreaux surrendered to the demons that had driven him since childhood.

An explosion of sound filled the bedroom. A scream which Allison knew was not her own pierced her ears as warm liquid sprayed across her face. Looking up, Allison saw Jefferson Boudreaux's contorted face seconds before his body slammed into her prone one.

Dimly, Allison was aware of men's hands roughly pulling Jefferson Boudreaux away from her. Violent shaking gripped her slim frame as adrenaline drained from her body. A voice that reminded Allison of her husband's Baliff assured her that she was safe. Gratefully, she felt a soft blanket cover her hurting body, and then the voice she needed to hear most of all whispered to her "Babe, I've got you." Smiling her reply, Allison let the darkness take her.

A soft humming slowly made its way into Allison's consciousness. Opening her eyes made her head hurt, but Allison was curious about the sound. As the room came into focus, Allison saw she was connected to several monitors, one of which was emitting the sound that had awakened her.

"Hey, sleepyhead." Allison turned her head towards the voice. "It's about time you came back to us."

"You look like hell" Allison croaked. Her mouth and lips were cracked and dry. "But boy am I glad to see you."

Gingerly, Jim perched on the side of Allison's bed. "How do you feel?" he asked before giving his wife a kiss. "Here, take a sip of water first" he instructed, placing a glass of liquid to his wife's lips.

"Like a Mac truck turned me into road kill" Allison replied after she swallowed several sips of water. "The entire front of my body hurts, and my right wrist feels like it's been set on fire."

"You're a lucky girl" Jim replied. "The cuts that bastard made on you didn't go too deep. Dr. Brien had to stitch a few of them, but mostly you're superglued."

"What?" Allison attempt at laughter quickly turned into a groan. "Superglued?"

"Yeh, the newest in medical advances" Jim assured his wife. Dr. Brien said scarring would be minimal."

"And Boudreaux? What about him?" Allison wanted to know.

"In custody. I tried to kill him, but Dickie Lee stopped me," Jim shook his head. "He said I of all people knew to let the justice system do its work." Jim lifted Allison's bandaged hand to his lips. "When I saw you, saw what he was getting ready to do to you, imagining what he might have already done, all I could think of was killing the son-of-a-bitch."

"I remember a gunshot" Allison looked at her husband. "Who shot him?"

"Dickie Lee" her husband replied. "Got him in the shoulder and took him down. If I'd gone after Boudreaux at that point, I'd have been guilty of first degree murder" Jim grimaced remembering. "My Baliff had a level head. I owe him."

"So, who has Boudreaux? The Feds or Toby?" Allison hoped wherever Boudreaux was that the jail cell was securely guarded.

"He's in custody in a Federal lockup in Birmingham. There's a DNA match on the Houma case, too. Came in this morning. Jake wants to get a Federal indictment for the Houma case, Mindy's case, and Marilee Wingo's murder and then try Boudreaux as a serial killer." Jim explained. "Toby is talking to the D.A. here about prosecuting your kidnapping and attempted murder on state charges.

If Jake gets his way, I doubt the state case will ever see the light of day – or need to."

Allison felt her eyelids getting heavy, but a thought prevented sleep. "How did you find me?"

"Frank" her husband replied. "In a room full of law enforcement officers, Frank was the one who thought about pinging your cell phone. When the trace placed you near the Fairchild place we figured that was where he had taken you."

"I'll have to bake him a pie" Allison murmured as she drifted off to sleep.

Jim smiled. Frank Martin deserved a lot more than a pie.

CHAPTER FIFTY-TWO

"Karma's a bitch" Allison toasted her partner with a cold Coke Zero, "or as my mother used to say, 'what goes around, comes around'.

"Isn't that the truth" David Jackson observed. "I'm sure Jefferson Boudreaux didn't plan on spending the Fairchild inheritance trying to avoid the death penalty,"

Someday, Allison told herself, she was going to write a book. First the McNair case, and now all the drama with Jefferson Boudreaux – Allison figured she had all the makings for a best seller. Maybe when she retired from legal practice she'd take a shot at becoming an author.

Representing Jefferson Boudreaux on the Will contest had turned into a big payday for Parker &

Jackson. After Boudreaux's arrest, and at his client's instruction, David Jackson had gone ahead with the Motion for Summary Judgment as planned. The indisputable DNA evidence that was properly obtained for the Will contest case established Jefferson Boudreaux as Rebecca Fairchild's son. Because Rebecca had never disinherited her illegitimate son, nor severed her parental rights to him, David had argued that Alabama law entitled Jefferson Boudreaux to his mother's entire estate. The Court had agreed and rendered judgement in favor of a now incarcerated Jefferson Boudreaux.

The disgruntled charities who found themselves on the losing end of the summary judgment filed notices of appeal, threatening to tie up the final disposition of Boudreaux's claim for another year or longer. Although neither Boudreaux nor the charities ended up completely satisfied, a generous settlement had finally been negotiated, and the Fairchild estate had been distributed giving Boudreaux ample assets with which to hire the best criminal defense lawyers money could buy. He would need them.

"Have you talked to Sarah yet?" Allison asked her partner.

"Yes." David replied. "She said this was my decision. That whatever I decided would be fine with her. What about you? What does the judge think?"

"I think he and Sarah must have traded strategies" Allison reflected on the conversation she had with her husband before leaving for the office that morning. "He said the firm earned this money in more ways than one, and what to do with the money should be a decision of the firm partners, not anyone else. That leaves the decision to you and me."

"A fifty million dollar fee seems obscene, even when it's a pittance compared to what Boudreaux recovered, and what the charities got in the settlement" David stated. "On the other hand, my client did try to kill you."

"And fortunately for me, failed" Although parts of her ordeal remained cloudy, Allison remembered more than she cared to admit. "I got a call from Rice the other day" Allison's change of topic took David by surprise.

"How's the chemo going?" David asked. "I know it's got less side effects than it used to, but it still can't be very pleasant."

"Rice is managing. Some nausea, some weight loss, but he has a good prognosis. He's keeping a positive attitude." Allison replied. "But talking to him gave me an idea about what we might do with some of that fifty million."

"And?" David waited for Allison to continue.

"I'd like to take part of that money and start a treatment facility here at Ft. Charles General. I've talked to the CEO, and with matching grants and some other private money, if Parker & Jackson commits to ten million, we can get a state of the art rehab facility and afford competent staff to run it." Allison raised her hand to stop David's reply. "If you don't want to be a part of this, or if you have another idea, I'm fine with using my share of the fee to do this. It's important to me."

David considered Allison's suggestion. He and Sarah had discussed setting up college funds for their children, and maybe taking an expensive vacation, but they had no desire for the kind of extravagant lifestyle their share of a fifty million dollar payday would provide. David knew Sarah would approve of Allison's proposal. "I agree" he replied.

"I've got another idea, too" Allison knew her staff would faint when they got the news. "I think we should close the office for two weeks, rent a couple of nice villas in the Caribbean, and take the entire office, plus families, on an all- expenses paid vacation. We ought to take Frank, too, seeing as how it was his bright idea that brought the cavalry to my rescue."

"I'll be right back." David disappeared down the hallway, calling for the firm's employees to gather in Allison's office. By the time the last straggler had wandered in, David Jackson appeared with a bottle of champagne and several of the firm's unmatched coffee mugs balanced on a tray.

"Are we having a party?" Donna Pevey asked watching David Jackson pour the fizzy liquid. "Y'all look like the cat that ate the canary."

Allison looked at people who worked for and with her. They were a team. A good team. Even though she chafed at times under the illusion that maybe she was tired of practicing law, she knew she had found her place. The fifty million dollar fee would allow Parker & Jackson to take cases based on merit rather than financial need. That alone would change the tenor of her practice.

Raising her coffee cup, Allison smiled at those around her. "Anyone up for a trip?"